W9-BEH-328

THE HIGHEST PRAISE FOR WILL HENRY,
"the greatest western historical
novelist of them all."*

"Humor, romance, gutsy adventure, realism, and
accuracy. That's the West of Will Henry."
—Don Coldsmith
author of *The Spanish Bit Saga*

"Will Henry combines the best talents of a natural storyteller with an inspired poet's glorious
use of the English language."
—Elmer Kelton
author of *Honor at Daybreak*

"Henry and his alter ego Clay Fisher have established a godhead of frontier lore that has changed
the course of the Western. His prose skirles off
white-ice mountain peaks and stings the nostrils
with the scents of burning wood and spent powder."
—Loren D. Estleman
author of *Bloody Season*

"His work . . . comprises some of the best writing
that the American West can claim."
—Brian Garfield
author of *Wild Times*

*Dale L. Walker, author of *Will Henry's West* and syndicated
columnist

"Henry is a creator of Literature. It is not only that he is a consummate storyteller, but his finely chiseled prose also sings with a lyricism that is as haunting as it is rare. His stories not only ring true, but also pull the reader feet-first into worlds that have vanished, except from the pages of books."

—*Santa Fe Reporter*

"The core of a Will Henry/Clay Fisher novel is historical bedrock, accurate in nuance and detail. History and heritage, spit and spirit; Will Henry sets the reader firmly in a time and place, in a context of drama, humor, tragedy and humanity."

—*The Californians*

"[Will Henry is] a born storyteller, a man strengthened with the uncommon melody of language, a literary outrider using his bent to describe in fiction the West that was."

—*True West*

"[Will Henry] is a splendid novelist...a superb craftsman of the short story. Henry has touched the Old West with an enduring storytelling magic that some authorities say deserves comparison with the best Western writing of Bret Harte, Mark Twain, Stephen Crane and Eugene Manlove Rhodes. This may seem like an exaggerated compliment if you have never read Will Henry...but it is one with which you will probably agree after reading... 'The Trap,' 'The Tallest Indian in Toltepec,' 'Lapwai Winter,' 'Sundown Smith,' 'Isley's Stranger,' and 'Not Wanted Dead or Alive.' If there is a Western Hall of Fame for writers, this is absolutely the stuff that belongs in it."
—*Stockton Record*, California

"A remarkable American storyteller...of unerring perception."
—*El Paso Herald-Post*

"Henry's writing style is a delight, and his characters are loveable, flawed, memorable people."
—*Texas Gazette-Enterprise*

Bantam Books by Will Henry

JOURNEY TO SHILOH
PILLARS OF THE SKY
ONE MORE RIVER TO CROSS
FROM WHERE THE SUN NOW STANDS
THE GATES OF THE MOUNTAINS
ALIAS BUTCH CASSIDY

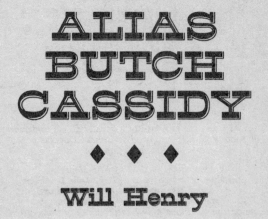

ALIAS BUTCH CASSIDY

◆ ◆ ◆

Will Henry

™
DOMAIN

BANTAM BOOKS
NEW YORK • TORONTO • LONDON • SYDNEY • AUCKLAND

This edition contains the complete text
of the original hardcover edition.
NOT ONE WORD HAS BEEN OMITTED.

ALIAS BUTCH CASSIDY

A Bantam Book / published by arrangement with
Random House, Inc.

PRINTING HISTORY

Random House edition published 1967
Bantam edition / March 1969
Bantam reissue / November 1991

DOMAIN and the portrayal of a boxed "d" are trademarks
of Bantam Books, a division of Bantam Doubleday Dell
Publishing Group, Inc.

Copyright © 1967 by Will Henry.
Introduction copyright © 1991 by Dale L. Walker
All rights reserved under International and
Pan-American Copyright Conventions.
No part of this book may be reproduced or transmitted
in any form or by any means, electronic or mechanical,
including photocopying, recording, or by any information
storage and retrieval system, without permission in writing
from the publisher.
For information address: Random House, Inc.,
201 E. 50th St., New York, NY 10022.

ISBN 0-553-24101-X

If you purchased this book without a cover you should be
aware that this book is stolen property. It was reported as
"unsold and destroyed" to the publisher and neither the
author nor the publisher has received any payment for this
"stripped book."

Published simultaneously in the United States and Canada

Bantam Books are published by Bantam Books, a division of
Bantam Doubleday Dell Publishing Group, Inc. Its trademark, consisting of the words "Bantam Books" and the portrayal of a rooster, is Registered in U.S. Patent and Trademark
Office and in other countries. Marca Registrada. Bantam Books,
666 Fifth Avenue, New York, New York 10103.

PRINTED IN THE UNITED STATES OF AMERICA

RAD   13 12 11 10 9 8 7 6 5

Author's Note

No man knows the true story of George LeRoy Parker, the Utah cowboy who became a legend in his own lifetime. No man knows where he was born. No man knows where he died. No man knows where he rode through all the outlaw years between. Even his real name remains in argument. He appeared; he ruled the Wild Bunch; he vanished. Now he is glimpsed on the famed bay, Kanab, thundering away to Old Mexico and eternal safety in Sonora, or Chihuahua, or Sinaloa. Or was it Coahuila or Durango? Again, it is in South America that he is seen, secure upon his secret rancho in the Argentine, or Bolivia, or Peru? Or could it have been in Colombia or Brazil? No matter. Always he is there, warm-hearted, gay, compassionate, brave. And always he is riding, on, and on, and on, into the sunset of the legend. Much is made by the minstrels of the middle years when Brown's Park, Hole-in-the-Wall and Powder Springs knew him well. Other strummers dwell upon the mysteries of the later years and that last great stand in the mule corrals of San Vicente near Grande River and La Paz. But the early years have been largely left unturned. What of boyhood beginnings? Of the fates, the places, the personalities which first sent him along the owlhoot trail? And how did he fare? And where? And with whom? The answers are not easy, for the dust of time lies deep. It is dim work to track such old signs—to total in some truth the tales of laughter, tears and tragedy; and to present at the last a reasonable sum of the unyielding spirit and iron flesh of the Circle Valley boy who began as the grandson of a Mormon bishop and ended as a Utah legend.

W.H.
Circleville

Introduction

◆

by Dale L. Walker

We do not know his name. He said it was George, his father said Robert. He worked for a time as a butcher in Rock Springs, Wyoming, and so we know him best as "Butch."

We do not know when or how he died. The legend (and the movie) has it that he and his partner, Harry Longabaugh ("the Sundance Kid"), died in a hail of bullets at San Vicente, Bolivia, early in 1909.

Or, some say, in the final moments of that battle with Bolivian soldiers, Butch may have killed the mortally wounded Sundance, then himself.

Or Butch, Sundance, and a third outlaw may have been killed at Mercedes, Uruguay, in December 1911 while trying to rob a bank.

Or Butch may have returned from South America, taking the name William T. Phillips, marrying, living in Globe, Arizona, working as a mercenary in the Mexican Revolution, establishing a manufacturing business, becoming a Mason and an Elk, and dying, in July 1937, near Spokane, Washington.

We do not know which, if any, of these is correct.

These things we do know: He was an outlaw—a cattle and horse rustler, a train, bank, and mine robber—but not a killer. "I have never killed a man," he said proudly, and there is no evidence that he ever did. There does seem to be general agreement among those who knew him that George (or Robert) LeRoy Parker—Butch Cassidy—had many fine qualities. He was, it was universally said, "good-natured" and "fun-loving"; he also had the virtues of generosity and truthfulness and he was "cheery and affable" with a "wild streak."

There is a famous studio photograph of Butch, Sundance, and their "Wild Bunch" cohorts taken "as a joke" in 1901 in Fort Worth, just before their dash to South America with the Pinkertons on their heels. Butch is seated on a wicker chair, scrubbed and manicured, a square-jawed dandy in a three-piece suit with a bowler hat tilted slightly over his left eye.

There is a sly hint of a smile on his lips and in his eyes.

The picture makes you want to know more about him: not so much his escapades as a rustler and thief—all of which have been well chronicled—but how he got that way.

Will Henry had a thirst to know more about Butch, too, and in *Alias Butch Cassidy* (originally published in 1967, the same year as *One More River to Cross* and its reconstructed life of Ned Huddleston, alias Isom Dart), he muses in his author's note that no one really knows Butch's history—where he was born, where and when he died, or precisely whom he rode with during his "owlhoot years." Where did Butch's beloved bay horse Kenab take him? From the Sevier River to Robber's Roost to Telluride to the Hole-in-the-Wall? To Sonora, Durango, Sinaloa, Coahuila, the Argentine, Brazil, Colombia, Bolivia, Peru?

And what of his boyhood? Especially his boyhood and the making of the man. What can it have been like?

This is the perfect Will Henry scenario: What is not known—and in the history of the Old West there is always a great deal that is not known—can be reconstructed in fiction grounded in meticulously faithful history, grounded in what *is* known.

He begins with a gentle tease in the title. The novel takes George (the author's choice over Robert) LeRoy Parker only five years along the trail of his life, from age sixteen up to age twenty-one, many years before the celebrated nickname came into being. (The name "Butch," in fact, is never mentioned in the book.)

What follows is a gripping, good-humored story with scattered moments of abrupt violence that is surely more truth than fiction. And there is a valuable additional ingredient—a deft message—that lifts *Alias Butch Cassidy* leagues above even the best of "good Westerns." University of Pittsburgh scholar Robert L. Gale (in his 1984 book, *Will Henry*) calls this between-the-lines signal a "mute moral," that "when a kid goes wrong he cannot turn the clock back to innocence."

In the beginning of Will Henry's wonderful reconstruction, we see George LeRoy Parker (Butch hereafter, anachronism notwithstanding), grandson of a Mormon bishop, eldest of thirteen children, as a gullible kid growing up on the Sevier Ranch—actually no more than a scraggle of stunted timber, rabbit grass, and sage-covered flatland—of his father, Maximilian Parker, in Circle Valley, Utah.

Butch, with his pony named Chunk, his fourteen-year-old brother Dan as his eternal shadow, his strongest oaths "by jings!," "lordy!," and "Jehoshaphat!," is "a boy born with the spirit of simple belief and the joy in his heart of honest innocence. He went to sleep each night dreaming of the wonders of tomorrow, never the regrets of yesterday."

Intruding into this halcyon life is Mike Cassidy,

an aging cowhand, ruffian, and expert with the "rustler's brush" (the running iron, used to alter brands) who is obsequiously trying to keep his job on the Parker ranch. (Will Henry has him saying to Maximilian Parker, "You know what I mean to say, as saint, sir; as a man of saintly compassion, of Mormon decency, divinity, and demi-tassity.") Cassidy gives the goggle-eyed Butch the benefit of his forty years as an open-range cowboy "in the stultritrifling limitations of the honest cow business," and some-time owlhooter with the "desperate McCarty brothers," blood brothers of the Jameses and Youngers.

Butch, who will soon take Mike Cassidy's surname as his own, loses his innocence forever when he takes part in Mike's plan to rob the bank at Panguitch, a town unfortunately within an easy ride of the Parker spread on the Sevier River.

Butch is naively looking forward to the time he will be the "outside man," the horse-holder replacing the late Babyfat Mattoon (shot up so thoroughly at Gloriosa during a bank job, Cassidy says, "they dug enough lead out'n him to start a new vein and sell stock"), but what neither he nor Mike can factor in is how Butch's younger brother Dan—the rambunc-tious, hero-worshipping Dan and his horse Spook, showing up again and again to remind Butch of the life he had left behind—is going to foul up their ill-laid plans.

The bank job is inevitably bungled, and Butch and his mentor are pursued for a time by Deputy Sheriff Orville Stodenberg. Mike Cassidy kills the deputy—the darkest moment of the novel—and takes Butch on a journey in the worst snowstorm in recent Utah history, up into the mountains to Rob-ber's Roost, a dry, rocky bench in southeastern Utah on the vast slope of Sam's Mesa overlooking the chasm of the Dirty Devil River to the west and Poison Spring Creek to the southwest.

By the time they arrive at the Roost in the winter of 1883, George LeRoy Parker has become George Cassidy, has followed a trail that has distanced his boyhood. He will soon reach the point where, in Will Henry's words, "He must travel on. His home was not here, but out there."

At Robber's Roost, Butch teams up with a fellow Mormon, Williard Christiansen, son of the bishop of the Nephi Stake, now known as Matt Warner, age nineteen and already a notorious bank robber, rustler, murderer, highline rider, and owlhoot legend. Warner, seen in Will Henry's depiction as the dark side of the man Butch could (but doesn't) become, is Butch's nemesis almost to the end of the novel.

There is a relationship between the characters of Matt Warner and Butch Cassidy in *Alias Butch Cassidy* and Matt Rash and Isom Dart in *One More River to Cross*, both novels published in the same year. All four are real characters from Western history; Butch and Isom are relatively harmless outlaws thrust among the worst of hardcases; the Matts, Warner and Rash, are harsh representatives to these babes-in-the-woods of the suddenness by which a man on the owlhoot trail cannot find his way back.

The best wisdom Butch ever gets is from the cranky old hermit and Colorado ferryman Cass Hite, and the great moment of truth in the novel—the one about turning back the clock to innocence—arrives when Butch fights the murderous Matt Warner and saves Hite's life on the Dandy Crossing of the Colorado.

"He was on the far side of a river which divided the desert wilderness," writes Will Henry at this critical stage of the novel. "On the far side was the old prophet, Nephi, advising him to return to the land of his people, to abandon the Satan with whom he had traveled while there was yet time, while he was still among the quick, instead of the dead."

Butch has gone too many miles down the trail to turn back completely, but he does follow the prophet Nephi's counsel to abandon the satan named Matt Warner and after Warner crosses the river alone, Cass Hite takes over where Nephi has left off.

Cass, his lonely life devoted to a study of the

men, mostly on the run, he has encountered at his stone-and-sod house on the ferry crossing, has parboiled all his observations on owlhooters and reduced their kind to two—"them as will kill you, and them as won't"— and has identified Butch as one who won't.

Says Cass Hite: "A man makes himself whatever he is. I don't have to be a loner and live out here with the snakes and kingfishers and coyotes. That just happens to be the way I want it. It's the trail I chose for myself. God didn't plant that decision in my daddy's seed. Folks are forever blaming somebody else for the bad they do in this life."

Butch knows he is not yet fully committed to the outlaw life and that he can take whatever trail he wishes, to the left or right.

History, of course, has settled which trail he took.

Alias Butch Cassidy ends in late 1887. Matt Warner has failed to involve Butch in a scheme to rob the ore wagon taking gold ingots from the mining camp in Telluride, Colorado, to the San Miguel Valley Bank. Butch wanders in and out of Brown's Hole, that spectacularly beautiful Green River area where Colorado, Wyoming, and Utah conjoin and which served as yet another Robber's Roost in its early history. Butch is involved in robbing a payroll train from Denver at Grand Junction and with stolen money and riding with his brother Dan—his earlier, innocent nemesis—crosses the Utah line.

They visit the lineshack in Circle Valley where Mike Cassidy killed Deputy Stodenberg, and at night Butch leaves Dan behind and rides on toward, but not to, home, all innocence and boyhood and commonplace existence beyond his reach forever.

Alias Butch Cassidy ends with the reader sensing the story has just begun—but what Will Henry has created will make the rest of the tale (no matter who is to tell it) more understandable.

Contents

PART ONE
The Bandits of Panguitch
1

PART TWO
The Ride for Robber's Roost
53

PART THREE
South Along the Owlhoot
107

PART FOUR
The Trial to Telluride
137

PART FIVE
Brown's Hole and Beyond
169

ALIAS BUTCH CASSIDY

◆ ◆ ◆

PART ONE

The Bandits
of
Panguitch

1

◆

The wagon crawled over the last rise. On the far side, out of the wind, the driver pulled in the team. The boy on the seat beside him shaded his eyes against the climbing sun. Far down the valley, on a bench rising to meet the right-hand range, the youth saw the gray-brown dots which meant ranch buildings. "That the place, Paw?" he said anxiously.

"That's it," nodded the man. "What you think?"

The wind swept over the rise behind them. It sent the sandy topsoil whirling under the team and over the empty flatness of Circle Valley. Despite the excitement of being first to see the new place, the boy shook his head. "Let's wait along to see it close up," he proposed. "This here sun is fierce. It ain't fair to judge against the light."

"I'll grant you it's lonesome," said the father.

"Well," said the boy, "I like the way it sets at the foot of that rise, the bench going up behind and right to the hills like it does, yet everything easy and flat around the house and so on."

"You don't need to like it, LeRoy," said the

3

man, slapping the reins on the horses' rumps, sending them on again. "Life ain't that simple that everything it brings us is going to turn out likingquality. I reckon God wouldn't have guided me to buying the old Marshall place unless He had something special in mind for us Parkers through the deal. He don't move his pieces about the board for no reason. You'll see, LeRoy."

"Sure, Paw, if you say." The boy, grandson of a Mormon bishop, the descendent on both sides of families which had made the great western trek, was, at sixteen, an agnostic. Yet he was respectful of his father's faith. And mindful, too, of is advantages in that very nearly closed society of Saints which was Utah in 1882. "By jings," he continued, "we'll bring that old place around. It don't matter what things was. What counts is what we make of them. Ain't that so, Paw?"

His father's face tightened visibly. "What you mean, LeRoy?" he asked, not looking at the boy. "Don't squeeze words under the fence. Say what's in your mind."

The boy had already said too much, and realized it. But he did not have the square jaw, red, sandy hair and clean-dancing blue eyes for nothing. Iron was in his character, no matter how hidden by the quick grin which chronically wrinkled his pug nose, turned up the puckish corners of his wide mouth. The question put, he would not ride around it.

"Well, you know what they say in Circleville, Paw."

"About the Marshall place, or about me buying it?"

"Oh, no, Paw, not about you buying it. But shucks, you know what they say about Marshall."

"Jim Marshall never made me his lawyer," said the man, slapping the team into a harness-jingling trot. "Neither did the Lord appoint me his judge. What they say of Marshall in Circleville don't smudge off onto me. I got the mortgage to his place through banker Puckett, and the title reads free and clear. I don't see where Marshall figures into it."

"It ain't so much him, Paw. It's the place."

"Go on, boy."

"Well, they say it's a regular outlaw hangout, Paw. You know that. I mean, it was, you know, before you bought it."

The man nodded, turned the team off onto the ranch road. "Whatever it was," he said, "needn't concern us. All that's important for the Parkers to know is that the place is paid for, it's got ample room for our big family, and it's deserted plumb empty. We can move in soon as you and me have give it the once-over."

The boy, peering ahead up the ranch road toward the house, straightened on the seat. "You're right, Paw," he said, "excepting for one thing." He gripped the edges of the seat with his hands, nodding the warning with his head, after the wary fashion of the country. "This here ranch ain't deserted."

2

◆

The man who stood waiting outside the house was not a young man. Neither was he tall, menacing or impressive in any way—not at a distance. He seemed only rumpled, short, thickset, poor. And one other thing; from the way that he stood, slouched yet ready, and from his rough clothing, he could not have been anything before he was a cowboy. The elder Parker drove up watchfully nonetheless. In that day and place, no one was approached casually.

"Good morning," he greeted the silent figure. "Was you looking for somebody?"

The raffish little man in the patched chaps nodded. "Was," he replied, in a soft brogue that was not Mormon and not Utahan, "and still might be."

"Anybody in particular?" The boy's father was watching the abandoned ranch house. He was feeling something he did not like. "Perhaps I can help you."

"Depends," said the man. The boy, studying him intently, now noticed the pistol butt protruding from the waistband of the faded overalls beneath the chaps. "Who are you?" the stranger asked,

6

cocking his head to one side and staring without a blink at the father.

The latter's first inclination was to tell the drifter to be on his way, to get off private property, and to get quick. But now he too noted the pistol's butt, and noted also the easy, accustomed way in which the tattered cowboy had slid the thumb of his right hand near the butt, and hooked the thumb in the overalls' waistband, ever so suggestively.

"I'm Maximilian Parker. Who are you?" he said carefully.

"Faith now, Mr. Parker, why didn't you say it was you?" The little Irishman's attitude changed coloring as swiftly as a chameleon sliding from rock shade to sunlight. "Of course you can help me. You're the man I was looking for."

"Who are you?" insisted Parker. He wrapped the reins, freeing his hands. "I don't recall seeing you around."

The aging cowboy scrubbed the bristle of his beard with the back of a sun-scoured hand. "You didn't see me when you drove up just now, either," he said. "Not till the boy spotted me. I don't make a career of being seen around, Mr. Parker. Don't believe in advertising my charms overduly."

The boy could tell his father was beginning to stew. A man of great physical strength and little physical fear, Maximilian Parker was slow to anger. But he lacked something in humor, and, like all serious or literal men, any inkling that he was being made sport of worked on him beyond ordinary measure. Now he got down slowly from the wagon and walked over to the bantam-sized rider.

"You can tell me your name," he said, "or be about your business. Which latter isn't on this ranch, in any event."

"Oh? Well, now, I'd say that was where you was wrong, Mr. Parker. You see, I sort of come with this ranch. When Marshall and the boys lit out, they left me behind. Too old for waving the hat, that's me. Leastways, they thought so."

The boy on the wagon seat was suddenly tense again. "Waving the hat" was an outlaw term. It referred to the common practice when strangers met in that desolate land. Rather than ride in close where either might recognize the other, and so be able to make subsequent identification under oath, the travelers waved their hats in an exchange of distant reassurance before resuming separate, distant ways.

"Gee!" said the boy. "You're one of them!"

"LeRoy, be still!" commanded his father sternly. But the little rider waved his hand airily.

"Let the lad talk," he said. "Faith, now, sir, how's he to learn if he don't inquire?" He turned to the boy. "You got a quick eye, LeRoy, and a mind to go with it. But I've no idea what you're following after. You say I'm one of 'them.' One of them *what*, now, may I ask?"

"Outlaws," said the sandy-haired youngster, his square chin thrust forward. "Rustlers, thieves and bandits, or whatever."

"Well, now, ain't you the wise little pecko," grinned the drifter. "But I reckon you're vaulting at shadows, lad. Why, a gentler, more law-abiding man than Mike Cassidy would be passing difficult to locate in these parts, I do declare and notary-ize. Now ain't that a fact, Mr. Parker?" he appealed to the father.

But George LeRoy Parker was not watching his father, or even thinking about him. Eyes and imagination were concentrating totally on the shabby little cowboy. *"Mike Cassidy,"* breathed the boy. *"The* Mike Cassidy?"

"As ever was," bowed the little man, sweeping off his hat. "In the flesh and not a tintype, nor a drawing." He ignored the boy as quickly as he favored him. "Now, then, Mr. Parker," he said, "how about that job? I know ever' coyote hole and jackass rabbit dropping on this spread, and for forty miles in any direction away from it—including into the hills yonder. What do you say, sir? I need the work and I'd be beholden to you for the chance. You'd never regret it."

Maximilian Parker eyed him. "Are you hinting that I might regret it, happen I don't hire you on?" he challenged.

"Oh, never!" avowed Cassidy. "Those translations are your own, and no shred of the truth. Please, sir, I can't find other employment, you know that. As a man of faith, of charity, of Christian mercy, sir, I appeal to you."

"*Christian* mercy?" said Maximilian Parker.

"Ah, 'twas a slip of the tongue, only," pleaded the rider. "You know I meant to say, as a Saint, sir; as a man of saintly compassion, of Mormon decency, divinity and demi-tassity."

"Cassidy," said the other, "get out."

The graying bandit, if indeed he were the desperado which local legend claimed Mike Cassidy to be, appeared to understand he had come to certain defeat. Sighing wearily, he gazed in farewell about the sunlit, silent pastures of the Marshall place.

"I've given the best part of my life to these here valley slopes and flats," he soliloquized. "This here Sevier River country has been kinder to me than any other. More kinder by far than I deserve. I thought I might stay on here for what little time is left me. I had it in my heart to help you and your folks get started here, maybe making up in such a way for some of the bad deeds I've laid my hand to. I heard you was a good man, Mr. Parker, sir, and would give an old outlaw the benefit of Mormon mercy. I prayed last night that you would let me stay on here. I love this valley. I'd hoped I might lay my last bedroll here. But I reckon what a man's done wrong will ride after him his whole life."

"I'm right beholden for the chance to talk out, sir," he said. "I'll get my pony and ride on, now." He walked over to the wagon, put a hand up to touch the knee of George LeRoy. "Boy, I'm special sad to be missing them days with you that I planned the minute I seen you coming up just now. I was thinking, just like the good Lord put it in my mind by magic to help me make amends for my many deep sins, that this old cowboy could teach a bright and quick young sprout like you more things of cowboying and horse and cattle lore, and hunting and tracking, all the things a lad yearns to know, more suchlike, I say, in a few months of chance granted by your good daddy, than you could come by in your lifetime, left to nature and them as ain't had my rich experiences in ranching and the range cow business. But then we all got our crosses to carry to Calgary. I ain't complaining. You just mind your daddy, boy, and don't bother none about this old cowboy."

He turned away, his bowlegged gait suddenly grown agonizingly worse. Each step seemed a torture beyond the bearing. He took only a minute to return around the house with his horse, a ratty white gelding as disreputable and unwashed as its owner. To watch him force his rheumatic joints up into stirrup and saddle was more than George LeRoy could sustain. The boy leaped from the wagon, ran over and seized the bridle of the white horse.

"Paw!" he cried, and stood there with an accusing look that demanded of the elder Parker amends for this almost-crime of dispossession, this heartless miscarriage of human justice and dignity.

Maximilian Parker knew that he was doing wrong. He also knew that he would never be able to explain to his friendly, bright-natured son any other course than giving sanctuary to this aging wastrel who called himself Mike Cassidy. Uneasily, he waved his hand and gave the decision. "All right, you can stay for a spell, Cassidy," he said. "We can use somebody who knows the place. Put your duffel in the log shack out yonder."

"Yes, sir, thank you, sir, Mr. Parker," said the little cowboy, knuckling his battered brow. "But sure the Lord told me right when He said to stay on, that He was bringing me work to do on this old place. Come along, lad. I'll show you the stock sheds and corrals whiles your daddy is inspecting the house. Boys don't care nothing about houses, now that's certain-sure."

"That's right!" enthused the square-shouldered boy, falling in to follow the old cowboy. "Where's your duffel, Mr. Cassidy? I'll tote it into the shack for you."

"Why, where do you expect it is, LeRoy?" said the other, winking and making a sign of private communication. "Didn't I tell you, you was a bright tad?" He rolled an eye to the rear, making sure the father had passed out of hearing. "I reckon you'll nail it to the fence with the first guess."

The boy also looked back to check on his father's whereabouts. He felt a bond forming between him and the scrubby rider, which was unlike any he had experienced with Maximilian Parker. The wise wink, the quick sunny grin, the absolute cocksureness yet adept cunning at talk and taking-on, all were familiar matters of communion to George LeRoy Parker. He knew that he, the Mormon bishop's grandson, and Mike Cassidy were of common faulty clay, and he nodded back to the bowlegged little man and said, blue eyes flashing, "Why, Mr. Cassidy, I knowed it all along; your things is already in that old shack: they never was no place else."

"They never was," agreed his companion. Then, softly, and with a nod all suddenly bereft of wink or grin, and innocent, too, of any playful guile, "Me and you will make a pair, boy. I wasn't lying back yonder. I will teach you more things about the cow business than your daddy ever dreamed was included in the price of this here ranch."

3

♦

That first happy summer on the Sevier River ranch, Mike Cassidy imparted to George LeRoy Parker the lore of forty years a cowboy on the open range. Cassidy was a working hand since he could recall, and he said he could recall roping and busting his first yearling at seven. The weathered drifter loved all cattle and horses, knew them as few men alive.

In the Parker boy he recognized a kindred soul. He gave his great knowledge to the lad as though he were bequeathing it. The boy, it appeared, was to be his heir. But if this were understandable, and even admirable, there was more which was neither: it soon became evident that his fond legacy to the square-jawed youth was to extend beyond what the little Irish outlaw called "the stultitrifling limitations of the honest cow business."

The primary step was to teach the boy the beauties and the dangers of "the rustler's brush," the so-called straight or running iron with which a good arroyo artist could reburn almost any brand

12

into almost any other brand, barring close inspection. However, merely being caught with such an iron on open range could lead to the long rope and the high limb sans legal discussion; therefore its use, its true high use, must do better than to pass a roundup glance through herd dust at fifty feet.

Mike taught George LeRoy to run over a brand so beautifully—the heat just so and administered through a wetted saddle blanket—that even a range court trial, where the suspected animal was killed and skinned-out on the spot, would draw blank. The work of the common wielder of the straight iron showed either no mark at all under the burned hide, or a scar mark which did not match the keloided tissues of the original burn or brand.

The risk was, of course, that the skinning-out by the irate rancher, or the local posse, would occur too soon after the added artwork, thus exposing a freshly healed scar ridge. But given a few weeks, the Mike Cassidy method (as the old outlaw called it) would result in an inside scar that would stand up in any range court.

They had used up six of the Sevier ranch steers to perfect this art in young George LeRoy, and this had concerned the boy. But Mike had told him not to worry; what the Lord took away, he would three-fold replace. As a matter of fact, such replacement miracles were the next order of learning. Throughout that autumn, when the cattle were fat and the trails dry and hard and at their best for not showing where two visiting riders had spirited away a few head of stock never bred near Sevier River—and when the first snows of winter could not be far away, snows which would cover all trails until the next spring—then it was that old Mike got back those six steers for the Parker spread. And not three times over, as he had promised. When he and George LeRoy turned out their hidden bunch on Parker grass, they had thirty-seven head of prime cattle, not one of which came from within Circle Valley, and not one of which came from more than a day's ride outside of it. They had been gathered three, four, five at a time, and with each trip the old rustler and the boy had not been away from the homeplace more than one night. Each gather was made in a different area, each planned a different way. But all the stolen animals had been put in the same high draw far back of the Parker place and held there until their new brands healed and they were ready to be scattered down onto the valley-floor pastures of Maximilian Parker's Circle Four Ranch on Sevier River.

The very name of the Parker place was taken from the fact of the good year, and good luck, which the new ranch seemed to have had under the foremanship of Mike Cassidy. The "Four" came from the number of letters in the reformed badman's first name; it was the idea of George LeRoy, the grizzled sinner's apt and eager pupil.

So the first winter began, and wore quietly along. No repercussions came from the stolen cattle, and young Parker was scarcely impressed with the dangers or disadvantages of permitting the other fellow to raise the calf and grow-out the steer for old Mike and himself.

When a boy as bright and quick as George LeRoy was could be shown that the natural rate of increase by the bull-and-cow method could be quadrupled, or double-quadrupled, through the man-made Mike Cassidy system of "moonlight multiplication," then the old-fashioned way of leaving things to God and some sore-footed old range bull became slightly ridiculous. Or at least most unreasonable.

That was the thing which really appealed to young Parker in evaluating Mike Cassidy's view of things: reason. Logic and common sense always had the greatest appeal for him. It was why the beliefs of the Saints, or the Shoshoni Indians, or the Catholic padres of the Church, which had spawned his bow-legged mentor, were beyond acceptance. They just didn't make sense to the grinning, infectiously friendly young cowboy from Circle Valley. Mike Cassidy made sense, however. And more than sense. Mike Cassidy made money.

So far, young Parker had not seen any of that money. The rustling they had done before that first winter lull enforced its snowbound halt had all been in the nature of experience, of teaching and learning, and of simply replacing the materials used up in the course by borrowing them from half a dozen ranchers within a day's "wide loop" of the Sevier. But now the methods had been shown and the first course completed. It was time to graduate, to pull off a money job and cash in on all the hard months of instruction and conditioning. Very soon now, Cassidy promised, they would get to serious work. The boy learned how serious that work would be one day late in February.

He and his next younger brother, Dan, aged fourteen, were cutting stovewood outside the Circle Four bunkhouse. They lived there with old Mike, as there was no room for them in the main house. Maximilian Parker had sired a notable brood, thirteen children, of whom George LeRoy was the eldest. The two boys led an almost independent life with Mike Cassidy in the rickety log shack, a fact which did not seem strange to them. In the Mormon scheme, closely colonized yet separate dwellings were commonplace, even though the Saints were as insistently individualistic as the Plains Indians. Theirs was indeed a tribal commune, much like that of the red man whose lands they had pre-empted and were seeking to make productive.

While both the Parker boys shared the bunkhouse with the one-time outlaw, Mike Cassidy neither approved of nor trusted the younger brother. Dan Parker was big and heavy framed, like his sire. He also had the elder Parker's plodding, all-serious outlook, but lacked his father's intellect and acuity. Cassidy, no less than most small men, resented

men of superior physical bulk and he transferred
the dislike to big stalky boys. Moreover, he insisted,
speaking professionally, that such "overgrowed stock
could not keep up with the herd." They could not
stand the gaff of trail and hardship that tougher-
made smaller men could.

Of these arguments George LeRoy was, of course,
not informed. Cassidy was much too smart to imagine he might safely discuss Dan with his older
brother. Blood, he knew, was a thicker bond than
the thin water of danger which held thieves together, or was supposed to. The risk was greater, as well,
in cases like these Parker boys, where the younger,
serious one was convinced that the older brother,
who was actually of wild and chancy character, was
the greatest thing to come down the long dusty
since the Angel Moroni, or at very least since
Bishop Brigham.

No, old Mike's opinions of young Dan were
held close, like the four cards kept when drawing to
an inside straight in a game where the stakes were
table variety and could go as high as a man might
care to back them. And old Mike was playing a high
game with the older boy.

George LeRoy didn't know it until that February morning when Mike Cassidy, looking toward
the sunrise over the snow-clad shoulder of South
Table Mountain, saw that the skies were clear as far
as the eye could reach into the eastern outland
stretches of Wayne County and the wild country.
He knew the trails would be open and hard-frozen,
and he knew, too, that this was the day for George
LeRoy's big test.

"George LeRoy," he said, after calling the youth
away from the woodpile were he and Dan were
working, "get rid of the kid as soon as you can. Me
and you are going for a ride."

The older brother first knew a strange excitement, for he could sense the vibrant tone in the
foreman's order. But then his square-jawed face lost

its bright grin. The blue eyes turned sober. "Dang it!" he said, "I don't know, Mike. Paw's told us to get in all the kindling we can whiles the weather holds. He ain't going to like it if I go to running off with you. How's about tomorrow, or the next day?"

Mike Cassidy rolled his rice paper cigarette around the perimeter of his mouth, settled it droopingly in the left corner. "LeRoy," he said, "at times you disappoint me."

The boy didn't care to do that, not ever. He began a defense of his argument, but Mike gestured him down.

"Ain't I told you often enough that ninety-eight percent of any job is laying it out right and proper?"

"Sure, but—"

"And ain't I told you that the two percent of pulling the job is like falling through a ready-cut hole in the floor? Now you think I done come out here and say to you to cut your choring and come along with me, without I've took good care of your daddy long gone?"

"I guess. I'm sorry, Mike."

"Sorry won't feed the sheepdog, LeRoy," chided Cassidy. "I told your daddy I needed some help to go up on the back range looking for any weak or snowbound stuff of ours. Said we'd lay out tonight in that old lineshack up there under Table Mountain. Be back late tomorrow. I calculate that ain't too much of a devious deposition. I like your daddy. He's square. Kind of stupid, but square."

"He's at least that," said young Parker. "But what about Dan? What'd you tell Paw for a stretcher to take care of Dan?"

"Dan is your part of the plan. I never said nothing to your daddy about Dan. Just me and you, boy."

"But Dan will want to drag along."

"Sure."

"Well, what'll I tell him?"

"Tell him nothing," said Cassidy, suddenly hardening. "If you can't get shut of a fourteen-year-old boy who's your own blood and trusts you, you ain't got no business going with me where I'm aiming to take you. Faith, now, and maybe I've made a bad mistake about you all along."

"But Dan's my brother. I'm supposed to look after him."

"Well, that's just fine. I hope you enjoy such work. Get in a lot of that wood, now, and make your daddy happy and your little brother love you." Cassidy turned away toward the corral and his saddled pony. "I'll drop by the house and call in to your daddy that you ain't in the mood for trailing-out snow-caught cattle," he called over his shoulder.

George LeRoy hesitated a minute, frowning. He didn't stampede. He didn't shout after Cassidy. He stood there only to think. Then he wheeled about and headed for the woodpile.

"Dan," he said, "Paw's ordered me to ride out with Mike and look out for them two-year-old steers up there in the high pasture timber. Wants them shoved down to the valley again. Thinks likely this last snow might have drifted some of them in, up there. Hate to quit on you like this."

The younger boy dropped his ax. "No need of that," he said. "Just hold on till I fetch my blanket and catch-up my horse."

"Can't be did, Dan. Paw says one of us got to stick with the kindling. Now you know that ain't no job for the eldest."

The other youth reached wearily for the ax. "I reckon," he said. "When'll you be back?"

"Tomorrow, late."

"You sure Paw said I had to stay and chop stovewood?"

"Only telling you what Mike said."

"Well, he don't always stick to the Bible."

"You want to check it out, Dan?"

"Well, not if you say it's so."

"All right, did I check it out when Mike told

me?" George LeRoy spread his arms with a purity of expression the devil himself could not have suspected. "You want to check up on me, you go right on ahead, Dan. I ain't got no Bible handy to go to vowing on, you know."

Dan Parker sniffed a bit, shook his head and turned back to the woodpile. "Golblasted kindling," he said, and began swinging at the wood before him as if to kill it piece by piece.

4

♦

George LeRoy stopped short, staring in surprise at the horses standing ready at the corral. His own cobby brown was already saddled for him. But Spook, the old white gelding which Cassidy ordinarily rode, was nowhere to be seen. In the gelding's place the little cowboy had saddled Escalante, another brown horse but no range-scrub such as George LeRoy's pony, Chunk, or Cassidy's disreputable Spook. Escalante was Maximilian Parker's number-two personal horse, and only Kanab, the big bay, could outdo him. And that brought the boy to the third horse, the one which Cassidy had rigged with pack-saddle and supplies. That was the real startler.

It was strange enough that old Mike had seen fit to take any pack animal at all along for such an easy overnight ride. But to put a top trail horse like Kanab under a pack was more than George LeRoy could accept.

"Mike," he breathed, looking toward the ranch house, "Paw will kill you. He will run you clean over the San Rafael Swell and into Green River.

Them's his best horses! And putting Kanab under a packfork! Mister, he won't kill you. He'll stake you down and torture you to death."

The little cowboy also eyed the ranch house. "Well, he might, at that," he consented, "providing you're going to stand there and auger it all morning. But if you'll leg up on that potbellied wolfbait of yours and heel him on out of here, I reckon we'll get by with it."

"Oh, no!" said the boy. "We don't take them horses without I know you got Paw's permission. Maybe you got other bed and board awaiting you, but I got to live here."

"Who says you do?" asked Cassidy coolly. He handed the boy the reins of the brown pony. "You'll be seventeen years old in another few weeks. Look around you, boy. This your idea of where you want to spend your declining years?"

George LeRoy took the reins. He glanced about the barren ranch yard, the icy corals, the square ugly clapboard specter of his father's house. He looked down the wandering wagonruts of the road toward the central flats of Circle Valley. Except for that scraggle of timber along the Sevier, there was no greater landmark or beauty dot than the occasional hummock of rabbit grass or stunt sage showing like a screwworm boll beneath the endless skin of the snow. The wind, prowling around the log wall of the corral horse shed, rattled the frozen leathers of his chaps, blew a dust of dry snow up his bare leg, under the cuff of his overalls. "No, sir," he said. "I guess not."

"Nor me," nodded Cassidy, swinging up on Escalante. "Come on."

The boy mounted up and followed Cassidy. They went skirting the corral and shed and then behind the rise beyond the ranch buildings to get into the river timber without being in direct view of the house, or the bunkshack, where Dan still flailed away at the stovewood pile. Staying with the river trail, they set out toward South Table Mountain and the upper pasture, which Cassidy had told Maximilian Parker they intended to check out. But where the land rose up to meet the Sevier Plateau, the little cowboy turned southward, taking a side-entering cattle track, which George LeRoy knew led neither to South Table nor the upper pasture. Kicking Chunk in the flanks, he moved him around Kanab and up to the side of Escalante and old Mike. "Where we bound?" he said.

Cassidy spat away the cold shuck of his dead cigarette. He grinned in that bright, quick way, so much like George LeRoy's, and winked broadly. "Got to make a little detour, kid," he said. "Traveling costs money and we're going to do some traveling. I figured to make a small loan from a feller I know in the banking business at Panguitch."

"Panguitch? That's twenty-seven miles from Circleville by the main road."

"Yep, and about thirty-five the way we're aimed."

"Well, good Lord, Mike, how come we need money to chase a few cows down off the bench? You got something in your mind that you ain't told me, much less my Paw?"

"That's right, LeRoy," agreed Cassidy. He halted his horse, got down from him and went over to Kanab. "Come on, give me a hand. We're going to switch this pack over to your scrub."

The boy dismounted and the changeover was made quickly. Remounted on Kanab, he and Cassidy rode on, the little Chunk horse bringing up the rear with the pack. After a mile of silence George LeRoy looked over at the old cowboy on Escalante.

"Mike," he said uneasily, "you mind telling me how come we got these here two top horses under us?"

Cassidy grinned. "Oh, two, three reasons," he said. "For one thing they're both everyhorse-colors, a brown and a bay, with no blazes nor tall socks to mark them special. For another thing they ain't ours, ain't yours and mine, that is, like old Spook and Chunk are. Number three, there ain't likely two other horses twixt hither and yon which can out-go them, happen we need to call on them. You know, this here's wintertime, boy."

"What the blazes you mean by that, Mike?"

"All part of the plan, boy, all part of the plan. You tooken a good look at that north sky since we set out?"

George LeRoy had not. But he noticed that the bright sun was now glazing over, getting that ice-filter look that it did when the weather was going to change and the air, curdling in front of the new storm's breath, was hazed with ice crystals over the high country. "By gum," he said, "there's a blizzard coming. And you knowed it all along. How come we are setting out when you knowed a big snow was coming down off the damned San Rafael? That ain't hardly like you, Mike, making a bad guess."

"It's like me, all right," said the little rider, "but it ain't scarcely no bad guess. It's more what you'd call a educated estimation."

"Like of what?"

"Oh, say of how long it may take us to get into and back out of Panguitch, as against how long it's liable to take that blizzard to whoop down off the Swell and go to piling deep enough."

"Deep enough for what?"

"To cover our track line."

"From who?"

"Try the Panguitch posse." He stared hard at the boy, then nodded to a clump of alder off the trail. "Tie your Chunk horse in there. We'll pick him up coming back, providing."

George LeRoy didn't flinch. "Providing?" he said.

"Yep, providing we come back."

"Oh." The boy led his horse into the clump, tied him, came back out. He stopped, looking up at

Cassidy. "In the dead of winter?" he said incredulously. "It ain't never been did!"

"Precisely," said the little cowboy.

"But, cuss it, them's our own people lives in Panguitch."

"Yours, maybe."

"Mike, it ain't right. A man don't take from his own."

"You ain't going to be taking, kid."

"But I'll be in on it!"

"Oh, you don't have to be," shrugged old Mike. "You can stay here with your horse iffen you choose." As he said it, he produced the long-barreled .45 Colt from beneath his sheepskin coat and looked it over. He put it back without another word or look, but George LeRoy was every bit as sharp and bright as the old bandit had thought him.

"I'll go," he said, and swung quickly up onto big Kanab.

The two horses broke into the rocking lope that such mustang-bred mounts could hold for miles without strain. Mike Cassidy flashed his tough, swift grin at George LeRoy Parker, and said, "Glad you took your smart-pills this morning, boy. For a minute, there, I thought I was going to need to give you a dose of something stronger."

"Shucks," said the boy, "a man's got to think. That takes time."

"Sure it does. I knowed that was all you was doing."

Cassidy winked as he spurred-up Escalante, and George LeRoy grinned back at him. But the blue eyes were not laughing and the short, square-jawed youth was still thinking. He had just seen how close together a grin and a gun could come in the outlaw business.

Old Mike could wink and smirk all he had a mind to, now. But back there a moment ago beside that alder patch, he would have killed George LeRoy

Parker if the boy had hesitated or given him a word of argument.

The boy had also learned that the side of that alder clump was way too late to be thinking things over. He had passed the going-back point with old Mike Cassidy that very first day on the ranch, when he had not told his father that the limping cowboy had never moved his duffel out of the Sevier River bunkhouse.

It had been a wink and a grin then, the same as snow. But meanwhile, something else had been squeezed in between the two. It was the old man with the scythe.

5

◆

"**N**ow," said old Mike, "here is the way it's set to work."

George LeRoy nodded, feeling his heart pound. They were just outside Panguitch, in a little draw which covered them from the road and the town. It was nearing midafternoon. The boy thought surely they were too late, but even as he fretted, old Mike pulled out his solid gold railroad watch and squinted at it.

"Two-forty," he said. "Just right. We won't miss a dime of the day's receipts. All right: I ride in and go direct to the bank hitchrack. I tie-up and go in. Inside, I yarn with the teller about the weather, and the road to the next town south. I'm a horse buyer from Salt Lake. I give the teller the bogus bank draft I showed you, and whiles he's taking it in to get it okayed, I go up front of the bank and pull down the shades to show she's closed for the day.

"Meanwhile, you'll have follered me into town by about five minutes—that'll be the time it takes you to count to five hundred at a fair pace—and will have tied-up at the saloon rail acrost the street from the bank.

"Now, when you see me pull them blinds, that's your signal to come over and untie my horse and hold him ready for me. I will be out that door with the money blamed near immediate, as I am only going for what will be in the cash drawers. This is a light strike, like I told you. The whole idea is to get in and out with only the bank folks seeing me, and the minimum of others give time to look you over, outside. You got it straight now, LeRoy?"

"Sure. But why don't you leave the watch with me so as I can tell them five minutes exact? That counting don't seem too precise to me."

"A fat gold turnip like this," said Cassidy, holding up the railroad watch, "makes no end of good impression on a bank clerk drawing six dollars pay a week. A man pulls out this beauty with just the right amount of flourish, he's established more credit in three seconds than he could in a month of honest residence. You got to have class in this game, LeRoy. It's why I've tooken you along. You got class, boy. That simple, happy face of yours would never put a honest sheriff in mind of something he seen on a Pinkerton flyer. I figure you to make the best outside man since Babyfat Mattoon."

George LeRoy had never heard of Babyfat Mattoon, but the reference to the latter disturbed him. "What you mean *since* this here Babyfat feller-er?" he asked.

Cassidy grinned and put away the gold watch. "Well, Babyfat lost his amateur standing last spring. Had to gun down two deputies outside the Gloriosa National Bank, over to Colorado. The gunfire drawed a crowd and quite a few citizens got too good a look at Mattoon. He ain't been much use since as a outside man. Too bad; he was a beauty. Thirty-eight years old and no taller than you was a last year. Something wrong with his innards. Never shaved nor growed old. Well, anyways, not till last fall."

"Oh?"

"Yep. Some of the boys got the bright idea to hit the Gloriosa bank again, figuring nobody would reckon they'd do it twict. Specially using Babyfat as a horse holder again. Well, somebody figured it. Mattoon aged quick. The citizens opened up with the biggest barrage since Shiloh or Cemetery Ridge. I hear they dug enough lead out'n Babyfat to start a new vein and sell stock."

"You mean they kilt him?"

"That was the rumor, LeRoy. Course the boys only read about it in the papers. They didn't linger to inquire."

"What boys was them?" said George LeRoy, beginning to cool a bit, and not alone from the icy whip of the wind up the draw.

"The McCartys. Now sure you've heard of them."

The boy had indeed heard of the McCartys. They were *the* bank and train robbers of the area. Rumored to be related to the fabled Jesse James and Cole Younger bands of Missouri, they were a blood brotherhood of the same clannish, tigerish breed as the Missourians. Or so ran the Utah, Colorado and Wyoming reputations of the "desperate McCarty Brothers," mention of whom had just now rewarmed George LeRoy's resolve.

"Jings! The McCartys! Say, don't tell me you have rode with them. With the *real* McCartys! Jings!"

"Naw," shrugged Cassidy. "*They* rode with *me*."

"Jehoshaphat, that's somewhat!"

George LeRoy breathed it more like a prayer than a statement of shivering fact. But the old outlaw beside him had no time left for amens. "All right," he said, wheeling Escalante, "I'm gone. Now make your count calm, and keep old Kanab down to a jingle-trot coming into town. Grin and nod, happen anybody on the street looks twict at you."

"Wait!" called the boy. "How about if I've missed the time a bit, or if you're slow in getting them blinds down? I mean, what if I got time to waste? I can't just set up there on old Kanab grinning and nodding at every tom fool comes along."

Cassidy checked his mount a moment. "Smart," he said. "I always knowed you was smart. That's how come I've already told the boys you'd likely do as our next outside man."

"Lordy!" said George LeRoy. "For the McCartys?"

"Why not? You'll beat Babyfat. He was stupid."

"Lord, Lord, the McCartys."

"Forget the McCartys, LeRoy. It's me and you that counts right here. You need something to do to stall in the street, you clean the snow out of your horse's hooves, you tighten your cinch strap, mess with the length of your stirrup leathers, anything that's natural twixt you and Kanab." He checked his own mount again. The animal was getting nervous. He pulled out the watch once more. "Blast it, we've talked four minutes over the plan. Now you'll go quicker on the count. Make it only three hundred. Watch sharp, leaving the draw here. Get on the road when nobody else is coming. Keep your side-eyes on them winder blinds. Hee-yah, horse, get out of here."

He was gone then; George LeRoy was left alone with his conscience and the cold wind of the draw.

"I don't know," he worried aloud to the big bay, Kanab. "It still don't seem right robbing your own folks." Kanab whickered softly and rubbed his head against the collar of George LeRoy's sheepskin coat. "Dang it all," said the boy, and began to count to three hundred.

6

◆

Robbing the bank at Panguitch was easy. The idea of taking it in February, with everything and everybody snowed-in, or assuming they were, was original thinking. Even George LeRoy had understood that. To knock over a bank in midwinter was unheard of. It spoke volumes for the professional skill of old Mike Cassidy. Or so George LeRoy silently prayed, as he headed Kanab down the main street.

Over at the bank hitchrail he could see Escalante tied, his bank humped to the whistle of the wind. Panguitch was no different than any Utah town. There was nothing in the frozen mud of the mainstem to stop the wind. Nothing, anyway, higher than the heaps of horse droppings which dappled the ridgy mud of the wagonwheel ruts. George LeRoy watched those horse droppings with a great deal of interest, and the scanning let him relax a little. He did not spot a single heap which was smoking. This told him that no one on horseback had gone by during the past few minutes. The street

30

was just as deserted as it looked. Good. He glanced again at Escalante and the bank's hitchrail. The brown gelding was humped to the wind like he had been there all day; his shaggy coat was burred with snow crystals, rendering his identity exactly the same as the half dozen other horses tied at various rails up and down the street. Say, wasn't it something to be in on a job with an artist like old Mike? This was really living. Spooky as sin, riding alone down that empty street, sure. But in a minute he would be turned in at the saloon, and Kanab would stand like Escalante was, quiet and snow-covered.

"Now, boy," he murmured to the big horse, and heeled him to the right. Kanab drew up at the saloon hitchrail and stood without command. George LeRoy sat him a minute, then slid off and stood by his side. His back was to the bank. He did not dare take a look around in that direction—not right off. But, oh, Lord, how he wanted to!

He fussed a bit with Kanab's bit chains, shortening them. The bay walled his dark eyes at him as though to inquire what the devil was wrong with those chains the way they were. George LeRoy stroked his muzzle and peeled some ice out of his nostrils, and the horse whickered in his throat and pawed with his off-forefoot to show his gratitude.

Two men came out of the saloon. Holy smoke! One of them was Sheriff Rasmussen of Garfield County. He knew Maximilian Parker and George LeRoy Parker, and they knew him. The boy squatted beside Kanab and picked up the off-forefoot with which the big bay had been pawing. The sheriff stopped and came over. There was a terrible silence behind George LeRoy while he crouched there, holding up the bay's forefoot.

Snow crunched behind him. The sheriff had stepped into the street, was standing squarely at his shoulder, stooping down. "Yeah," the boy heard the familiar deep voice say, "got snow-ice caked in the frog, eh? Well, dig it out of there, boy. Don't want nothing to lame-up a nice horse like him." He straightened and slapped Kanab on the rump.

George LeRoy buried his face in the collar of his sheepskin, straining to lower his voice. "No, sir," he said. "Sure don't." He didn't dare say another word, and he was lucky. He didn't need to. The sheriff crunched on away. But, suddenly, the man wasn't going back to the saloon side; he was angling across straight toward the bank! George LeRoy could watch him go, still crouched at Kanab's feet, looking under the horse's hairy belly. Now what? Did a boy cut and run on his own? Did he shag after the sheriff and take him up in smalltalk, revealing his identity in the act? Oh, Lord, it was too late for anything: the lawman was heading straight for Escalante. He had spotted the strange, unattended mount in front of the bank, and was going to check him out. George LeRoy got up and grabbed for Kanab's mane to vault up in the saddle. Then he and his runaway heart got a reprieve. Sheriff Rasmussen crunched right on past Escalante. He went down the boardwalk, south of the bank, and disappeared in the stormdoors of a hotel.

George LeRoy let out a breath, which he must have been hoarding a minute and a half. "Lord God," he sighed to Kanab, "I don't need another squeak like that this afternoon." His eyes went to the bank, his heart beginning to pound again as he saw one of the shades in the front windows go down. He pulled Kanab away from the rail by the reins, got a foot in the stirrup, eased up on him and started him across the street toward the bank hitchrail and Escalante. The schedule was moving. From the elevation of the saddle he could see into the bank; old Mike was walking toward the other window shade. The outlaw had not yet pulled his gun. The bank was quiet; no other people were moving about in the front of it, anyway. Evidently the clerk had done exactly what Mike had predicted—gone back to the rear office with the draft Mike had presented for cashing. Say, this was easy after all. It made Mike look better and better. Another minute or two and ...

"Hey, LeRoy! Hey, George LeRoy! Wait up, it's me!"

It was a dream, a nightmare. He was hearing things. He had to be. But he turned and looked down the street toward where the dream-shout seemed to be coming from, and then he wasn't only hearing things, he was seeing them. For a dread instant, George LeRoy hesitated.

In that instant he saw two other parts of the nightmare come together. Down at the hotel, Sheriff Rasmussen was coming out onto the street again, toward the bank. Inside the bank, old Mike was reaching for the second window shade, and the clerk was returning from the banker's office waving the bad draft and saying something testy to Cassidy. The little outlaw dropped his hand toward the long-barreled Colt, which George LeRoy knew lay just under the sheepskin coat. The sheriff was thudding up the boardwalk. And that third thing, that bad-dream voice, was yelling closer now from the middle of Main Street, "Hey, ain't that you, George LeRoy?"

George LeRoy did not think. He just jumped off Kanab in one leap that landed him on the boardwalk, where two more jumps put his pug nose right up against the bank's other window, just as Cassidy's left hand laid hold of the shade to pull it down. The old cowboy had his body turned away from the window to face the upset clerk, and his right hand was continuing that long slide toward the Colt's handle.

"Mike!" bellowed George LeRoy against the frost-rimmed glass.

The little outlaw swung around, away from the clerk, facing the window and the street. The boy outside only pointed desperately up Main Street, twisting his short, thick body to hide the gesture from the approaching sheriff.

Mike, with the true predator's instincts for survival, never questioned the lookout's hand signals. He shot his own faded blue eyes up Main Street in one smooth stab, and saw what George LeRoy had seen in his nightmare. Only the old bandit knew it was no nightmare, no bad dream, but only one of the worst-crazy breaks of outhouse luck ever to hit a bank heist in mid-stretch. For the shouter was much nearer to the bank hitchrail now, and there could be no doubt of his identity or of his bloodline.

That was young Danny Parker jogging up to his brother at the hitchrail of the Panguitch Bank of Commerce. And he was jogging up on Spook, Mike's old white cow horse, known in all of South Utah and ten counties of Wyoming and Colorado; behind Spook, he was leading Chunk, George LeRoy's pony and sometime packhorse supposedly tied short and hard back in an alder grove beside the Sevier Plateau trail.

But old Mike had class. He sharked away from the second window shade, bathing the irate bank clerk in a buttery grin. "The slant of that late sun is something fierce," he said. "I trust you don't mind me pulling that south shade, mister teller. Now dear me, I can see from your face there's trouble. Don't tell me, it's that pesky Salt Lake City draft. Am I right? Of course. I knowed it the minute I let that Kansas City drummer pass it on me."

The clerk had other thoughts. He had seen Sheriff Rasmussen pull up outside to talk to the Parker boys, and he was of a mind to clear the bogus draft and its would-be passer with the law, direct. Mike was a mile ahead of the teller. The outlaw seized the draft from him and raced out the bank door, yelling for the sheriff. He started to run right on past him, waving the draft and galloping for the jail office across the street. It was George LeRoy who reached out and caught him by the arm and told him where the sheriff was. Mike recovered gallantly, and before the bank teller could even clear the door, he was urging the Panguitch officer to get out a Garfield County bench warrant for the rascal from Kansas City. Rasmussen, kind but firm, was explaining the difficulties involved in a citizen of Cassidy's record signing a complaint against anybody, when the teller panted up to the group and made his play to incriminate old Mike.

It was too late in the afternoon for that.

After giving the sheriff a description of the Kansas City drummer, Cassidy and the two Parker boys were released and advised to get on home before the big snow set in. The clerk was advised to cease and desist in his defamation of the Sevier Ranch cowboy's intent: it was one thing to make such allegations about the old drifter, but these here were Bishop Parker's grandsons with him, and their paw was well known to four counties roundabout, and personally to Sheriff Rasmussen for the hog's share of sixteen years, give or take six years, so scat and shut up!

It was nonetheless a grimly silent expedition which set up the Circleville road for the return to the home ranch. George LeRoy was scarcely any more entertained than was Mike Cassidy by the details of Dan Parker's remarkable ride to catch up with them.

The younger boy, however, insisted on explaining how he had discovered that old Spook was still at the ranch, and how he had thought of borrowing him. This was, naturally, only after he had gotten permission from Maximilian Parker to join Mike and George LeRoy in their hunt for the snowbound cows. And then he explained how he had so luckily spotted old Chunk tied in the alder clump and knew right off that the little horse had somehow gotten loose from them; he thought that some friendly passing rider had caught him up and tied him there for his owners, so that when they should come back looking for their lost horse, old Chunk would be there for them. But then Dan had figured, all on his own, that he would just unrope old Chunk and lead him on along with him, so as to save Mike and brother LeRoy the need for looping back to pick up the little horse, the weather having turned off so miserable and mean, and all.

"Dan," interrupted George LeRoy at last, his blue eyes as fish-cold as those of old Mike Cassidy, "you say one more word and I will shove it so far down your gullet it will come out your ventpipe. Don't think and don't talk. Just ride along and stay quiet."

7

◆

The story which Maximilian Parker got was simple. Mike and George LeRoy had found the cattle they had thought to be stranded in the high pasture along the upper river instead. So rather than turn back to the ranch, they had decided to ride in and look around Panguitch, neither having been to town in three weeks. They had left Chunk in the alders just to spare the little horse from use, intending to pick him up on the way home, or to send Dan out for him from the ranch. The mix-up at the bank was passed off as a cowboy joke that Mike pulled on both the banker and the sheriff, one which had worked "near as good as if they'd cashed the draft." The elder Parker was neither amused nor convinced. Young Dan did not tell exactly the same story, and there was no need to borrow Escalante and Kanab for the original trip to the high pasture. But Maximilian Parker was not a hasty man. When he had time to go to Panguitch, he would have a talk with his old friend Nils Rasmussen. Maybe old Mike Cassidy had reformed. Maybe the bogus draft was a bad bunkhouse joke. But even a simple man with little humor could see that something was crooked in the story other than the back-way track line laid by his son and the old outlaw.

Mike Cassidy understood this very quickly. "We been smelled out," he told George LeRoy. "If that knucklehead Dan wasn't your brother, I would part his hair with the posthole auger. Your paw ain't stupid. He knows I aimed to knock over that bank. Likewise he knows you wasn't along for the exercise. Tonight, boy, your uncle Michael is moving on."

"Where'll you go?" They were brushing out Escalante and Kanab in the horse shed. Through the open door of the shed they could see Dan at the woodpile. His orders were like theirs: clean up your day's work. What you start on this place, you finish. Dan had a lamp to work by, as they had in the shed. There would be no supper for any of them until six hours of work had been put in. It was eight P.M. and they had four hours to go. Mike and George LeRoy had to curry out and clean the hooves of every head of using stock in the home corral—twenty-three horses. Understandably, then, old Mike was in no haste to reply to his young companion's inquiry about his traveling plans.

But neither did the lateness of the hour leave the old outlaw undue time for contemplation. "Where'll I go?" he repeated, turning Escalante loose and shaking out his frozen halter rope to catch-up the next horse. "Hell, where can I go? Sheriff is sure going to find out I didn't get that bogus note off no Kansas City drummer in Salt Lake. Banker is sure going to make him do something about that. Your paw sure ain't going to deny them hot coffee and a hard-boiled hearing when they show up here. So where's that leave old Mike?"

"That's what I asked you," insisted the boy. "Where?"

Mike tied the other horse and began stabbing at

him with the curry-comb. "The Roost, I reckon,"
he said laconically.

"Naw," George LeRoy came to stand close to
him, his eyes darting to the open doorway. "Robber's
Roost? Up there crost the swell? You actually know
the trail?"

Mike Cassidy also checked the open doorway.
"There's three ways into the Roost," he said. "I can
ride any one of them backward and blindfold through
a blizzard."

"Jings!" George LeRoy listened a moment to
the cry of the wind outside the shed. "Happen this
storm keeps making like she is now," he said, "you
mighten have your chance to try it that way—through
a blizzard, I mean."

"Come on, kid," said Mike. "We got twenty
horses to go. I can't set out without something hot
in my belly. No, wait a minute. Maybe I can."

He was suddenly intent. George LeRoy, following the direction of his gaze, saw the riders coming
up to the ranch house. A moment later, Maximilian
Parker came out of the house, holding up a lantern
and hallooing the horsemen.

Cassidy pulled the lantern off the shed wall and
blew it out. "LeRoy," he said, "you know them
fellers?"

"Not from here, Mike. Big one looks like
Peterson, the one owns the next place south. Little
one could be that deputy from Circleville. Ain't
sure, but he's the right size and stands hump-
shouldered like him."

"There's telegraph wires in Panguitch, from
Salt Lake."

"Yeah, but none in Circleville."

"Don't matter. They've had time to ride it up
from Panguitch, happen it's us they're looking for."

"*Us,*" echoed George LeRoy, his throat con-
stricting.

"*Me,*" corrected the graying outlaw. "You can
claim you was led by the nose. LeRoy," his voice

took on the buzz it did when he was going to move, "you get on down there to the house. If you can learn what they're up to sneak out and pass it to me. If you can't get away, stall them long as you can. You haze Spook into the shed with the rest?"

"Yes, sir. He's agin the far wall."

"Where'd Dan dump my saddle?"

"I put it away for you; on its right peg in the bunkhouse."

"Get it, whiles I neck-rope old Spook."

George LeRoy started out the shed door, but froze in midopening. "Mike," he called back in the shed's darkness, "lookit yonder." Behind him, he could hear the outlaw run up and stand poised. The horsemen hadn't even dismounted. They were coming up the slight slope to the horse shed, walking their horses quietly. Behind them came Maximilian Parker, his lantern blown out and smoking in the cold air.

"Lordy, Mike, they got you. That *is* the deputy from Circleville."

"I know the little banty rooster," said Cassidy calmly. "Now listen, LeRoy, they ain't coming here to the shed. Their angle is on the bunkhouse. That's the only lamplight left, and they're figuring to jump us in there. They're onto us, that's certain."

"Maybe they ain't. They might be bound on some other business. Might just want to ask some questions, perfectly innocent."

"Maybe, kid. But that ain't Peterson with the Circleville deputy. It's that raw-bone buzzard from Panguitch, that big dumb cuss of a deputy of Rasmussen's. What'd he call him? Orville?"

"You're right, it is Orville!" breathed George LeRoy. "They really are a'coming for you."

"Well, they ain't on no church social with them Winchesters out of the scabbards and barred acrost the saddlehorns, boy."

"Lord, Lord, what'll you do, Mike?"

"Easy, boy. The minute they disappear inter the

bunkhouse, I'll slope out of this here shed on old
Spook and be long gone before they discover they've
jumped a empty nest."

"Without no saddle, nor nothing?" said the boy.

"Hardly without nothing, LeRoy," grinned the
ragged bandit. "I'll go with thirty years experience
and a good start. Funny," mused the little outlaw, "I
was just your age, coming seventeen, when I went
on the dodge first time." He slipped away in the
dark, returning almost instantly with the old white
gelding. The horse was neck-roped only, but was
owlhoot-trained to run bare of any tack, like a Ute
or Shoshoni buffalo horse. "Get back agin the wall
and stay out of the way, LeRoy. This looks like it's
going to go all right, but you never know. Tighten
up, now, they're pulling up at the bunkhouse."

George LeRoy tightened up, but not to the
stimulus of Mike Cassidy's injunction. Rather it
was to the shrill croak of Dan Parker's changing
voice raised in friendly greeting to the silently
approaching lawmen.

"Well, howdy there, deputy. You all a'looking
for George LeRoy and old Mike? They're yonder to
the horse shed. Ain't nobody in the bunkhouse but
the bedbugs. Ha, ha, ha!"

"Look out, kid!" hissed Cassidy at George LeRoy,
and went aboard the old white horse and drove him
out the open doorway of the horse shed. George
LeRoy, knocked down in the rush out the narrow
opening, hit the frozen earth hard. Before he could
regain his feet, the thunder of gunfire and the lance
of orange flame were splitting the ranch yard gloom.

8

◆

Through the dark and the drift of the gunsmoke, George LeRoy saw his father on the ground. Beyond his father, the big deputy, Orville, was still on his horse. Between Orville and his father, the small deputy, Charley Peel, sprawled with arms outflung, one boot heel still hung in his saddle's right stirrup. His horse, an old cow pony, stood tense but did not break. Somewhere across the yard and lost in the night, the thud of Spook's retreating gallop still echoed.

George LeRoy ran out of the shed to his father's side. But Maximilian Parker was already getting to one knee, unharmed. He had hit the snow, flat, at first gunshot. "Get holdt of Charley's pony," he told his son, and George LeRoy did so. His father followed him. "All right, Orville," he said to the big Panguitch lawman. "He's gone. You can get down now."

It sounded like sarcasm and would have been from any man save Maximilian Parker. For Orville Stodenberg was as frozen in the saddle as though iced there by the increasing wind. He had not fired

42

his Winchester, had not even lifted it or his hands from the saddlehorn.

"Orville," repeated George LeRoy, reaching up and tapping the deputy on the knee. "You all right?"

"He's all right," his father answered for the deputy. "But Charley ain't. He's bleeding bad. Damn you, Orville, get down and help me with Peel."

It was the only time in his life that George LeRoy had heard his father use profanity. It was probably the first time Orville Stodenberg had been cursed of late, too, for he had the reputation of being as mean as he was big. The combination, in any event, proved effective. The raw-boned deputy dismounted and carried little Charley Peel down to the main house. There they got him cleaned up and found he had been hit twice, the second shot having severed an artery in his leg that could have bled him white in ten minutes if left unstaunched. As it was, he would live, but he would not want to be traveling that night. They put him to bed in the back bedroom and he expressed his gratitude for the help, especially with the shutting off of the bleeder in his thigh. The nasty scrape along his forearm bone was not dangerous, but it would serve to remind him not to pull down on the outlaw likes of old Mike Cassidy at handgun ranges. Not while Charley Peel, or any other lawman, was trying to put his horse between Cassidy and where Cassidy wanted his own horse to go. Especially not on a dark night with snow blowing and by kerosene lamplight.

Indeed, such was the measure of his debt to Maximilian Parker that the Circleville deputy said that he would request Orville Stodenberg to stay over at the ranch until morning.

When the elder Parker wanted to know what was so gracious about that, the little deputy whispered to him—while Orville was eating in the kitchen— that the other deputy had been instructed by Sheriff Rasmussen to arrest and bring in both Mike Cassidy and George LeRoy Parker for questioning and possible charges of the attempted holdup of the Panguitch Bank of Commerce. Now perhaps by morning Stodenberg would have some kinder thoughts about arresting the boy, particularly since he had lost the main bird, and would agree to forget about taking the lad in.

This seemed eminently fair to Maximilian Parker, and he asked that nothing be said to George LeRoy until it was seen how things would work out. Charley Peel agreed, and called in Deputy Stodenberg. The latter grumbled a bit, but the blizzard was coming on fiercely outside and he had no noticeable stomach for bucking the drifts back to town that late at night.

"We'll leave it lay till daybreak," he grudged, "but I'm saying here and now that the kid will go in. He was in this thing up to his ears, and had he been anybody else's son but yours, Mr. Parker, Sheriff Rasmussen would have jailed him sure. He knowed the boy and Mike meant to take the bank; he just figured to let it go since no harm was did. It was me that wired Salt Lake and got the facts."

Maximilian Parker nodded. "I reckoned it was you, Orville," he said. "You always been quick to come down hard on the easy side of the street." He went out to the kitchen, the deputy trailing after him, demanding angrily to know what he meant by that remark. "Nothing," answered the rancher. "You'll bed down with the boys up to the bunkhouse. Coffee's on by five, bacon and beans by six. We don't waste the daylight hereabouts. You ain't up on time, you don't get fed."

Stodenberg glared at him. He took hold of George LeRoy, who came into the kitchen just then. He spun the latter around hard. "All right, badman," he growled at the boy, "forward march. Lead out for the bunkhouse."

Maximilian Parker stepped in fast. His hand came down in a chopping arc on the forearm of the

deputy. Stodenberg released the boy, bellowing in
pain. The youth's father pointed out the door. "The
bunkhouse," he said. "And keep your mouth shut
until morning."

For a moment it seemed the Panguitch lawman
would tackle the older man. But Maximilian Parker,
if not as big as the deputy was, was as tough as the
deputy was supposed to be. Orville seemed to understand that. "You didn't need to go cracking my
armbones," he complained. "All you got to do is
talk out. I can hear, you know; I got ears."

"I'm glad," said the rancher. "Goodnight, George
LeRoy."

"Goodnight, Paw. I'm sorry things got clabbered
up."

The boy and the Panguitch deputy went across
the yard together toward the bunkhouse. The youth's
mind was leaping ahead of their crunching boots.
Like Orville Stodenberg, he had ears and he could
hear. He had been eavesdropping at the bedroom
door and picked up every word between the deputy
and his father. Now his thoughts were trailing far
out into the night, after the vanished form of old
Mike Cassidy. How he wished the outlaw were
there to tell him what to do. One thing the boy felt
very certain of, though, and that was the risk in
letting himself be taken in. It was all right as long
as they were still on his father's ranch, and maybe
all right as long as they were still where little
Charley Peel could call the tune. But how about
after that cussed Orville had got on down the road
past Circleville, and into Garfield County, where
Charley couldn't gainsay him? Orville was mean,
even if he was yellow. Something told George LeRoy
Parker that it wasn't a good thing to go with the big
deputy tomorrow.

But where else was there to go? The answer
seemed to come with the lonesome shriek of wind
and the driving cut of the snow across the empty

ranchyard, and it was no answer at all. No place, it said; there was no place else to go.

But there was.

As they came up to the bunkhouse, the glow of the lamp from within cast itself out across the clean-swept snows of the yard. Off to their right, where George LeRoy had last seen the ghost form of old Spook skitter and go off whinnying wildly into the night, the boy now saw something else.

Under the slash marks of Spook's hooves here the old gelding had made the sidejump—there was something dark there. It looked black in the lamplight, and was like a spreading, seeping stain, with a splatter to begin it, then a line of splash drops, and then faded off into the darkness.

George LeRoy had seen such marks on snow before, and by lampshine. Those stains were red, not black—they were blood. Ole Mike, or maybe Spook, had been hit in that gunfire. Either way, that blood trail gave George LeRoy his answer.

He knew now where he was going, what he must do. As long as there was the chance the blood was old Mike's, no true friend of the little outlaw could remain safe and warm in the Sevier River bunkhouse. Somewhere out there, Cassidy could be lying helpless. His horse might be hit and down, and himself wounded, or even dying, and no one could do anything for either man or beast—not even pray.

It was the owlhoot code, old Mike had said, that no man left a wounded brother for the law. George LeRoy did not know about that. But he had his own code. Owlhoot or otherwise, the smiling, square-jawed youngster had never shirked the hard trail, nor sought the soft. Nor would he ever in his life.

They were almost to the ground rise in front of the bunkhouse door. It must be now. George LeRoy made a sudden move toward the woodpile. "Lord amighty!" He gasped and stood stock still, pointing behind the corded stovewood. "I can see a man's boots sticking out yonder, behind the pile!"

"What's that you say?" said Orville, edging about.

"Charley Peel must've hit old Mike," said George LeRoy. "Somebody's down and stiff, yonder."

The Panguitch deputy pushed past him, his Winchester poked forward. The boy reached down and picked up a piece of hard and heavy yellow pitchpine. The piece was two feet long, with a knob on the end where a branch had healed over and humped the wood. It made a solid, very absolute *thunk* when it hit the back of Orville Stodenberg's black Stetson. The big deputy went down meek as milk. He rolled over once and came to rest, face up, with his boots sprawled out behind the woodpile. George LeRoy nodded soberly down to him.

"Leastways," said the boy aloud, "I ain't a liar. I told you I seen boots a'sticking out, and I do."

9

◆

The boy's next concern was brother Dan. But a glance in the cracked-pane window of the bunk-house showed the younger lad motionless in his bunk. Whether or not he were asleep would have to be gambled for the moment. George LeRoy went quickly over to the horse shed, but he did not run. There he found the pack of supplies which Mike Cassidy had made up for their trip to the upper pasture. It was still where he and Mike had dumped it. Whatever food and utensils the little cowboy had put up for them might now make a world of difference. George LeRoy's schedule could not possibly include any visits to the main-house kitchen.

Luckily his Chunk horse was in the loose herd near the shed. He whistled him in and put the pack on him. Next was Kanab; the boy believed he must have the big bay and no other, not even Escalante. Escalante didn't have Kanab's soul. You couldn't sweet talk Escalante, whose eyes didn't shine with Kanab's inside fire. Kanab was Morgan and Arabbred, with some Standard Trotter for size and speed. He was the best horse George LeRoy had ever seen. Kanab could do anything—and in the run which the boy was now going to try to make, he might have to do just that.

He got the rangy horse into the shed with halter rope only, something not every cowboy could do in the middle of a winter night without stirring up the rest of the herd. But George LeRoy had the softest hand with a horse in Circle Valley. No one less than Mike Cassidy had said that, and Mike Cassidy was the acknowledged top-hand horsebreaker in South Utah.

Kanab never made a louder sound than a grunt; George LeRoy had him under saddle, with Chunk roped on behind, and led both of them past the bunkhouse inside of ten minutes.

But just past the bunkhouse, the boy stopped them. Dropping Kanab's reins, he said, "Stand easy; I'll be along in two shakes." Both horses only pricked their ears to follow his course back to the bunkhouse. Neither moved a step. They understood George LeRoy; he could talk to horses.

As for George LeRoy, he understood many things about men, as well as about horses. He understood that if you left a man unconscious out in winter weather like this arctic night, that man would never wake up. He had to get Orville Stodenberg in out of the cold, and he knew only one way to do it. He certainly couldn't move the deputy himself. Orville stood six-four and weighed two hundred and thirty pounds. George LeRoy was stout, but not all that stout. Moreover, even at pushing seventeen, life—life and old Mike Cassidy, that was—had taught him that more mountains could be moved with brains than could ever be budged by muscle.

A few seconds later, Dan Parker was sitting up in his bunk, rubbing his eyes. A terribly concerned George LeRoy told him that Deputy Stodenberg must have fallen over the woodpile in the dark. Old Orville was bad hurt out there. He was knocked colder than a pole-axed market beef, as a matter of fact. While George LeRoy got a blanket out to him, Dan must race down to the main house and fetch Maximilian Parker.

"No time for putting on nothing but your boots, Dan'l," the older boy told him. "Just figure how you'd feel if old Orville was to freeze solid because you tooken that extry minute to rig yourself out comfortable for the trip down to the house."

Dan was not only a serious boy; he was slow of mind. Now he only gulped and groped for his boots. Jamming them on, he fled the bunkhouse in his nightshirt, convinced that he was on the greatest errand of alarm since Paul Revere outfooted the British.

George LeRoy waited only for his brother to be three or four jumps gone. Then he grabbed Mike's saddle and bridle from their wall pegs and lunged out the bunkhouse door. Going around the corner of the little building, he broke into a weaving run, awkward under the burden of the heavy stock saddle. Coming up to his waiting horses, he threw the saddle on top of Chunk's pack and tied it in place with a calf-roping piggin string, which he had already prepared and carried into the bunkhouse in his teeth. The saddle secure, he leaped aboard Kanab and drove his heels into the big bay.

Kanab responded with a snort and a jump that nearly beheaded the dozing packhorse, Chunk. The latter managed to recover and get into stride, although badly over balanced by his topheavy load. Before Dan had awakened the lower house, George LeRoy and the two horses had disappeared over the rise into the river timber.

By the time that Orville Stodenberg was carried into the bunkhouse and revived enough to tell the story of what had brought him to such low station,

George LeRoy was not only twenty minutes on his way, but the blizzard had begun to really bellow. Stodenberg was plainly in no condition to ride, and somber Maximilian Parker quietly refused to go after his son, either then or later.

"LeRoy will come back," he said. "He always has."

PART TWO

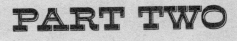

The Ride
for
Robber's Roost

10

♦

Through the thickening fall of the snow, George LeRoy saw a dark patch lying in the snowbank beside the river trail. At first it looked so small that he would have ridden by it, but a second glance showed him that the dark object was the huddled form of Mike Cassidy.

The next moment he was kneeling beside Mike, trying to arouse him. As he pleaded for the little cowboy to awaken, he heard Kanab whicker softly. At once, he was alert for pursuit. But Kanab's whicker was answered by another whicker, and it was only old Spook ambling up to inspect the newcomers from the refuge he had sought in the nearby willow thicket.

"Wisht you could talk," George LeRoy greeted him. "But leastways you've give me a good idea."

He took Cassidy by the feet and began sledding him over the snow into the willow thicket. Unbidden, all three horses followed. The boy knew that he must risk a fire now to boil some water and make coffee. Getting something hot into old Mike was the first, life-saving thing. Not only was the

stimulant of the dark brew vital, but without fire-
side warmth he would not dare undress the man
enough to locate his wounds.

Outside the thicket the wind was building gale
force. The boy had covered five or six miles since
leaving the ranch. It was yet another five or six
miles to the South Table lineshack, where George
LeRoy had already planned ahead to take Mike,
should he find him alive. What they would do once
that retreat was reached, he had not figured out.

He got his small fire lit swiftly, and soon had a
warming blaze lighting up the naked-trunk walls of
the thicket. In the pack on Chunk, he found the
coffee and the burned-black pot in which to boil it.
Before long, he had a vicious brew bubbling and was
forcing a tin of it down the reviving outlaw's throat.
With Mike conscious, he was able to peel off his
coat and shirt and get down to the inner layer of the
little cowboy's long-handled winter underwear.

The wound was painful and a considerable
bleeder—a raking shot across four ribs on the right
side—but had clotted already. With the coffee in
him and the warmth of the rescue fire, Cassidy
might be able to make it on to the shack.

"Easy, kid," the white-faced fugitive grinned,
"I've rode out worse storms than this, and I've cut
myself worser shaving. This ain't nothing. If you'll
boost me up on Spook, yonder, we'll be on our
merry way."

Once mounted on the white gelding, however,
the outlaw was forced to clench his teeth and claw
his hands desperately around the horn. "LeRoy," he
gritted, "you're going to need to lace me on. I can't
guarantee to take top money in this here ride, less'n
you do."

George LeRoy understood. He tied old Mike's
feet fast together with a rope passed under Spook's
belly. He also roped the little outlaw about the
waist and bound him hard to the saddlehorn. He
might be bled dead by the time they reached South

Table, or have his head caved in by a branch-stub hitting him along the trailside, but he would reach South Table in the saddle, and that was all either he or George LeRoy could hope for at the moment. They had to kick out the fire and get on. From here, it was the boy's stumpy strength and great courage, together with the heart and intelligence of the horses, that would see them safely to the lineshack, or dumped motionless into some drift on up the mountain, there to lie until spring brought the thaw, or the law.

Neither the boy nor the old outlaw joked about it. Once the last cherry-red coal of the fire had been sizzled into a black chair beneath the kicked-over snow, and George LeRoy had swung back up on Kanab, the time for laughs was past.

"Now, big horse," he said softly to the bay, "leave us see what you can do. Once out yonder in that full bow, it's going to be you against the mountain. I can point you up the South Table trail, and that'll be about it. From there, you make it on your own. Hee-yah!"

Kanab went out of the willows, into the deepening snows of the trail. Upward he forged, pulling behind him both Spook and Chunk, the white gelding roped to Kanab's saddle, the pack pony in turn tied to Spook's saddle. For two or three miles George LeRoy was able to discern the South Table trail and could know that big Kanab was not faltering or straying in the climb. But then the piling driftsnow blended with the new fall; it was all one whiteness. "Big horse," he said, "she's all yours."

Kanab seemed to comprehend the transference of full responsibility. He increased his lunging gait. He broke the drifts apart, climbing upward, neither hesitating nor wandering nor backing off, but going straight up old South Table. And in this way, unbelievably, through the worst snowstorm in recent South Utah memory, he came to the top of the rising bench behind the Sevier River ranch. He stopped at last, head down and blowing out thin blood through nostrils belled with exhaustion.

At first George Leroy thought the big bay had quit on him. He did not curse the horse, however. He leaned up along the drooping neck and whispered to him, "Never mind, old boy, you done your level best."

But Kanab, who understood this boy who talked to horses, lifted his head enough to roll a dark eye backward and whicker a querulous complaint against George LeRoy's flagging faith, before dropping his dark muzzle once more to the groundsnow.

"My God," said the youth, "you ain't done; you're just at the end of the run."

He slid stiffly down and stumbled forward through waist-deep snows, the going as blind as if into a white wall. But what he brought up hard against within three lurching strides was no white wall but the split-plank door of the South Table lineshack, and what he had gasped out the moment before was true; Kanab had not quit; he had just stopped because they were at the end of the trail, and they were saved.

Half an hour later, George LeRoy had the injured Cassidy in bed and a good fire warming the little plank and tarpaper shack. In another half an hour, he had the three horses stabled in the lean-to of bullpine logs and mountain-sod slabs, which attached directly to the shack.

He fried some fatback and made more coffee. The aroma in the little cabin was almost grand, and George LeRoy began to know some relief. He did not think anyone would follow them up the mountain that night, and with the morning they could make new plans. Mike seemed to be in good shape. He knew there was hay for the horses, because he and Dan had put in six summer weeks cutting and stacking the mountain fescue and timothy for the lineshack and for riders such as themselves, who might need to sleep up there during the winter months. So with the stock hayed down and old Mike fed and coffeed and gone on to sleep, a Circle

Valley boy might well take the time and pleasure to borrow the outlaw's tobacco pouch and rice papers and roll himself a reward-smoke—and maybe to grin a bit at how easy it had all been. This outlawing business might not pay as well as old Mike had advertised it did, but it was every bit as easy to pull off as the little cowboy had said it was. Nobody had gotten bad-hurt either. Why, heck, George LeRoy had seen more blood at a calf-castrating and more busted bones at a branding fire. There was really no reason at all, except for bad luck, that, with the same scratches and bumps, he and Mike couldn't be here in the same shack with a few hundred hard dollars, of Panguitch Bank money withdrawn the easy way, by Colt pistol passbook.

The boy's square, good-natured face lit up at the thought. It had not occurred to him down there in the willows. Or back at his father's horse shed, with the guns going off. Or when he had seen the dark stains of Cassidy's unknown wound spreading in the snow outside the bunkhouse, or Deputy Stodenberg's stiff boots protruding from behind the woodpile.

But now, with all that risk behind, George LeRoy sucked headily on his rice-paper cigarette and savored the victory of his first brief dash along the owlhoot trail. He did not remember the cigarette going cold between his lips, his tousled blond hair falling sideways, his muscular bowed legs and bone-weary arms going limp in sleep. All he remembered was that when he woke up, hours later, the gray light of day was staining the shack's tiny grease-paper window, and things had changed a great deal during the dreamless night.

11

◆

Old Mike's wound had reopened; he had bled all over the bunk and was as gray as a grilled fish. George LeRoy could not arouse him. All that he could do was to get his undershirt opened and then, when he saw the wound still seeping blood, take his knife and cut the shirt away. From there he had to treat the little outlaw no better than a lamb or calf which would not stop bleeding after castration. Building up the fire, he put his knife into it to heat the blade to cherry red. While the knife was in the fire, he went outside and up the slope to where some bullpines and small cedars stood sentinel above the shack. He scraped the lichen-like moss off the north sides of several trees, until he had gathered a hatful of the soft tissues. Then, sliding and leaping, he went down the slope again.

With the hissing knife blade he cauterized the gaping bullet slash in old Mike's side. The outlaw regained consciousness, moaning pitifully from the intense pain. He did not open his eyes, but gritted the tobacco-ruined stumps of his teeth and said,

"Burn it deep, LeRoy; you won't get another swipe at it." He meant that he was going to die if this treatment did not stop the flow of blood. George LeRoy knew this to be the truth, too. In his hard ranchboy's life he had seen both men and animals bleed to death. He understood that he must not let mercy interfere with his work.

Three times he reheated the knife. When at last the burning left no red flesh on the wound, and all of the tissues were literally cooked gray and blood-less, he packed the little bandit's side with a com-press of the moss. Over this he put a pad made by folding and refolding his own shirt. Then he bound the pad and the moss to the cauterized wound as tightly as he could, using strips cut from the lineshack blankets and wound completely around Mike's body and cinched down hard. "There she is, Mike," he said. "Don't move and don't breathe no more deep than a hibernating bear. I think we got her shut off."

All day the outlaw lay half-conscious. That night the boy sat by his side until the gray of the new day returned to the greasepaper window. It seemed that all had been for nothing, so quiet had the wounded man become; his color was pale and poor in the cold light of the dawn. But when the sun came a little later, while George LeRoy turned away from the bunk and wept from weariness and bitter disappointment, the outlaw opened his eyes.

"LeRoy," he said, "what you sniffling about? You catch a cold a'setting up with this old serpent?"

The boy turned around, hardly daring believe his ears. But his hearing was not playing him wrong. Old Mike Cassidy was grinning. He still looked whiter than a bellied-up trout and it would be a spell before he took to wrestling any bears, but he was grinning and he would get well.

"You know, kid," he said, the words costing him gasps of pain beneath the grin, "you want to kill a snake, you got to cut off his head. You can't just go busting up a few bones and blood tubes.

Remember that next time you want to bury yourself a badman."

George LeRoy made himself sneeze three or four times to take advantage of the excuse Cassidy had offered him. "By God, if I do catch cold, I will kill you," and went on to fry fatback and some bannock bread for the outlaw's breakfast.

When they had finished eating, old Mike wiped his mouth and lay back with a great sigh. "LeRoy," he said, "I owe you one."

It was all the reference he made to the fact that the boy had saved his life two times over. But he was not grinning when he said it. Come the time, far up the trail or over the mountain, where George LeRoy Parker would need to have the debt repaid in kind, it would be repaid.

It was the way of the owlhoot breed.

12

◆

The boy knew that no deputies would be out on horseback in that weather. The snow had continued to fall during the two nights and the wind stayed high. Drifts would be over a mounted man's boots. A search by his father might be made, but it would not go far. Where would the searchers look, once they had quartered the vicinity of the ranch house? The first night's snowfall alone had covered all tracks that he, Mike and their horses made in getting away from the homeplace. Even if Maximilian Parker should think of checking the lineshack, how would he get up South Table's base? Kanab had barely pulled them up there the first night, when the trail was only beginning to get deep. Trying to come up that mountain this second morning, a man would need to be a bird or a blamed fool. And besides, he knew his father.

"Paw won't come up here," he said to old Mike. "He won't come after me."

"How you so hard sure he won't?" It was noon-time now. The outlaw had awakened from his nap

63

feeling still better, but he was worried about pursuit. "I'd come after you if you was my boy."

"Ah," murmured George LeRoy, "that's just the difference. Paw raised me hard. He never saw no fun in life. He said, 'LeRoy, if you dig a hole and then fall in it yourself, you'll have to scramble your own way out of it. Elsewise you won't learn nothing about holes.'"

"So what?" frowned old Mike. "I don't foller you."

"Paw knows I dug this here hole we're in. I heard that damn Panguitch deputy telling Paw all about you and me and that bank job. The deputy had wired Salt Lake after Sheriff Rasmussen turnt us loose."

"Oh. So they found out there wasn't no Kansas City drummer?"

"Sure."

"That mangy Orville. Wouldn't it be just what he'd drool over, to stick me with that stupid Panguitch job? He'd been after the old sheriff's star for the past five years. You know something, LeRoy? I'll kill that outsize orangutan if he goes to pushing me again. We don't need no sheriffs like him. Old Rasmussen's all right. He knowed just as well as Orville did that we was going to heist that bank, but he's a man of reason and light. He figured it didn't make no sense trying to prove we was a'going to do something we didn't get done. But that Orville, I'll dot his eyes for him next time he so much as looks my way." He paused to regain his breath, still weak from loss of blood. "You know something else, LeRoy? If that blasted little brother of yours wasn't that blasted little brother of yours, I'd of knocked his head in with a ditch shovel first chance I got after we was home from Panguitch. I don't have no use for a stupid kid, no more than a stupid man. Him and that Orville ought to be kin, not him and your paw."

George LeRoy grinned. It was good to hear old

Mike hunching up his back and pawing the ground again. Moreover, there were times when he himself would have liked to use a shovel on his brother Dan. "I know what you mean," he said. "But I reckon we don't need to fret none about Dan and Orville, nor Paw neither. Them deputies was going back to town yesterday. And I'm dead certain, like I told you, that Paw won't trail me."

"You still say your paw will leave you in this here hole without even lacing on a snowshoe to cruise the lower slope?"

A moment's lull in the outer wind brought the mountain's silence heavily into the shack. The greasepaper windowpane ceased its hollow drumming. The plank door no longer rattled and banged against its warped frame. George LeRoy's voice sounded strangely loud in the unexpected stillness.

"Paw will leave me here," he said. "He wouldn't set foot to snowshoe, nor finger to lace-straps, to come after me."

The door of the shack flew open with a splintering crash, kicked-in from the outside. In its opened jaws stood Deputy Orville Stodenberg, his Winchester Carbine leveled at the astonished George LeRoy.

"Well, kid," said the giant deputy, "I ain't your paw, and here I am, snowshoes and all."

George LeRoy could see that. But it wasn't the fact of Orville having snowshoed up the mountain and sneaked in on them under cover of the blizzard's yammering which shocked him. It was the identity of Orville's happy-faced guide, standing now behind the deputy and waving a gloved hand in proud greeting, which completely unnerved the Circle Valley boy.

"Howdy there, LeRoy," announced brother Dan. "I told old Orville I could find you. I knowed percisely where you'd go."

George LeRoy groaned. He looked around at old Mike in the bunk behind him. The little outlaw was crouched as far back in the bedclothes as he

could get, his blanket gripped hard. He looked to
George LeRoy as though he was in the last throes,
where but the moment before he had been as chip-
per as a snow bunting rustling bread crumbs. The
grizzled rider now weakly gestured with his left
hand, the right hand being limp beneath the blanket. "Stand aside, LeRoy," he said. "It ain't no use
to try nothing. The deputy knows I'm bad-hurt, and
can't do nothing to side you. Come on in, deputy,
this here boy was only trying to help a poor old
cowboy what got hit and was bleeding-out fast. He
ain't no bandit, nor no bad man. I'm your bird for
that. I surrender."

Deputy Stodenberg stomped into the shack,
brother Dan following cheerfully. "I reckon I don't
need none of that bulljuice, Cassidy," scowled the
lawman. He heeled the door shut, keeping the
Winchester on the little outlaw. "Unlace my snowshoes," he ordered Dan. The boy kneeled quickly to
obey.

"Gosh, LeRoy," he beamed up at his older brother, "how come you ain't happier to see us? Heck's
fire, when old Orville told me you'd been bad-hit in
the gunfire and had surely run off to lay-up and die
like a crippled coyote, hell, I just told him to cease
off his worrying. 'Ain't but one place old LeRoy
would hole-up hereabouts,' I said. 'And I can guide
you up to it afoot, happen Paw will loan you his
snowshoes. I can borry old LeRoy's, seeing's he ain't
here. Ha, ha!'"

George LeRoy looked at his younger brother.
He was remembering old Mike's idea of the ditch
shovel in the head. "Glad you was thinking so clear,
Dan," he said. "Ha, ha."

"Shut up, the both of you," snapped Deputy
Stodenberg. Dan had by now freed him of the snowshoes, and he stepped around George LeRoy toward
the bunk and its pale occupant. "Cassidy," he warned,
"don't try nothing. You ain't got a chance."

As if to give the lie to his hard words, his

glance went nervously around the shack, and he stopped in midstride as though reminded of something. He knew that George LeRoy was unarmed, because Dan had already informed him that the older brother did not own a pistol and had not taken the old bunkhouse Spencer Carbine. But for a fateful moment he had neglected to locate Mike Cassidy's weapons, assuming that they were hung up out of the play. Now something cold had suddenly invaded his gut, and he was not so sure.

George LeRoy's eyes leaped to follow the big deputy's. Both glances pounced at the same time on the wounded outlaw's gun belt, where it hung over the back of the shack's only chair. Then the boy went tense and tight: the gun belt was still there, but its holster was empty.

In the remaining fragment of time, George LeRoy knocked Dan Parker to the floor, sheltering him with his own body. He did not see old Mike's hand move; the long-barreled Colt simply appeared above the blanket. The boy realized, even in that suspended fragment of waiting, that during one of the catnaps he had taken from his nursing of the wounded outlaw, Mike Cassidy had managed to get his weapon from the gun belt, not even trusting George LeRoy Parker.

Across the room, Stodenberg was whirling to bring his Winchester back on the bunk's supposedly helpless occupant. But the instant of carelessness was his last lesson on the long road to get Sheriff Nils Rasmussen's star. Watching from the shack's rammed earth floor, George LeRoy wondered at how things seemed to move as if in a dream. He had known the same feeling of unreality at the hitchrail of the bank in Panguitch, when brother Dan and Sheriff Rasmussen were bearing down on him, and old Mike was still in the bank pulling down the shades. Orville moved as if suspended in a bowl of molasses. At the bunk, old Mike behaved with the same fluid grace. It was like a dance, slow and graceful, yet strained in some terrible way, and that was right, too, for he was watching the dance of death.

He saw the spurt of flame lance from Mike's pistol. Almost as swift, the fire leaped from Orville's Winchester. But the deputy's shot went high into the sod roof over the bunk, and the outlaw's shot went home. Orville let the Winchester slide from his hands; his arms dropped slowly, straight down. He brought the empty hands back up to his face and placed them against his forehead. His movement was spasmodic, like a killed animal will lash out with a forefoot, or hitch up a hind leg, even though life is already gone. George LeRoy knew what had happened. He didn't look at the huge deputy when he sagged to the floor and lay face down, still pressing his forehead with both hands. He looked instead at the bunk across the room. The smoke was still weaving its thin blue coil upward from the muzzle of Mike Cassidy's gun.

"My God," said the boy, "you hit him square where you said."

Young Dan Parker got to his feet in the stillness and gawked down at the dead man. There seemed neither surprise nor revulsion on his slack-jawed face, only curiosity mixed with the same cautiousness with which a shot snake is approached by a boy with a probing stick. Young Dan squinted closely at Deputy Stodenberg. Reaching gingerly, he pulled the hat away from the lawman's head. Only then did he turn a little white, stand up, and step away.

"Gawd amighty, you've kilt him," he said.

Neither his brother nor the old bandit replied. They only looked at each other and then back at the stupid boy, who had brought death to Deputy Orville Stodenberg.

13

◆

Dan revealed that Maximilian Parker knew nothing of the snowshoe expedition to the South Table lineshack. Deputy Stodenberg had proposed the idea to the youngster as a rescue expedition to save the life of the supposedly wounded George LeRoy. How the latter had been wounded, or where he had been caught in any gunfire at the ranch, were not explained by the deputy, nor asked after by young Dan. The slow-minded youth had fallen in with the dead lawman's scheme, and Stodenberg warned him that his father would surely stop them were he to know of their journey. Again, no story had been needed to cover this threat. The mere thought that brother LeRoy was lying wounded and helpless on South Table's icy slopes had been all Dan required. The fact that George LeRoy had fled the ranch to escape the law, the same as old Mike Cassidy, was not the sort of negative thinking to which Dan Parker's mind was victim. He never did seem to understand that his own clumsy good intentions had set the fatal stage in Panguitch to begin with, and at the

South Table lineshack to end with. Both his older brother and Mike Cassidy knew better than to tell him this. The boy grieved even while thinking he had been a hero; let him know what a fool he really was, and God alone could guess at what idiotic thing his faithful brain would produce by way of amends.

When they had finished digging out of him all the information they might, they knew three things that could not be ignored: Stodenberg told Maximilian Parker that he meant to go to Circleville and send out help for Deputy Charley Peel, whose now infected wound needed medical attention; the injured Charley Peel had advised Parker (his own refusal to go after his son notwithstanding) that he, Peel and a Wayne County posse would have to follow George LeRoy as soon as the weather lifted. The toughening in the Circleville deputy's attitude came about at the news that George LeRoy had taken his father's best horse and lit out for parts unknown, thereby incriminating himself. To this, Maximilian Parker had finally nodded and said, "All right, Peel, I'll side you, and at the same time I'll see my boy don't get no bad treatment. He ain't done nothing that's a crime. You'll see."

The story of his father's loyalty brought a lump to George LeRoy's throat. For a brief time, he considered returning to the ranch and going in on his own, the way Maximilian Parker believed he would. But when he voiced this impulse to Mike Cassidy, the old outlaw pointed to the lineshack's other bunk. There, hands crossed on breast, boots laid straight, bloody face covered by wide-brimmed hat, lay Deputy Stodenberg, made as decent as the strong arms and hasty respects of the Parker boys could manage.

"What you going to tell your dear paw about *him*?" the little cowboy asked.

"Well now, I didn't wing him," said George LeRoy, honestly enough. "What's to hide?"

"Oh?" said Mike. "So you wasn't the one fired the fatal shot, eh? I see. And where was you when that shot was got off? What was you doing to help the deceased at the time of his taking? You got a witness seen you try to help him?"

"What you getting at, Mike? You ain't making sense. You done the killing."

"Ah," smiled the little outlaw, "and ain't that the cat, though. Faith, now, LeRoy, if it's the law you're a'scowling over, forget it. Old Mike writ the book. You are what's referred to in jewresprudments as a accessory after the fact."

"A what?" said George LeRoy, his frown darkening.

"A feller stands by and watches another feller knock over a deputy sheriff, which same deputy sheriff this here other feller had already heretofore told the first feller that he aims to knock over next time that deputy sheriff gets afoul his gunsights, that's what," answered Cassidy.

George LeRoy nodded slowly. "You're saying that because I was with you of my own free choice when you kilt a man, then I'm as guilty as you? Is that it?"

Mike Cassidy sighed and lay back wearily on the bunk. "That, LeRoy," he said, "is it."

Dan Parker stood bravely forth. "Don't you listen to him, George LeRoy," he bleated out. "Hell, he's weaker'n a gunshot cat. All we got to do is leave him lay there and croak."

"Sure," said the older boy. "And supposing he don't croak? Then what's your next-best bright idea, Dan?"

"Wait'll he goes to sleep and get the pistol away from him."

"Good, then what?"

"Croak him with it."

The stillness returned to the frosty air of the little shack. George LeRoy looked at his brother. Old Mike Cassidy looked at them both. Finally,

George LeRoy nodded sorrowfully. "Dan," he said, "you don't know nothing. Go fetch some snow and boil a pot of coffee. Me and Mike has got to talk. Bucket's there ahint the door, where you was standing when the brains was passed around."

14

◆

or ten days, while Mike Cassidy's wound crusted over and set, the blizzard continued. When at last it was blown out, gusting on down to whirl around and die somewhere across the lonely Kaiparowits Plateau, the little outlaw was, fortunately, fit to travel. With the end of the storm came one of those strange warm chinook winds wafting out of Montana, or Idaho. South Utah seldom saw such thaw winds. They weren't called chinooks there; no one in Wayne or Garfield counties understood them by such a name. But the effect was the same. Beginning in the high country, they literally melted the snowpack overnight. Creeks and streams frozen near-solid the day before were rotten honeycomb ice within twenty-four hours and, within forty-eight hours they were broken open and booming. Winter floods hit the valleys, marooning stock and ranchfolk only then digging out of the blizzard's pack. Avalanches rocketed down the mountain, undermined by the deep melt. Trails and forests and slides exchanged locations in chunks hundreds of yards wide and long. Within three days the wind had wandered on and was gone as mysteriously and quickly as it had come. That night the temperature dropped. After seeing to the horses in the lean-to shed, old Mike Cassidy came in, blew on his reddened hands and sent Dan Parker outside to chop firewood. When the raw-boned younger brother was gone, he turned to George LeRoy, who was busy frying the night's meat.

"LeRoy," he said, "she's a'dropping out yonder like a cannonball kicked off a cliff. Come daybreak, all them trails made mud and slush of by this crazy melt will be refroze harder than arrowflint. Likewise they will be dry. The Injuns say these here hot winds in winter are always trailed-up immediate by hard freezes. I seen three like this in my years in this country. I'll tell you, them redskins know what they're talking about."

George LeRoy speared the mule deer steaks out of the skillet. He forked them onto the willow bark slabs whittled for platters. "That may be so," he agreed. "But that don't mean that I know what you're talking about."

"Traveling," said the little outlaw. "That plain enough for you?"

"I reckon. You think the posse will be along up from Circleville, eh?"

"It ain't that. Posses don't stampede me. But, LeRoy, me and you have got to travel on. Out yonder in the horse shed, froze stiff but beginning to soften up, lies a dead deputy. Your brother Dan seen me kill him. There ain't no way around that except to kill the kid, and you know that ain't my line."

George LeRoy nodded; he was thinking. In the square face, the blue eyes were held steady and the wide mouth still lifted its corners cheerfully. But George LeRoy was not smiling. "Mike, I'll level with you. I reckon I got a option, where you ain't. Dan seen me when you killed Orville, and he seen I had nothing to do with it. It may be true that they might jail me for helping you get away. But you know and I know that I ain't going to be tried for murdering Orville Stodenberg."

"I ain't never said that you was," objected Cassidy. "I only told you that you was in trouble, too."

"No, you said they'd hold me guilty same as you."

"Well, boy, that was a stretcher."

"I figured it was, Mike. But me and you been friends a long time. You taught me plenty, always treated me square. I reckon you was only trying to say we was in the thing together—win, lose or draw."

"Something like that," admitted the outlaw. "What about it, LeRoy? You agree, or you going to cut out on me and extracize that there option? I'll grant you, you got it, boy. You can go with me or with your idiot kid brother. You can take your chances on the jail or on the trail, but old Mike's choice ain't all that salubrious. With me its, 'How'll you have it, Cassidy, long drop or short?' And I'll tell you, LeRoy, I ain't waiting for the question."

Again the valley youth nodded. "Heck," he said, grinning suddenly, "how can I say who I'm aiming to go with when I don't know where you're heading?"

"Where I'm heading is into the high rocks, LeRoy. You heard me speak of the Roost. Ain't no place left for me to run but there. If I can make it into the Roost, ain't no posse in Utah going to come after me. Then when spring comes along, I can drift out the other side and head for new country." He paused, the look of the wanderer putting its restless glow on his drawn face. "New country, LeRoy," he said. "I reckon there ain't no grander kind. Places no horse, saving your own or some Injun's, has put a hoof. Places other men ain't built a fire in. Places where the grass will curry the belly of a tall steer, and where the deer and elk graze like cattle, they're that tame, and where firing a shot would be like insulting the Lord in church. Places, LeRoy, so high and dizzy even the eagle ain't perched on them. Meadows and streams and benches and slopes, canyons, high pasture, lakes, overlooks, painted cliffs and spires, why, my God, boy, there's places off over there across the Swell and beyond the Roost that would make you weep, they're that grand and lonesome and silent-lovely."

The light faded from his eyes; the words trailed off. "Forget it, kid," he said, turning away with his willow bark platter of fried deer meat. "You go on home with your brother Dan. Make it up to your paw. Do what time you must. There ain't no place out there for you."

He sat down on his bunk, staring dully at his food. But the stare was not fixed. Out of the corner of his shadowed eye he watched George LeRoy, and saw what he hoped to see. If the nomad's glow had left his own seamy features, it had been transferred to the broad and pleasant planes of George LeRoy's shining face. The boy's blue eyes were seeing the silent, lovely places of the little outlaw's farewell. He was viewing the spires, the battlements and crags, of the canyons where no horses had yet trod before old Spook and big Kanab, and his ruddy color grew higher still.

"By God, Mike," he said, almost prayerfully, "I'm a'going with you to the Roost. We'll send Dan down the mountain with my Chunk horse first thing in the morning. Me and you will ride along together. We will winter in there with your bank robber and cattle rustler friends. Come spring, like you say, we'll go and see them lost, lonesome places where there ain't been nothing but the eagle and the elk. By God, we will do it, too. Me and you, Mike. And nobody else."

Old Mike Cassidy sniffed, and then he sighed. He was affected, that was certain. And restored. Suddenly, he fell upon his platter of deer steaks with a wolf's hunger.

15

◆

They went up the Sevier River trail past South Table mountain. At Otter Creek they branched off and went up the smaller stream, north. After a time they turned east and climbed to the Awapa Plateau, crossing it toward the Aquarius Plateau; there, through a saddle lying between two landmark peaks eleven thousand feet high, they could glimpse, far off and hazy in the sunset glow, the fires of color staining the twenty-mile upthrust of the great Capitol Reef.

"These here guardian peaks," said old Mike, "are Thousand Lake to the north and Donkey to the south. Tomorrow we will go on through and foller down the foot of the Reef to where a branch of Fremont River breaks through, flowing east."

Gazing at the distant rampart of the Reef, George LeRoy shook his head. "Lord, Lord," he said, "ain't that somewhat."

"You wait," nodded his companion. "When you see the Reef close up, you won't believe it. I told you I would show you things see'd only by the birds and Injuns. Ain't six white men alive knows that

Little Fremont Canyon trail where we're a'going through the Reef. I was showed it by a old Paiute chief name of Jack Rabbit. Far as I know, old Jack Rabbit may still be living somewheres over yonder among the high rocks. Happen we might even meet up with him."

George LeRoy was going to be seventeen years old in a few days. But he was a boy born with the spirit of simple belief and the joy in his heart of honest innocence. He always saw the trail leading ahead. He went to sleep each night dreaming of the wonders of tomorrow, never of the regrets of yesterday. He and old Mike Cassidy were creatures of that bond stronger than any sire's seed. They were not father and son, not brother and brother. It was a far deeper thing than that. And the thirty years which stretched between them made no difference. Because they were boys together, they were friends like men cannot be friends. They had begun that way, and so they would end.

"Mike," the Parker youth now said, "don't never think you done wrong to bring me with you. Outlawing ain't nothing to do with it. It's just to be away off in this lonesome country, a good pal by your side, good horses underneath you, nothing but the rocks and the sky betwixt you and the next day's ride, no towns, no roads, no wagonruts even; just two friends pushing on, passing through, wanting only to see over the next rise, to build one more fire, roll one more smoke, and then to travel on."

The old outlaw sniffed and looked away from the boy. He dabbed at his eyes with the frayed cuff of his sheepskin winter coat. "This switchy sundown wind," he said, "cuts like it was honed on the north pole. It ought to be arrested for carrying a knife. Come on, the camp is yonder in the pine."

16

◆

Shortly before noon the next day, they came to the Reef and turned south along its base. George LeRoy could not believe the great rampart. The result of untold centuries of erosion by wind and water, the towering upthrust was a procession of scarps, pinnacles, gorges and goblin rocks of incredible fantasy. The rock strata ran in temples, walls, bridges, arches, both vertically and horizontally. They unified the giant sculpture of the monolith, yet divided it into a thousand layers, bands and ribbons of formations. The colors made old Mike's stories of the wonders seem almost pale. Great stripes of raw blue, purple, lavender, orchid, vermilion, orange and green banded the full twenty miles of the Reef. The buttresses of the main upthrust, the spilling slides of talus from the weathering of the mammoth top, faded from the brilliant, pure pigments to the dust-grayed muted tones, and seemed like enormous folds of velvet shrouding the shoulders of the rearing giant. For over one hour after

79

starting along the base, neither Mike nor his young
companion spoke a word.

Then the cowboy stopped his horse and pointed
to the view which unfolded before them. "That
there white Navaho sandstone dome topping them
base buttments of the reddish-brown stone is what
give the Reef its name, LeRoy. You recognize what it
is?"

"No, sir," said the youth. "Except that its stag-
gering gorgeous. It ain't as blazing bright as back
yonder, but it is grand, yes sir. What's it supposed to
be?"

"That there," announced his guide proudly, "is
the living image, white dome and all, of the U.S. of
A. national Capitol at Washington, D.C.!"

"Naw!"

"As ever was, you betcha. Course, you got to
realize I ain't never been to the national Capitol.
But it beats hell out of the Mormon temple up to
Salt Lake, or the county courthouse, either one. So I
reckon it stacks up fair-even with the Capitol in
Washington, D.C." He made allowances for George
LeRoy's lacks in higher learning. "Uh, that there
D.C.," he amplified, "it stands for the District of
Hail Columbia. That's in Washington, which is
back East somewhat past Kentucky."

"Boy!" said George LeRoy. "What's the 'Hail'
for?"

Cassidy frowned quickly and shot a suspicious
glance at his companion. "What the deuce you
mean, what's the 'Hail' for? If a boy your age don't
know what the answer to that is, I ain't going to
stoop to tell you. Let's get on along."

They came to what Mike called the Little
Fremont Gorge in mid-afternoon. Turning east, they
began the tortuous trip through the narrow cleft. At
first the going was only twisting and tiresome. But
then it climbed up out of the stream's bed level and
soared along the sheer canyon wall hundreds and
hundreds of feet above the jagged rocks below. Any

horses but the mountain-bred likes of Spook and Kanab would have gone over the edge within the first rising mile. Even so, hairpins and jumpoffs and talus dips in the dizzy track put George LeRoy's stomach up into his throat time after time. He was determined not to complain, however, or even to hint to his leather-faced guide that he was half sick and wanted to quit. After what seemed like a month, and was about two hours, they came to a little turnout of grass—a place like a pocket or nest plastered to the wall of the gorge—where they could dismount and let their horses breath and blow out.

"You want to see something, boy," old Mike said. "Come over here to the edge."

George LeRoy did not want to go near that edge, but he was as bulldog-stubborn as he was unquenchably cheerful, and he went over to join the little cowboy. He even forced himself to take a look down into the canyon, to pretend that it didn't affect him any more than standing on the bunk-house landing. He was instantly knocked away from the edge by Mike's back-swung arm. "Don't never just walk up and peer over a deep hole like that," he scowled. "Don't you know you'll get drawed right over inter it? You got to look at such pits sideways, then they don't bother you none."

In the moment of his downward glance, George LeRoy had indeed felt some great force pulling at him like a magnet, making him want to leap over the edge, or spread his arms and dive down into the depths. It was a scary thing, and he nodded soberly and thanked old Mike and edged back from the precipice.

"Now," said the little outlaw, "what I want you to do is look out eastward through the gorge. Tell me if you ever in your life seen anything to match it."

The boy did as he was told, his blue eyes widening.

"On a quiet, clear evening like this here one,"

said Mike, "you can see clean to Robber's Roost from this here Taweep Lookout."

"Lord, God," murmured George LeRoy. "It seems like you're looking over the edge of the world!"

"It's an eighty mile arrow-flight to the canyon of the Colorado, one hundred and forty mile to them far, far ranges crost the river. Them's the Uncompahgres, in Colorado. Twixt here and the river, nigh straight along the line we look out'n this gorge, lies the Roost."

"God, it's wild-looking country," said the boy.

The little cowboy shook his head. "It ain't just wild looking, LeRoy. It's wild. You don't never get used to it." He turned back to the horses. "Come on, boy," he said. "Trail heads down again, just past this point. We camp on the bottom by the stream tonight. Happen full dark catches us not yet off the cliff—well, never mind. Just don't waste no time. We got to drop about seventeen hundred feet."

The descent proved much easier than the climb to the rim, however. They were down to the stream, had their bedrolls spread and the coffee water boiling by six o'clock. It was pitchblende-black in the lower gorge and much warmer, because more wind sheltered, than the high country. It was thus a cheery camp, with the great blank walls of the canyon rising sheer on either side of the water, their tiny meadow cove of shore sand and cured winter hay snugged at either end by vast, house-sized boulders, and the red shadows of their driftwood fire dancing all about. The camp was one of the memories which George LeRoy would put away deep inside the war bag of his mind, keeping it there like others kept money or jewels or gold against the time when limbs grew slow and eyesight dimmed, when old times were the only times which counted.

Mike Cassidy could play the harmonica sweeter than the prairie's breath, more sad and poignant than the whippoorwill, and George LeRoy owned a rich and honeyed singing voice—one would never

expect it from the vibrant, stinging way he laughed
and talked, or from his short, square frame of muscle and smiling puckish face.

George LeRoy also played the harmonica, one
which Cassidy had given him the first summer on
the Sevier. The boy had never grown as artful as the
teacher, but he could play along with Mike's lead in
harmony to put the gooseflesh up the spine of soft
and hardcase alike.

Now as the fire died and the tired bodies relaxed to the music of the river riffling past, the little
outlaw brought forth his harmonica and tapped it
on the heel of his palm. Across the fire, George
LeRoy dug out his instrument and made it ready
without words.

"What will she be, LeRoy?" asked Cassidy.
"Something sad I'd say, but something that looks
away and away."

"I think so, too," said George LeRoy. "How
about 'Shenandoah'?"

Mike began to play softly, plaintively. The
boy played to the lead, a perfect haunting counter-
point. But then, on the second chorus, he let the
harmonica fall away and sang in his clear voice.
The words, and the refrain of Mike's playing, were
pitched to the key of the river and of the night
wind sighing where the cedars grew down to the
willows' edge.

> Oh, Shenandoah, I long to see you,
> Away, you rollin' river;
> Shenandoah, I long to see you,
> Away, we're bound away, across the wide
>   Missouri.
>
> Oh Shenandoah, I love your daughter,
> Away, you rollin' river;
> For her I'd cross the rollin' water,
> Away, we're bound away, across the wide
>   Missouri.

The words and the thinning notes of the harmonica faded and fell still beneath the rush and
rustle of the river, the lone, sad whisper of the
wind. Old Mike was looking into the fire, his head
down. George LeRoy was looking up at the night
sky and the far stars.

"Tomorrow," said the outlaw, after a long, quiet
time, "we will make Hanksville."

"Hanksville?" echoed the boy, alerted by the
name.

"Last stop before the Roost, LeRoy." Old Mike
paused, his sharp glance holding on the boy's face.
"Last chance to turn back," he said. "Once we leave
Hanksville, we'll be under watch. No changing your
mind then."

George LeRoy grinned. The moment of camp-
fire magic induced by the sad notes of "Shenandoah"
was dispelled. "Heck," said the boy, "you don't need
to fret about me. My onliest fear is that *you* will
decide to shy off. After all," the grin widened, "I
ain't got nothing but your word for it, that you'll be
greeted with any long-lost brother celebrations."

"True," nodded the little outlaw, his own quirky
grin replying to the boy's. "But two nights from now
you can be asking about my credit at the McCarty
National Bank in Roostsville."

George LeRoy looked quickly at him. But his
companion was not joking—it was his usual way of
putting the ring of knife steel into words, which,
taken straight, would sound like banter or bulljuice.
"You mean," he said, "that the McCartys are in the
Roost?"

"I wouldn't want you to gamble my word on it,
LeRoy," answered the other. He fished a frayed piece
of paper from inside his coat and handed it across
the fire's winking coals to George LeRoy. "Here.
Borrowed this off'n the wall in Sheriff Rasmussen's
office while's we was there," he said. "It ain't a bad
likeness of Bill and George, but it don't flatter Tom
none."

George LeRoy unfolded the paper. It was a reward flyer put out by the Pinkertons: *Wanted for Bank Robbery and Assault—Notorious McCarty Brothers.* It was smudged and smeared, torn and tattered, and half dark red with Mike Cassidy's blood, but George LeRoy could read and he could decipher the words *$5000 Dead or Alive*, and he could make out what was left of the smeary photoprints of the three desperate men, even by faint, dying firelight.

"Lord Amighty," he said, "it's them."

"Keep it for your proof," said old Mike. "You don't know it's them. Save it and show it to them when we get to the Roost. They'll sign it for you. After all, you ain't got nothing but my word for things, so far."

Chastened, the boy nodded, but then grinned defiantly. "Well, cuss it all, wasn't it you told me never to trust nobody?"

"If it wasn't," answered the outlaw, "it ought to have been. Now shut up and leave me sleep. Long ride tomorrow."

17

◆

Hanksville, entered at dusk, was a sight to unsettle the spirits. Coming down its frozen-mud main street from the west, George LeRoy and Mike Cassidy were the only human beings in sight. A few horses stood at hitching rails, their rumps to the cut of the fierce wind. Two wagons stood in front of the feed store. Here and there, in the saloon, the general store and the "hotel," oil lamps burned. Otherwise the town lay dark in the icy winter twilight. Not even a cur dog ran out to greet or challenge the two horsemen.

"Jings," muttered George LeRoy, "I seen welcomer sights in a cemetery."

Old Mike sniffed and angled Spook toward the windswung sign which read: *The Hanksville House, Rooms.* "Maybe that's because there's more people been buried in this burg than in most graveyards," he said. "I told you this here was the saddlesore of the San Rafael Swell."

The Hanksville House was a hotel only because the proprietor said that it was. There was no entry hall or office, neither a desk nor a letterbox nor a brass spittoon. There wasn't even a potted rubber palm tree. There was only a coal-oil stable lamp hung by a nail on the wall; beyond that, a narrow, bare hallway ran off into the gloom with unpainted doors spaced along its drafty spine. As George LeRoy shivered, Mike led the way to the first door. He kicked it open, peered in, doffed his hat and bowed in response to the vile curse which greeted him. Then he said politely, "Oh, goodness gracious, excuse me, friend. I didn't have no idee they would be tourists in town this time of year."

He started to turn away and go on to the next door, when a monstrous fellow in a nightshirt but still wearing his boots loomed in the violated door-way. He seized Mike from behind by the nape of his neck and lifted him three feet off the floor. The giant, at least six feet eight inches high and full bearded, swung the little cowboy-outlaw around and drew back his free hand to smash Mike's head off. All this occurred before George LeRoy could yell a warning, or even spin about to run and save his own life. But the blow was never struck.

The vast fellow stopped in mid-shot. He brought Mike closer into view, directly under his huge, bulbous nose, and peered at him with a bearlike squint, which betold his obvious short-sightedness. "Gawd awmighty!" roared the monster, his voice shaking the thin walls of the hall. "It's you!"

Mike was mad. He was red from his neck to whatever else he had worth getting bloodshot. George LeRoy watched fascinated.

"You!" Mike sputtered at the hairy giant. Hanging in mid-air as he was, his boots treading the empty space beneath them, the small man still whipped out his long-barreled Colt and planted its muzzle between the peering eyes of his assailant. "Set me down this instant, you crazy ape," he demanded thickly. "If my feet ain't feeling a solid ground inside two ticks of my pocket turnip, I'll drill you a third eye so's you can see good enough not to go assaulting your betters!"

"Mike, little old Mike," crooned the creature. "Lawd, Lawd, Mike, now you know old Grizzly wouldn't never lay handt to you in anger. Ain't it wonderful to see you again, though, you hairy-eared watchfob, you!"

The giant carefully put Mike back upon his feet. He was as careful resettling the little outlaw's hat on his head, apologetically dusting snowflakes off the latter's sheepskin winter coat, restraightening the set of the coat deranged by his gargantuan grasp, and in general showing all signs of respect for the stumpy outlaw.

For his part, Mike Cassidy did not press the advantage. "George Le..." he began, clearly intent upon introducing the Circle Valley boy to the huge brute with the beard. But he seemed taken with some caution and began again. "Grizzly," he said, "I want you should meet the new horse holder I told the boys of. This here is my onliest living nephew, George. George, shake hands with Grizzly."

The giant took hold of George LeRoy's hand, pumping it like a jack handle. "George," he vowed earnestly, "I like you. We ain't had a kid in the Roost for a long spell. I like kids."

George LeRoy thanked him, not knowing whether to wonder how he liked his kids (well done, medium or blood-rare), or to accept the monster's simple statement at face value. While he was pondering, Grizzly put both hands at his waist and lifted him up off the floor to have a closer look at him.

"Yes, sir," he nodded, satisfied, and held George LeRoy up to the light. "You're a fine-looking boy. You got any more name than just George, George?"

"Cassidy," broke in old Mike quickly. "Uh, I ain't never told the boys, but I had a brother, older brother, dearly beloved by all, name of George LeRoy Cassidy. This boy is named after him, but he don't cotton to George LeRoy, so's we all just call him George, or Kid. My old daddy's name was George, too. Oh, of course, onct in a spell we forget and call this here lad George LeRoy, but he don't hold it against us for long. Do you, *George*?"

"Uh, no, sir," attested the boy. "George Cassidy, that's me, Mr. Grizzly. How about setting me back down?"

Grizzly seemed not to hear him. Putting George "Cassidy" under his arm, he turned and began to talk of old times to Mike. It was only when he stopped to draw breath that Mike was able to get the giant's attention back to the newly christened boy.

Grizzly, reminded, at once put George LeRoy back onto the floor. The boy was turning blue and would not have lasted another fifteen seconds, but he managed to stagger around a few steps and stay upright. Old Mike herded Grizzly back into his den and closed the door on him with voluble promises that they would all meet for breakfast in the morning.

Going on down the hall, Mike opened a second door, only to be answered by what sounded—although, of course it couldn't have been—just like a girl's giggle, followed by a thrown bottle of whiskey. The bottle smashed against the jam alongside Mike's intruding head. "Forgive it, brother," said the little outlaw. Then, tipping his hat, "Amen, sister."

The third door was locked. The fourth door had a light shining under it. At the fifth door Mike decided to knock before entering; he was answered by three shots fired right where Mike's head would have been had he not been born so short.

"You see what manners gets you," the outlaw growled to George LeRoy, and went to the last door down the hall.

Fortunately the sixth room was unoccupied. When they were in the straw-ticked iron bedstead, trying to find a valley between the reefs and mesas of the mattress, old Mike said, "LeRoy, from tonight you'd better remember who you ain't. There's no use dragging your folks inter whatever mess you make of things along the way."

"Thanks," said the boy, simply. "That was surely quick thinking when you told Grizzly I was your nephew George."

"It was done to keep your paw's good name clean," replied the little outlaw. "Your paw is a man I respect. Taking to you as I do, LeRoy, I could hope that you'd be like your paw. But you ain't. You know it; I know it. So I reckon we'll agree you're more my kin than his'n."

"That's so," said George LeRoy. "I knowed it from the first time I seen you."

"Some are born to sweat," said the little bandit, "and some to rustle and rob. Each kin knows its own kind."

George LeRoy lay thinking about that. There was no question of the way he was drawn to old Mike Cassidy. The attachment was so close that when the little man had told Grizzly that the boy from Circle Valley was his nephew, George LeRoy had felt proud. Yes, and the name sounded natural. "George Cassidy" had a ring to it, when taken as old Mike's favorite and only nephew. It made a boy think that he amounted to something in the world. He didn't feel awkward or wrong in taking old Mike's name, or in being called "his kind" by the bowlegged outlaw. And yet, and yet...

"Mike," he said, "you still awake?"

"No, bless you, LeRoy, I'm sound asleep."

"Mike, how come you gun down Deputy Stodenberg like you done?"

There was a long silence. The boy could hear Mike breathing; he could feel the tremble of anger in the bed beneath them. But he waited, his jaw hard-set in the darkness.

"That's been sticking in your craw all along, ain't it?" the wizened cowboy accused his companion. "I've see'd it in your eyes every mile of this here ride." He paused, his breathing more easy, his voice losing that flint-edge it could take on so swiftly. "LeRoy," he said, "answer honest; you want to turn back?"

"I don't never turn back," answered the boy with no hesitation. "But you can answer honest, too; why'd you kill Orville when you didn't need to?"

The old outlaw soberly explained his action at the lineshack at some length. He said that he had long ago made the outlaw oath never to be taken and never to do time in jail again. With his record, and with the law wanting to see him behind bars, to let Stodenberg take him in would have amounted to an automatic sentence, and likely to a long term served in the Laramie Penitentiary in Wyoming. That, he assured George LeRoy, was no place for any man to be put into without a fight. He also alleged that, as he had always warned the boy in training him to handle the six-gun, no man on the dodge ever tries to bluff another man—especially a lawman—who has a weapon ready. "When the other fellow has you covered, you don't ask him any questions, LeRoy," he concluded. "You can't question and beat the odds, or stay out from behind the bars or the pine box. You shoot or you shut up. It ain't no complicateder than that."

George LeRoy nodded in the dark. "Sure," he said. "But how come you kilt him?"

"Boy," said the outlaw, "you never shoot to do nothing else in this business."

George LeRoy's blunt jaw grew more stubborn yet. "I don't believe it," he said quietly.

"You'd better believe it," said the other, just as quietly. "Either that or turn back tomorrow morning. And I mean early."

"No," said George LeRoy, "I ain't turning back." He paused, then added, talking between set teeth. "Nor ain't I going to take to killing folks in cold blood, neither. Not ever."

Old Mike Cassidy thought about it for over a full minute. George LeRoy thought he had gone to sleep. But the old outlaw had only gone back along the trail a long, long way, to far before he had ever heard of George LeRoy Parker, and, indeed, to when he had been the same age as the square-jawed boy. Finally he bobbed his head. It was a gesture of unspoken agreement, preceding the words.

"Happen you're right, LeRoy," he said, his voice very low. "When I told you I knowed you was my kind, I didn't mean it to say you was exactly my kind. You got something I ain't never had. You ain't afeered of any man that walks, yet you don't hate nobody, nor call them scum. You know something, boy? I believe you when you tell me you ain't going to kill nobody a'purpose. You ain't going to back down to them, neither. That's the blasted part of it that you don't seem to get set straight in your mind. But then's when you'd best listen to old Mike, boy. Because then's when the guns go off, whether you like them to or not. And when powder burns, lead flies. *Somebody* stops it. However, leave it lay for tonight, eh, kid? We can augur it first thing tomorrow. For now, this old hoss is tuckered and puckered. I couldn't be rode another forty feet. Don't hog the blanket, hear? Goodnight, LeRoy."

The boy lay a moment. His frown eased, unlocking the obstinate trap of his jaws. "Goodnight, *who*?" he grinned.

"Oh, Dear Lord," groaned the little outlaw, brave beneath the burden of his new nephew. "Goodnight, George."

18

♦

The chill atmosphere of The Hanksville House was the same by night and by day. In the gray, cold light, Mike Cassidy and his "nephew" shivered into their overalls, boots, hats and sheepskin coats—all they had removed the previous night. It was too cold to talk. They went down the icy hall out into the blast of a sleety wind, which Mike cursed and likened to an ice-coated sandstorm. The town had no restaurant. In a lean-to of the livery barn where they had left the horses, a one-eyed man with no visible teeth divided his time between swamping out the stalls of the barn and serving up "hash" to the boys. The sign on the lean-to announced that the filthy shed was, in truth, *The Chez Fremont*, and claimed to serve *jenuwine home-cookt meels*. The one-eyed chef was known only as Frenchy, and was rumored to have been on the long lope from the Canadian Mounties by way of original recommendation. Whatever he was, or wherever from, his talent lay in cleaning stalls, not in cooking. Even Grizzly, who joined them in the *Chez*, and who was not precisely a cosmopolite, suggested that the eggs had been laid by a buzzard, the bacon cured from the carcass of a polecat and the coffee made by a grind of rat filings and road apples. But none of them wanted to hit the trail unfueled, and they ate.

It developed that Grizzly was in town with three packmules to "refurbalish," as Mike put it, the outlaw brotherhood's supply of staples: beans, flour, coffee, salt, and the like. The giant announced that he would be pleasured to have their company on the ride back. This way each man could lead a mule and better time could be made. Also there was the matter of the comradeship of the trail, an important item, particularly in ice-bad weather such as the present spell.

Mike Cassidy growled aside to nephew George that he would prefer the company of a real grizzly to that of the bearded behemoth, but that the big man was inordinately fond of Mike and insisted upon "protecting" the latter, whether he wanted the service or not. "The leetle feller," Grizzly called the gray-haired outlaw, and chaperoned him unmercifully. "If he was a road agent, rustler or bank heister like the rest of us," the banty-legged cowboy explained, "I'd long ago have put him under on some lonesome trail, or turnt him into the law, or plugged him twixt the blades during some bank shoot-out. But, pshaw, he's the camp cook up to the Roost, and the man who lays a finger onto the cook—well, now, I'm telling you; you know the rules, LeRoy."

"*George*," corrected the straight-faced youth.

Cassidy frowned anew. He glanced over to where Grizzly was wrangling the last of the mules up to the tie-bar of the barn. "LeRoy," he said, "I can't get used to calling you George. It don't fit you no more than Clarence, nor Cuthbert. We got to agree on something else. How about just 'Kid'?"

"George 'Kid' Cassidy," mused the boy. "Not bad, Mike."

"No thanks," grimaced the little cowboy. "Forget the whole thing. Yonder's old Grizzly a'waving for us to come along."

"I'll call me George, you call me Kid," suggested his companion, "and you can be George LeRoy instead of Mike. How's that take holdt of your tongue?"

"I'll take holdt of *your* tongue," promised Mike, glowering. "I'll unreel it about a yard and wrap it aroundt your throat so's you can choke on your own guff. Lay off the bright comment, you hear?" While they made a play of looking to cinches and cheek straps on Spook and Kanab, the little outlaw continued his side-mouthed warning to the boy. "You draw a line with a ruler on a map due east of this burg and to the Colorado, or better yet to the Green. Then draw another line due south of this same burg down to the Henry Mountains, and afterwards you take all the country inside them two lines, south and east, and you get some idee of where you'd best keep your mouth shut. Every foot of that there territory is owlhoot country, and the man you meet in it is not the one to make bright remarks with, you get me? Me and you, boy, we've had it clost and happy, and we can josh and joke and make a grin do half a day's work for us. That's just fine and dandy— for me and you. For the likes of Grizzly, yonder, and anybody else we see or speak to southeast of Hanksville, you keep your mealy mouth shut."

He broke off and swung up on Spook. "Coming, Grizzly!" he called out to the huge man who had started over toward them. "Had to check the kid's rigging for him. He's valley-bred and ain't no useful idee what's ahead of us today by way of trail."

Grizzly had by now come up to them. Nephew George had not gotten started fast enough and was still afoot, standing beside Kanab. Before he could object, the giant had seized him by the waist and hoisted him to saddle, much in the manner of an ordinary man putting a four-year-old child on its first pony. "There you be, boy!" the outlaw cook boomed. "Now mind you, the leetle feller's right. We'll go places today a cat would claw to get up, and wouldn't never dast to try to get down out of again." He paused, eyeing the new recruit. "Unless, of course, he was to be shot down out'n of it," he said.

Mike Cassidy's nephew of convenience was small for a boy pushing seventeen. He was sturdy and as strong as a bull calf, though. And he did not like being picked up and handled about like a baby. It was an unsettling experience. That and the fact that the huge camp cook's tiny, deep-set eyes were boring into his made the new George Cassidy glad old Mike had been smart enough to drill it into him about getting careless or free "southeast of Hanksville." He had the sudden feeling that Grizzly was not nearly as stupid or animal-mannered as his name and behavior might lead some valley kid into thinking. He also got the feeling that he was being watched, and watched hard, and not alone by the hairy-faced Grizzly. The boy had heard the expression that the walls have ears, but he was now uncomfortably aware of the fact that they might also have eyes.

He forced the grin with which he answered the bearded giant. "I reckon," he said, "that with the likes of you and Uncle Mike to help me, Mr. Grizzly, I won't get myself clawed up into no places where's I'll need to be shot down out'n them. I'll learn, you'll see, sir."

Grizzly nodded and turned to Mike, who had uneasily drifted back to side his nephew. "Ain't he grand and polite, though?" he said to the little outlaw. "You hear that? *Mr.* Grizzly, and *sir*, even." His small, inky black eyes darted again to the boy. He put a hand the size of a #6 baitpan trap on the latter's shoulder. "George," he said, "you'll do." He blinked and turned away, then halted and shot a look back at the boy. "Mebbe," was all he added.

19

♦

From the local legends, which even then were building about the sinister haunt known as Robber's Roost, the boy had always believed that the outlaw lair lay "at the very top of the San Rafael Swell." A forbidding mass of black rock reaching toward eight thousand feet in elevation and spanning some eighty miles in the form of a wide horseshoe, the Swell was the desolate, waterless heart of a region where, as the handful of white men living in its perimeters said, "hell would have felt right at home." More important to the boy from Circle Valley, however, was that he believed this storied Satan's hole to be due north from Hanksville. Imagine, then, his surprise when Grizzly led the little cavalcade out of the ugly town in precisely the opposite direction. Moreover, the huge rider did not, as the boy kept expecting him to, circle about and swing north, once out of sight of the settlement. He continued across the broken and unwatered highlands west of the deep canyon of the Dirty Devil, mile after mile after mile. Mike

Cassidy said nothing, and so his nephew wisely did the same. By noon they had been in the saddle six hours. Halting on a high point which hung dizzily above the depths of the main canyon, they made coffee.

"Well, kid," rumbled Grizzly, swishing the thick grounds of the vile poison about the bottom of his tin cup, "what you think so far?"

"You mean about the trip or the coffee, Mr. Grizzly?"

"No choice there," interrupted Mike. "They're both hell."

Grizzly frowned at the little outlaw. "That's a joke," the latter instructed him carefully, and the giant broke into a hee-hawing roar that shook the canyonside. Mike looked at the boy and rolled his eyes upward helplessly, as though to say, "Well, what can you do?" The boy had to admit with an answering uplift of his hands that he had no rightful idea what you did about a human animal the size and uncertainty of this monster camp cook.

"Naw," Grizzly finally explained, wiping the merriment from his pinpoint eyes, "I mean about the ride inter the Roost. You enjoying it, kid?"

Old Mike's nephew nodded slowly and with exaggerated conviction. "Yes, sir. It's surely some humdinger of a trail, Mr. Grizzly. But I don't let it spook me none, long as I can see you leading on like as though it weren't nothing. I reckon with somebody like you to foller, ain't no boy going to fear harm nor suffer hardship. Leastways, not this boy."

Grizzly nodded, then knocked the coffee grounds from his cup into the palm of his hand, tossed them into his mouth, and began to chew them up with relish. "Tarantula juice," he said, spitting a lance of the black fluid at a pert snowbunting hopping too near. "Ain't nothing to touch it for salubriating the brain." He got up and put his cup away, Mike and the boy following suit. They mounted up, wrangling the packmules into line. When everything was set to Grizzly's taste, he waved the start. After they had gone but a few rods the huge guide, without looking at his companions, and as though merely announcing it to the barren rocks, boomed out into the frost-cold air, "I recommend you take up the habit, *George LeRoy Cassidy.* You're a'going to need the stimulashun where we're bound."

Mike and the boy exchanged glances behind Grizzly's back. Mike nodded not so much to agree with the big man's advocacy of tarantula juice, but to warn the boy that he could take Grizzly's odd announcement as proof that this outsized, seemingly simple-minded brute was anything but dumb. "You see?" Mike's look seemed to say. "What did I tell you? You've got to be careful with this customer."

To hide his uneasiness, the little outlaw replied aloud: "Now you hear, George? You just listen to old Grizzly. He's telling you straight. You got to look sharp and to keep your mind clear, happen you're going to ride with the likes of me and him."

"Yes, sir, thank you," said the boy, and let it go at that.

But it wasn't that, and he knew it wasn't. Grizzly was warning him that he knew his name wasn't George Cassidy, and that, if he, George LeRoy, was going to get on in the Robber's Roost society, he would have to quit being so flip and fast, to keep a sight quieter than he had up to now. Grizzly was warning him to keep his eyes and ears open and his mouth sealed tight. He ought not to have needed to be told that. South Utah of his day was not all that haired-over and gentled-down that a boy, born there and raised more or less wild, had any excuse for shooting off his mouth in grown-up company. The boy had only five grades of education, and those five were so shot-through with hookey-playing and honest missing through ranch chores that they didn't amount to much more than three years. And in the Circleville School they surely had not taught him anything about keeping healthy through dumb answers. Well, now he had been warned. It was up to him to profit by it, whether by chewing cold coffee grounds, or just by limiting his answers to "yes, sir" and "no, sir." Called by any name, George LeRoy, Kid, or George Cassidy, he was going to have to watch himself.

This sober resolve was well cemented by the adventure of the next five miles of trail. Only minutes from the noon halt, Grizzly seemed to disappear over the lip of Dirty Devil Canyon. Following him, his stomach in a sudden pinch, the boy discovered that the mule track switched back upon itself and plunged down into the gorge along a cliff which seemed to lean outward from the bottom. Perhaps it only seemed to because the bottom was not visible, and because the trail was formed by the detritus of centuries packing into a gigantic fracture in the cliff's face; a hairline crack, it ran from top to bottom of the gorge as if a crazy bolt of lightning had emblazoned it on the canyon wall. Repeatedly it seemed that their animals must go over the edge, or that the track ahead broke and hung in empty air. But after an hour of unrelieved nerve strain, they were on the bottom, had made the river crossing, and were "resting out" on the far side of the Dirty Devil.

"From here," old Mike reassured the wind-chilled youth, "it gets interesting."

They went on, doubling back north up the east side of the steam, but staying at stream level. Now and again, seemingly at every turn of the tortured river, a dry canyon would come in from the rifted and broken rock of the plateau above to join its riven fissure with the greater fracture of the Dirty Devil's eroded slash across the stark desert. These sidebreaks were pure hell to negotiate, being choked with a litter of boulders, talus, water sludge and decomposed sandstone drifts. At last the travelers came to one such side-canyon bigger than the rest, and more Stygian, more dismal of scarp and rockslide and gargoyle boulder, than anything so far encountered.

"Happy Creek," vouchsafed Mike Cassidy to the boy.

The latter looked up the desolate stream bed of bleached silica, which was the water of Happy Creek. "Beautiful," was all he could think to reply.

"Glad you like it," said Mike between chapped lips. "We turn off here."

The boy thought he was joking with him. He nodded with a knowing grin and said, "Oh, sure, sure." But the next moment he saw Grizzly swing his shaggy brute of a plowhorse to the right, hard up the fossiled spine of Happy Creek Canyon. Cassidy and the boy followed after him, too weary even to trade glances of disgust.

Not far up the tributary gorge, Grizzly went over the dry steam bed and past a rotten stench of sulphur springs to the north wall. There, to the boy's amazement, another lightning-stroke trail zigzagged upward and was lost in the overhang of the cliff. By now it was late afternoon, and before they negotiated the north-wall ascent of Happy Creek Canyon, the sun was gone. When at last they broke free of the frightening dropoff and were on the solid welcome ground of the plateau, only the brief, cold translucence of the winter twilight lingered. The boy shook his head in disbelief at the awesome loneliness about them. There wasn't any place made by God that could be so utterly devoid of warmth, of color or of life. It stunned the mind.

Old Mike kneed Spook over to stand closer to Kanab, as Grizzly signaled the halt for blowing-out the livestock, after the lung-bursting climb. "Yonder," muttered the little cowboy, pointing across the black gap of Dirty Devil Canyon, "is the place we boilt our coffee at noon. If we was fresher and the wind was just right, we could spit on it from here."

The boy nodded, overwhelmed. Five hours of heart flutter and horse lather, of constant, tense gluing of eye and nerve and muscle to the simple matter of staying upright on a mount on a rock ledge only wide enough to breathe shallow on! And they were within honest, high-arched pistol shot of where they had nooned. Little wonder, he thought grimly, that sheriffs, stock association men, tax collectors, or even the Pinkertons, seldom troubled to follow their shadowy birds past Hanksville. It was too wild, too hard, too unbelievably tricky and treacherous. Old Mike had not been lying when he had said he would show him places where only the eagle perched. Or maybe not even the eagle.

As if reading these thoughts, the little outlaw caught his eye and nodded. "Yep," he said, "she's the high lonesomes, sure enough."

"Lord," shivered the boy, "ain't she, though?"

"That crossover we made," said Mike, "is the onliest way to get over Dirty Devil betwixt Hanksville and the Henry Mountains; forty-five miles, boy, without no other chance." He paused, pointing upward from the rim upon which they rested. The land rose in an unending incline of red and russet sandstone toward a fluted scarp, which seemed, in the eerie twilight, to vault upward ten thousand feet. It was a trick of the strange light, of course, but to the tired youth it seemed no trail could surmount that elevation, could possibly arrive at that castellated aerie floating in the turquoise green of the evening sky. "Yonder," said Mike Cassidy softly, "is the Roost."

"That?" queried his companion. "That's the Roost? On top of that God-awful high rock?"

"No, the scarp is the foot of Sam's Mesa. That's

the high point of the swell down this way. The Roost is over on the far side of it."

"Lord, Lord," sighed the youngster. "Not only up but over."

Grizzly guided his stocky mount over to them in time to hear the remark. "You complaining, boy?" he growled. "Lemme tell you suthin, we ain't hardly commenced to climb yet."

They set out, and for another two hours and until the arctic-white moon had risen, no more was said. About eight P.M. they topped the scarp. Before them lay the roughs of the tableland called, in those times, Sam's Mesa. It was the real landmark of the real Roost, the legend of the San Rafael Swell notwithstanding. So said old Mike Cassidy, and the boy believed him.

They pushed on now, their mounts and packmules showing that quickening for home, which is the instinct of such owlhoot stock. In another hour they came into a stunt cedar break and wound down through it. Grizzly's horse began to snuffle and roll his bit. The mules flagged their ears. Ahead the cedars thinned. They emerged on a bench of mountain hay. Below, by easy trail clearly seen in the moonlight, lay a rocky garden of great boulders, sandstone walls and open runs of dry sweet grass. In and among the great rocks, the welcome cheer of lamplight beckoned and winked from no less than a score of cabin windows. Up to the watchers on the bench drifted the pungent smell of wood smoke, the incense of clear, dry pine and the perfume of red cedar, foretelling of warmth for their bone-chilled bodies and of food for their empty bellies. It was an unforgettable moment.

"*The Roost,*" breathed the boy. "*Robber's Roost!*"

Beside him, Mike Cassidy checked old Spook for just an instant, his voice low with warning. "It sure ain't Circleville, LeRoy," he said. "Watch yourself." Then Mike was gone on down the slope, catching up to Grizzly. Left alone, the square-jawed youth tightened his hold on Kanab's reins. He patted the tall bay on the neck, pressed him with the knees and touched him with the heels. They went silently down toward the outlaw settlement, and toward the new life that waited for George LeRoy Parker, the boy from Circle Valley.

PART THREE

◆

South Along
the
Owlhoot

20

◆

The morning after his arrival at Robber's Roost in the winter of 1883, all the rules changed for George LeRoy Parker. From that day he was George Cassidy for real. The summer years of childhood lay as far behind him as the Sevier River ranch of his devout Mormon father. Nor did fate keep this fact long from him.

He and old Mike had dressed and come out of the latter's cabin. They stood a moment in the frost of the mountain air. The sun was just tipping the rim of Sam's Mesa, spilling down into the outlaw lair. Its warmth at that thin altitude was quick and welcome, thawing eager youth and middle-aged man. The comrades lingered, looking below. By daylight, Robber's Roost was scarcely the grail of adventure it had been by the shadow lantern of last night's moon. Nephew George winced and shook his head. "Jings," he said softly.

"Lovely, ain't it," answered Mike, and fell silent.

The roost was a dry, rocky bench on the vast slope of Sam's Mesa. It overlooked the chasm of

Dirty Devil River to the west, that of Poison Spring Creek to the southwest. Northwest loomed the twin pilot knobs, which, in the legend, landmarked the Roost when approached by the trail from Green River. To the left of the pilot knobs the Dirty Devil twisted up toward Hanksville and its confluences with the Fremont and the Muddy. Eastward, hidden by the forbidding north shoulder of Sam's Mesa, ran the Orange Cliffs, buttressing Cathedral Canyon and the Colorado River.

The bench jutted in shelflike manner from the mesa to provide the characteristic "overlook" of the outlaw hideout. This vast panorama spread for a day's ride, or longer, in three directions from the Roost. The fourth direction was walled-off forever by the impenetrable fortress-palisades of the Orange Cliffs, needing no overlook, nor outpost. The cover of the bench was a hardy, highland grass, low sage, stunt cedar, and dwarf pine. Three good springs of sweet water fed it all by sub-irrigation and provided drinking and household water. That, beyond the walls of sandstone and the floors of desert sand, was the extent of the Roost's natural and utilitarian beauty.

The score of cabins which young Cassidy thought he had seen in the moonlight of the previous night were reduced by harsh day to a dozen shacks, dugouts, soddies and such assorted mud-and-log hovels wherein nested the robber birds of the Roost. The pole corrals, hayricks and feed sheds evident at every dwelling bespoke the intensive horse-keeping culture of the settlement. A dirt track ran down the center of the cluster of huts, beginning nowhere and ending the same place. To George Cassidy, the high and lonesome bench of Robber's Roost seemed to have but one way in and no way out. He looked uneasily at Mike.

"Well?" demanded the latter. "What do you think of it?"

Send for your FREE
Hardcover Collector's
Edition of
Louis L'Amour's Sackett!
FREE BOOK
BONUS FREE GIFT
RISK-FREE PREVIEW
(SEE INSIDE)
NO RISK!
Accept our invitation to receive your *free* copy of *Sackett*, the premier volume in the *Louis L'Amour Collection*. Here's your chance to hunker down with one of the greatest Western adventures ever. It's our way of saying "Welcome ..."
SEE DETAILS INSIDE!

Saddle Up For Adventure With Louis L'Amour!

Free Book! Now you can read and enjoy the classic Western adventure *Sackett.* It's yours to keep, because we have a FREE Collector's Edition of this great Louis L'Amour story reserved for you. It's our way of saying "Welcome to the Louis L'Amour Collection."

Louis L'Amour—Master Storyteller. No one captures the smell of a mesquite fire, the sound of the wind across the open range—or the glint in a gunfighter's eye just before he draws—the way Louis L'Amour does. Every story is so real you'll feel like you're part of the action!

Handsome Books You'll Be Proud to Own. Each volume in the *Louis L'Amour Collection* is beautifully bound in rugged, simulated leather of sierra brown—made all the more elegant by a deep "brand-embossing" of rich golden lettering on the spine and cover.

These are substantial books built to last, with the fine, "weighty heft" of a trusty Colt revolver. Just the kind you'd find on the library shelves of an old hacienda or the big house on a wealthy ranch.

Try Us Free! If you're the steady hand I think you are, you'll fit right in with the cow-punchers, desperados, dandies and loners that you'll find in every Louis L'Amour story.

But seeing is believing. So I'm inviting you to try us out for *free.* Mail the card to the right without delay. Here's what you'll get:

- A FREE copy of *Sackett*—the first volume in the Louis L'Amour Collection.
- A RISK FREE PREVIEW of *Flint*, book 2 in the Collection. It's yours to enjoy for 15 days, so you can decide if you want to remain a subscriber.
- The FREE BONUS GIFT described below.

NO RISK! If you keep *Flint*—under the terms described on the order card—we'll send you future volumes, about once a month, on the same 15 day free preview basis. Keep only those you want. There's no minimum number of books to buy and you may cancel at any time.

FREE! Get this mighty fine calendar, too! Experience the raw West at its best every day of the year with this full-color Louis L'Amour Calendar. Bold, exciting art of scenes from the most popular L'Amour stories. And it's yours to keep, even if you cancel your subscription.

A Fair Deal No Matter How You Cut The Cards!

1. Get *Sackett* FREE! It's the Collector's Edition. And it's yours to keep no matter what!
2. FREE! The latest Louis L'Amour Wall Calendar with exciting, full-color art.
3. RISK FREE PREVIEW! Get *Flint* free to read and enjoy for 15 days. There's no obligation to buy!
4. Always Great Value! Keep only the books you want. Build your Western adventure collection one book at a time!

MAIL THIS CARD TODAY.

Ride With Sackett
FREE!

Send my Collector's Edition of *Sackett* FREE to keep, and sign me up as a subscriber to The Louis L'Amour Collection. I'll also receive, *Flint*, the second volume in this matched set. It's mine to read and enjoy FREE for 15 days. If I like it I'll pay just $11.95 plus a modest shipping and handling charge. Future editions will be sent about once a month—each on a 15 day free preview basis. I'm not fenced in, 'cause there's no minimum number of books to buy, and no obligation to remain a member. *I may cancel at any time.*

IL56   31427

• Orders subject to approval. Prices subject to change. Residents of NY & Canada subject to sales tax.
• Prices in U.S. dollars. Outside U.S. prices are generally higher.

Name _____

Address _____ Apt. _____

City _____

State _____ Zip _____

☑ BONUS FREE GIFT
Receive the full-color Louis L'Amour Calendar when you sign up now!

Every Slap-Leather Word Guaranteed to Please!

Every Louis L'Amour story is filled with the sights, sounds and action of the Wild West. No other author captures the spirit of Western adventure better. As a subscriber to the *Louis L'Amour Collection* you are *guaranteed* the best Western adventure every time. Each book is sent on approval free for 15 days. Return any that don't catch your fancy. Keep only those you like. Cancel at any time—no strings attached. Welcome!

Detach here. Send no money now, but please do reply today. Thanks!

Stake your claim to this free book offer. Send for your Collector's Edition of *Sackett, and* your free Louis L'Amour wall calendar. Try the Louis L'Amour Collection with *no obligation*. See details inside.

DETACH HERE BEFORE MAILING.

FREE BOOK OFFER

BUSINESS REPLY MAIL
FIRST CLASS   PERMIT NO. 2154   HICKSVILLE, NY

POSTAGE WILL BE PAID BY ADDRESSEE

The Louis L'Amour Collection

Bantam Doubleday Dell Direct
PO Box 956
Hicksville NY 11802-9829

NO POSTAGE
NECESSARY
IF MAILED
IN THE
UNITED STATES

"It's grand," said his square-faced nephew. "Just grand."

"Last night," said Cassidy, unperturbed "me and Grizzly talked about you and what you could do in here. We decided Grizzly could use you down to the store. What you say?"

The "store" was a log shed set at mid-settlement. It was more of a supply dump for the owlhoot trade than a mercantile center. Grizzly did not keep regular hours or operate for profit, but he was the storekeeper. That was what he did to earn his outlaw keep, and the hard-eyed denizens of the Roost held him accountable for the service. His title of camp cook was bestowed because highline riders passing through stayed with Grizzly and were fed by him at outlaw expense. The work could become considerable in season, and Grizzly had been without an assistant since the demise of the late lamented Babyfat Mattoon. The prospect of replacing Babyfat as Grizzly's flunkey did not match precisely the image of the owlhoot life which old Mike had conjured up and sold to Nephew George in the beginning.

The latter now scowled and stalled. "What you reckon old Grizzly has got figured out for me to start at?" he inquired. "I ain't too graceful at inside chores, you know. Me and long-handled brooms don't mix."

"How the deuce do I know what he'll put you to?" defended Mike. "But I do know you had best shag on down there and find out what it'll be. Work won't kill you, boy. But at this here altitude, idleness just might."

"Lead it back past me, real easy," suggested the youth. "Maybe I'll be able to read the brand second time around."

"What I'm a'telling you," said his mentor, "is that iffen you set around up here doing nothing, the questions will commence. Folks will want to know who you really are. How come me to bring you in here. Just what it might be that you're aiming to accomplish in the Roost. Things like that."

"So?"

"So, on the other hand, you go to work and stay to work down there with old Grizzly, nobody asks nothing. They can see what you're doing. Hard work's the best alibi in the outlaw business, kid. Now get."

George Cassidy did not get. Instead, he jutted his blunt jaw at that familiar angle, which showed that he was about to demur. "Just advise me as to one little thing," he said, "before I report to the chief cook and bottle washer. Whatever happened to that there horse holder job with the gang? When the devil do I get to meet the McCartys?"

Mike was not comfortable. He shifted from standing hipshot on the left leg, to stand hipshot on the right. "Well, uh, that's what I was going to tell you, kid," he mumbled. "It seems the McCartys ain't here."

"They ain't here!" It was an accusation of betrayal, but old Mike stood to it honorably.

"No, they ain't," he answered. "Don't nobody seem to know where they might be, neither. Some say that George he's give up outlawing and aims to go straight. Others say Bill he's gone back east and went to working with the James and Younger gangs a'robbing trains. The McCartys and Jameses is said to be blood kin, you know. Anyhow, Tom's the one you want, not George nor Bill."

"Well, where's Tom at?"

"Good question," said the little cowboy.

"You mean you don't know?"

"I mean nobody don't know. Story is the Pinkertons got to closing ground on him for that Gloriosa job. They say old Tom lit out south. But there ain't nobody as knows." Mike made an apologetic gesture with his hands. "Your guess is as good as anybody's, kid."

George Cassidy nodded ruefully. "My guess is

that I've been sold short," he said. "All your grand
talk about the high, lonesome country and holding
the horses for the likes of the McCartys, and what
do you really deliver? A damned coyote farm set up
here on the shoulder of the most godforsaken mesa
in South Utah. A scant dozen broke-down shanties
squattering in the rocks. A chance to be a runny-
nose general store swampie for a bunch of deadbeat,
two-bit crooks. And a long-chin yarn from my dear
pal and favorite uncle about how's his famous friends
and feller bank robbers, the Great McCarty Brothers, have just so happened to fly the coop right
before we get here. Well, I will tell you something,
dear Uncle Mike: I reckon you are full of thornbush
beans. Happen I had wanted to be a pushbroom
jockey, I could have rode inter Panguitch, or over to
Beaver, or up to Price, and got paid for shoving out
the sawdust and the dead flies."

Old Mike regarded him with new eyes. "My
God," he announced with unabashed admiration.
"Maybe I have had you pegged wrong all the while.
Faith, now, and I should never have tried to make a
honest cow thief or bank lookout out'n you. I'd
ought to have run you for Senator or Governor. I
ain't heered nobody can equal you at blowing off
elegant without a prepared orryashun. I'd ought to
rent you out by the hour, boy. Or maybe by the yard.
The yard of tongue or lip, that is. Now leave me
advise you of something solid, Nephew George.
Shut off the steam and get yourself the heck down
that hill and to helping old Grizzly with whatsoev-
er it may be he's got for you to do." His address
broke off in mid-lecture, his alert glance shifting to
the steep hillside trail which climbed up to his
shack from the settlement. "No, set tight," he
decided. "We got company."

The rider coming up the trail seemed to be
little more than a boy. But when he drew nearer
there were lines in his wind-burned face not found
in the faces of boys. When he drew nearer still, the

friendly blue eyes of one of his watchers widened in surprised recognition. "Williard!" George Cassidy called out to the newcomer. "Williard Christiansen."

The dark-faced young rider came up to them and stopped his pony. He peered hard at the square-jawed boy who had called to him, and who now stood grinning ear to ear. Then his own eyes lost their narrowness of suspicion, and opened the least bit. "George LeRoy," he said quietly. "Wherever on earth did you spring from?" Then, laughing suddenly, and too loudly, "By Brigham, another Saint gone sour! How do you like that!"

21

♦

Williard Christiansen, like George LeRoy Parker, was of Mormon origin. His father was the bishop of the Nephi Stake. The youth had been born in Ephraim, Utah, in 1864, two years before the Parker boy, and he and George LeRoy had known one another through church and family gatherings in their earlier boyhood. They had never been close friends—a hundred miles separated Ephraim and Circleville—but their similar larkful, high natures had drawn the two boys together at the infrequent clan meetings.

Both, at these times, had spoken of "getting together" when they were older, and of "doing something." After the manner of small boys, these vows were nebulous threats to "get back" at a life of discipline and dullness, which was hardly suited to their wild, overly-spirited characters. "By jings!" the agreement had run, "me and you has got to figure out something and then go and get it did!" But, again after the manner of small, rebellious boys, nothing had come of the mutual urge.

Then, at only thirteen, Williard had struck another boy in the head with a rock during an argument over a girl. The other boy had been so seriously hurt that it was not certain whether he would live. Williard, understanding that his age would not save him in that rough frontier society, quietly took to the out-places and was seen no more in Ephraim, Utah.

While the Parker boy had not forgotten his sometime friend of the Nephi Stake, the intervening years, when Williard seemed to have been swallowed up by the back country, had certainly dimmed the memory of the former meetings. Now the two boys stood face-to-face again.

Old Mike Cassidy could sense the awkwardness between them, once the first rush of youthful good feeling had subsided. At the same time, the little cowboy outlaw knew much more of Williard Christiansen than did his new nephew, George. He knew that their visitor and his protégé from Circle Valley might faster and better catch up on their lives without the presence of an elder to slow their remembrances. "Boys," he said, "you got some touching up of old times to do. Likely, I'd best run on down and tell Grizzly you'll be a mite late to work, LeRoy. Meanwhiles, you and 'Williard' had best begin by getting each other's names straight. Allow me—"

He broke off, eying them both. "Matt," he said to the newcomer, and inclined his head toward George LeRoy, "meet George Cassidy. George, you shake hands with Matt Warner."

Matt Warner! The Parker boy's eyes now really opened wide. This Mormon lad named Williard Christiansen, whose own father was a high bishop in the church, *he* was Matt Warner? The bank robber? The rustler? The murderer? The highline rider, who, even at nineteen years of age, was already mentioned in equal link with the likes of Sam Carey, the Taylors, Jim Warren, Wilcox, Denslow and the others of the outlaw elite who made the Roost their Utah home and hideout?

But young George Cassidy was quick to recover. He did not blurt out his surprise. Beyond that first big blink, he did nothing to disclose his astonishment. As old Mike Cassidy had observed on first meeting with the sandy-haired, blue-eyed youth, Maximilian Parker's oldest boy had a quick eye and a mind to go with it. Now he only grinned and put forth his hand again. "Glad to know you, Matt," was all he said.

The other youth nodded and took his hand. "Likewise, George," he answered. He turned to old Mike. "Did you say you was going down the hill?" he demanded suggestively.

The gray-haired outlaw bristled at once. "Why?" he demanded. "You got something to say to the kid, you ain't ready to have me hear?"

Matt Warner shook his head. "Not necessarily."

"What does that mean?"

"Down to the store, they told me you was looking for Tom McCarty."

"So?"

"So how come you was looking for him?'

"The kid, here; I told Tom he'd make into a good horse holder in place of Babyfat Mattoon. That's why the kid come along with me to the Roost. He's the one really looking for McCarty."

Matt Warner nodded. "Then he's the one I want to see," he said. "Get along." He gave it like an order; to young Cassidy's amazement, old Mike accepted it that way. Well, he almost did.

"You've come up a long ways, since last time I seen you," the old outlaw said. "You hand out directions like you was appointed chief at the last war stomp. You sure I heard you right?"

"That's up to you," answered the youth. "I said it plain enough."

Mike studied him a moment. "Sure enough you did," he agreed, and grinned and tipped his hat and went off down the trail toward the settlement. When he was gone, his nephew George looked at the older boy and said, "You et yet, Matt? If you ain't, come on along in, and I'll fry you some meat."

Matt Warner watched old Mike Cassidy going down the mountainside for another moment, then answered, "No, I ain't et yet, George. Thanks. You fry, and I'll talk. Maybe me and you will go somewheres and get something did, after all."

22

♦

The boys wolfed down the fried beefsteaks, gulped the bitter coffee, chewed hard at old Mike's saleratus biscuits. As the food went down, the talk sprang up.

Matt Warner said that his sister, Teenie, had died recently, and that was the reason for Tom McCarty's disappearance. Unknown to many folks, the young outlaw continued, his sister and Tom McCarty were married. The girl's death had put the noted bandit off the deep edge, and Tom had sworn to forsake the country and make another start somewhere where her memory wouldn't linger in everything and everybody he saw. This loneliness and sorrow was the reason McCarty had said nothing to his outlaw pals about his whereabouts. He had wanted to grieve by himself, and he still did, evidently, for there was no word or sign that he intended ever to return to Utah.

But Matt had just risked a stolen visit to his family up in Sanpete County and learned some things. The boy he had hit on the head with the

rock was daft and never would be right, and this
served to keep the homeplace stirred up against
Williard Christiansen's return. Matt had left quietly
and in the middle of the night, just as he had six
years before. But he had not gone without some
news that brought a release of gladness to his wild
heart. There was a letter at the homeplace for him,
and it was from Tom McCarty. That letter had
brought Matt Warner back to the Roost, and was
going to take him right back out of it the minute he
could make arrangements.

What those arrangements were he did not say,
suggesting instead that it was George Cassidy's
turn to fill in the back trail.

The latter did so quickly, beginning with meeting old Mike at the Sevier River ranch, ending with
the Panguitch bank job, the wounding and escape of
Mike Cassidy, and the subsequent murder of Deputy
Orville Stodenberg. It was a rough and stupid story,
and young Cassidy made no effort to cast it otherwise. His listener appreciated the honesty.

"Don't blame yourself," he said. "Mike's getting along. He don't think too good. Moreover, he
wasn't never much of a bank or train man. Mostly
rustling."

"He's tremendous good at that," said young
Cassidy.

"Sure, nobody no better that I know of."

They made cigarettes, Matt got out a ragged
letter. He opened the grease-stained envelope and
unfolded the paper within. "Want you to listen to
this," he said:

> . . . and while things ain't the same, and
> never will be, with Teen gone, a man has
> got to do something, or go bust in his
> head. I have figured out a little thing down
> here, but need some help. Have one fellow
> with me. If you'd like to come here, do it,

*and bring with you somebody for lookout
and who can handle horses. . . .*

Matt Warner put away the letter, sucked on his
cigarette to get it going again, then looked hard at
his companion. "Postmark on that envelope is Fort
Wingate, down to Arizony. You ever hankered to
hold horses down thataway?" he said.

The other boy's square face, intently frowning
as he listened to the excerpt from Tom McCarty's
letter, now lighted up. "Lord, God," he said, "you
mean you're asking me to go with you? To side you
and Tom McCarty? *Me?*"

Matt looked around the cabin's one room. "I
don't see nobody else in here with us," he said.
"You're elected, if you want to be."

As he was to prove all of his life, George Cassidy
was an essentially calculating individual. "Why?"
he said.

Matt Warner had not expected this directness.
For a moment it appeared as though it angered him
and harm would come of it. Then his dark face
relaxed. "Two reasons," he said. "Mike Cassidy has
spread it up and down the owlhoot that you're an
absolute top hand with horseflesh. Other thing is
that we're Mormons, me and you. That counts.
With me it does."

Young George Cassidy nodded. "Thanks," he
said. "Me, too, I reckon."

"Well, what about it?" Warner was watching
him again, and it unsettled him. Matt had changed
in the lost years. He no longer was just wild—he
was dangerous now. It came off of him like a scent,
something keen-nosed creatures like George Cassidy
could pick up without it being baited out, or put
down heavily in the wind. George chose his words.

"You know I'm hankering to go," he said. "But
what about Mike? He's been like a second paw to
me. I can't just up and ride out on him."

"You can, if you're going with me."

"I don't know, Matt. Damn, I sure do want to go."

"Where's your horse?"

"Pole corral, yonder in the pines."

"He a good one?"

"He'll use with any of them."

Matt Warner nodded to this information, and looked up at the morning sky through the shack's window. "Going to be a good day. No wind. Still early and she's quiet below. Time to go, George LeRoy. You got a gun?"

Young Cassidy could feel his nerves tighten. They sang like telegraph wires. "No," he said.

The other youth crossed the room. He reached and took Mike Cassidy's old Model '73 Winchester from its spikebuck hooks above the rock and mud fireplace. He tossed the weapon completely across the room to the startled George Cassidy. "Now you have," he said. He went quickly to the door and looked out. "Coast is clear," he announced. "Let's go."

The swagger of his pose in the doorway, the laconic crackle of his words, the lean, dark look of his hard face, the beckoning blue of the mountain sky seen beyond him, the sudden thin, far cry of an eagle circling Sam's Mesa to the south, were too much for George LeRoy Cassidy.

He took a belt of ammunition for Mike's carbine, threw some beef, biscuits, sugar, salt and coffee into a flour sack, rolled his blanket and was ready.

"Hightail it," said Warner tersely, his eyes narrowed on the settlement below. "They're moving around down yonder."

The other boy nodded and got his saddle from the lean-to. He ran with it across to the pines and the hidden pole corral. Behind him, Matt Warner swung up on his muscular thoroughbred. He minced the horse sideways toward the corral, his eyes never leaving the trail down the mountainside and the settlement below. Presently, George Cassidy joined him on Kanab.

"That was quick," said Warner. "You may do."

He turned his chestnut up the hill, to put the pine clump between them and the cabins down the bench. Young Cassidy sent Kanab after the first horse. The big bay snuffled and rolled the bit and pricked his ears at the chestnut.

"Good-looking horse," said Matt Warner, turning in the saddle. "I reckon he'll do, too."

"Do?" said George Cassidy curiously. "Do for what?"

The dark-faced youth threw him a tiger's smile. "For getting us shut of the Roost short of gunsmoke," he said. "Getting in is easy; getting out, they like to take a vote on it. And you ain't registered. Plain enough?"

George LeRoy Cassidy bobbed his sandy thatch. "Plain enough," he said, blue eyes dancing. "Let's get up the mountainside!"

23

◆

They went over the mesa and down into the Happy Canyon depths with no sign of pursuit to that point. "Forget it, now," said Matt Warner, eyeing the rim far above. "If they ain't showing on top from here, they ain't a'going to take us."

Issuing from the lateral canyon, they crossed the Dirty Devil and climbed the lightning bolt trail to the western plateau. Pausing only to rest the horses, Warner led the way south toward the five dark peaks of the Henry Mountains.

"Heading for Trachyte," was all the information that the older youth gave, but it was enough.

George Cassidy knew that Trachyte Canyon was the last of the three known entrances in the Roost. He had been on the Hanksville–Dirty Devil route. The Green River route was much longer but more open, even if its last day's ride was straight up and over the San Rafael Swell without one drop of spring or rock-tank water the entire way. But old Mike had told him that the Trachyte Canyon trail made the hellish ride from Hanksville seem like lady's day at the pony ring.

After an hour's hard going, in which the trail angled away from the canyon of the Dirty Devil, they climbed down into and back up out of the west-entering gorge of Poison Spring Creek. Here, the trail struck off to the west over a high desertscape as gray and dreary as the shadow side of the moon. Patch snow and sheet ice encased the land. No elevations over fifty feet high presented an obstacle to the winter wind, which was now on the rise.

Young Cassidy, although warmed by the coffee they had stopped to boil, found himself shivering. "Matt," he said, "where's she go from here?"

"To the head of Bitter Canyon. It'll take us down to Hog Spring in the North Wash. Camp there."

Warner, unlike the friendly Cassidy, was not a talker. He brooded a lot, and had a habit of compressing his lips and shaking his head silently while on the trial, as though life were one too many for him. Or perhaps he was considering different ways of doing in the comrade he had with him at the time, and was rejecting one idea after the other, until he came to the right one. It was not a cheering thought, but the latter possibility did serve to keep the other fellow on the qui vive, young Cassidy decided.

"How far will that be?" he asked. "To Hog Spring, I mean."

"Dunno," said the other. "Let's ride."

The camp at Hog Spring was cold and sleepless. One of them had to be up all through the night to forage for desert drift to feed the fire, which fought off frostbite and boneache for the weary riders. Breakfast was a burned slab of beef and more coffee. They were in the saddle while it was still black.

In about ten miles they struck Trachyte Canyon and the trail which followed its southeast course to join the Colorado at Dandy Crossing. The sun was just tipping the high roughlands of the Manti-La Sal and Elk Ridge country across the big river. Its wan beams warmed Matt Warner enough to let him point toward the morning's light and announce, "Thirty mile down the Trachyte we hit the Colorado. We got to cross there. Happen old man Hite ain't to home, we'll need to swim it."

"Old man Hite?"

"Runs the ferry over the river. Ain't no other crossing."

They rode on, making the Colorado at sundown. There was still light and time to get over the river, and Matt Warner meant to cross it. "It's like trailing stock," he said. "You like to camp across the water, not just shy of it."

"Sure," said young Cassidy. "That shines."

In the sunset, the approach to the crossing was spectacular. To the north the great bent bow of the Orange Cliffs were dyed a fiery crimson. Southward the eight-thousand-foot guardian rampart of Mount Holmes reared snowcapped in a sky of wild pink and blue clouds floating against the twilight green of the winter day's end. Across the river, the great wash of White Canyon's mouth spewed itself into the Colorado, building the footing of unseen sand and rock, which here widened and slowed the larger stream. The site was the best of all four natural crossings of the mighty Colorado. On the western shore, where George Cassidy and Matt Warner now rode, the entire cliff formation of the main canyon drew back like some gigantic sandstone stage drop, to disclose the awesome stillness and majesty of the fabled crossing. "God," said young Cassidy, "ain't that something!"

"Yeah," answered his companion. "It's Dandy Crossing."

They rode on down to the stone hovel where old man Hite was known to make his den, summer and winter, since the early seventies. The ferry raft lay silent at its cabled mooring. Soft waves, back-lapping from the slowed current, made strangely loud and resonant sounds against the steel drums lashed to the hand-sawed log and plank decking of the ferry. Old man Hite was nowhere to be seen.

Matt Warner slowed his mount and pulled his Winchester from its saddle scabbard. "Old man," he called, "come out."

There was no reply from the stone hut. But from the boulders behind the two young horsemen issued an order understood without debate along the owlhoot. "Heist 'em," said the reedy voice.

Matt Warner mumbled a curse. Slowly and with professional cleanness, he restored the Winchester to its scabbard and elevated his hands. George Cassidy had long since dropped the reins on Kanab's neck and eased his stout arms skyward.

"Get down off your horses and turn around," instructed the voice. Again, the two young riders obeyed. "Stand away from them," said the voice, and the ambushed pair stood away. Only then did old man Hite rise up from the rocks. Squinting at Warner, he said in plain disappointment, "Oh, it's only you."

"You crazy crackpot old fool!" shouted the Mormon youth. "Who the tunket you think it might be, Bishop Smith? Colonel Fremont, maybe?" He reached for his horse's trailing reins. "Leave me tell you something, old man," he grated, his face harder than the rock of the river. "Next time you pull down on me, you'd better mean it."

The ferryman nodded and came forward, still holding his rifle on them. He looked to young Cassidy like some ancient prophet out of the Book of Nephi. The wind, the sun and snowglare of that desolate place had seared his skin until it was blacker than the hide of a Ute Indian. His hair fell long to the shoulder; his beard tumbled nearly to his waist. Both were as white as fine-bleached muslin. He was not halt or infirm of gait, like so many with the full span of the Old Testament upon them.

He went quick and sure, the way a young man might. His eyes, a memorable frost-blue in color, were clear as a boy's. He did not in any way appear afraid of Matt Warner; he only watched him with a hunter's care, and kept coming on. When scarcely the reach of the rifle's barrel from the glaring outlaw, he stopped. "Man's got to be keerful in my business," he told Matt Warner. " 'Specially of the snakebite kind, like you."

George Cassidy believed his companion would leap at the old man then. Matt's eyes blazed. The cords on his neck, and the veins, stood out like those in the neck of a blown horse. But the young bandit was looking into the bore of an old bronze-frame Tyler Henry .44 Short. And he knew what the stubby cartridge's thumb-thick slug could do at shirt-burning ranges. He also knew that as many as sixteen of those fat, deadly little pills could be loaded into that old Henry. The veins in his neck went down.

"We only want to get over the river," he said.

"Fine," answered the old man. "That's what I'm here for. You boys got any money?"

"Money?" said Matt Warner.

"For fare," said the old man.

George Cassidy had made his calculations of the stand-off by this time. He flashed his bright grin and shrugged his broad shoulders. "Me, Mr. Hite," he said, "I ain't got a dime. Not for fare, not for nothing else. What can we do to help you around here? You know, work our way acrost."

The old man grounded his rifle butt. He stood a moment as if at parade salute, then turned slowly to look at the Circle Valley boy. "*Work?*" he said incredulously.

Cassidy broadened his grin. "I'll admit it's a frightening thing to say," he nodded. "But Matt tells me we got to get acrost the river. Them as can't pay, works. That's what my paw always maintained. I never argued it."

"What's your name, boy?"

"Cassidy, sir. George LeRoy Cassidy."

"You a Mormon?"

"Yes, sir."

"Ummmm—" Hite seemed to be thinking it over. He scrubbed at his beard with his left hand, relaxing his grip on the rifle with the right hand. It was the signal that Matt Warner had been looking for. He leaped at the old man with no warning, no sound whatever. Seizing the patriarch, he kicked the grounded rifle out of his grasp, whirled the old man about, took him from the rear. George Cassidy saw the boy's left arm bar itself across old Hite's throat, saw the gleam of the knife blade arcing back in the right hand to bury itself in the old man's kidneys. His own leap was instinctive, and only in the glint of time. His thick-set form hurtled into the lean body of Matt Warner, just as the knife reached Hite's straining backbone. The blade ripped sideways instead of driving inward. It tore the old man's coat and drew a thin line of blood across his tenderloins, but that was all. In the next instant Matt Warner, still clutching the knife, was on the ground with George Cassidy sprawled on top of him. Without hesitation, Warner twisted violently and tried to drive the blade into the other youth. Cassidy hit him full in the face with his balled fist, and felt some of the soft bones give under the blow. Matt fell back, dazed and hurt. His companion picked up the nearest cantaloupe-sized rock and struck his knife hand with it. Warner cried out and dropped the weapon, which young Cassidy retrieved.

"Sorry, Matt," said the boy, low-voiced. "I tooken a vow I'd never stand by and see—well, never mind, it don't matter. You all right?"

The other youth did not answer him. He got slowly to his feet, feeling his bloody mouth with the back of his hand. He began to nod and compress his lips and look from George Cassidy to old man Hite, and still uttered not one word. Of a sudden, young Cassidy wished that he were far away from the friend of his Mormon boyhood. Evidently old man Hite shared the impulse. He picked up his fallen rifle and leavered a shell through the action to see that it had not been sanded by its skid along the ground. The bright metal case spun out tinklingly into the nearby rocks, and the old man nodded. "All right," he said. "March."

"Where to?" asked Cassidy. Matt Warner still was silent, still darted his dark eyes from one to the other.

"The ferry," answered the old man. He looked at the short, square-jawed boy. "You just paid the fare for both of you," he said. "Get your horses."

They loaded Kanab and the chestnut on the raft, and the old ferryman cabled them across and set them ashore. He also set ashore their rifles, which he had kept for them while going over. He told them not to try and pick up the weapons until he was well gone. He took his own Henry, and whirling without seeming to aim, shot the head off a black mud coot paddling in a quiet pool no less than fifty paces off. Convinced, the two young riders edged away from their beached rifles, nodding in agreement. Matt Warner still had not uttered a word.

George Cassidy thanked old man Hite and expressed the hope that the river would stay down that spring, and that Hite would have a good summer at the ferry business.

At this unexpected politeness, the bearded boatman, not yet out into the current, shoved his long guidepole into the sand of the bottom and held the raft steady. "Boy," he called, "you still hold with hard work?"

Young Cassidy sensed that this was not the casual inquiry it might seem. Old Hite was holding out a lifeline to him. He licked his lips. He knew Matt Warner was watching him, but he was smart enough not to watch back. He only grinned and

waved at the old man, and asked him what he had
in mind.

"Got a hunch you may be right," the old fellow
yelled back. "Business going to be on the boom this
year. Reckon I could use a bright, strong boy here at
the crossing."

George Cassidy thought he knew where he
was. He was on the far side of a river which divided
the desert wilderness. On the other side was the old
prophet, Nephi, advising him to return to the land
of his people, to abandon the Satan with whom he
traveled while there was yet time, while he was still
among the quick, instead of the dead. Behind him,
silent and still and dark, a young devil waited. The
time for decision was slipping past.

"Boy? What you say?" The old man's call was
imperative.

Young Cassidy waved to him, then turned to
Matt Warner. "So long, Matt," he said. "It's too far
back along the trail that me and you was friends.
We'd never make it to Fort Wingate. Not together."

Matt Warner nodded in chill agreement to the
allegation.

Cassidy picked up his '73 Winchester and led
Kanab down to the water's edge. Old Hite poled the
ferry in, the boy loaded the horse and they shoved
out into the current. Behind them, Matt Warner
stood without moving. Only when the raft was
small with distance over the great river, did he
come down to the shore rocks and retrieve his rifle.
He stood a moment, lips moving but making no
sound. Then he went over to the chestnut thoroughbred and swung upon the lean-bodied racer,
and rode out swiftly into the settling darkness,
southward.

24

◆

Young Cassidy's guess about the humanity of the old hermit, Cass Hite, proved correct. "Boy," said the bearded ferryman, when they had moored the craft, "you was burning a short fuse. Happen you'd ridden on down the trail with that one, you'd have been blowed sky high and left to bleach where buzzards wouldn't even find you."

"I reckoned you was giving me the high sign," said the youth. "I'm beholden, Mr. Hite."

The old fellow nodded. "Come on," he said. "We'll eat some supper. I shot a bighorn sheep this morning. First yearling ram I've see'd this winter. He'd ought to eat mighty easy."

The stone house at Hite's Ferry was windproof and weatherproof. Its doors, built of drift lumber, were expertly fitted and hung. The roof was not of poles and leaky sod, but of beams and sheeting and heavy wood shakes; these were hand-split from big cedar logs brought down from the high timber country by the Colorado in flood. Cass Hite was a craftsman of the pioneer order, with nothing but time to prove it to himself. Young Cassidy had not felt so warm, full-fed and safe since leaving the Sevier River bunkhouse of his father's Circle Four Ranch.

"Mr. Hite," he sighed, pushing back from the table to roll a cigarette, "maybe I kept my friend from putting you under, and maybe I didn't. But I'll say one thing, as to the other way around. I surely do owe you one for this fine supper and the God-blessed snugness of this here first-class rock home of yourn. Right now, I figure I'm going to live till morning, and I wouldn't have give nobody odds on that, hadn't you throwed me that job offer over on the other bank." He paused, cocking his head. "How come you to do that, Mr. Hite?" he asked.

The old man told him that charity work was not in his regular line. However, he said, he did owe his life to the boy's interference with the deadly intent of his recent companion. Knowing the owlhoot breed as he did, having ferried its kind over the Colorado since the early seventies, he understood all too plainly that the likes of young Matt Warner were not born to bluster. When George Cassidy had attacked the other youth, he had violated the code.

"You can't turn on a pal in the outlaw trade," Hite admonished his listener. "The word goes up and down the line, from Sonora State, down to Old Mexico, to the Canada border up north. The boys are given your number, and then that number ain't no place else but up. You take my advice, boy, you'll get a good night's sleep, and bright and early in the morning you'll saddle up that there stout bay horse and you'll ride out of here on a different trail than you come in on. You foller my drift, kid? You ain't like that one we put ashore on the other side. A man lives alone like old man Hite, he gets to see them all. Sooner or quicker, they all ride through here, getting out of the country or coming back inter it. The breed comes in two varieties only— them as will kill you, and them as won't. You learn to spot it fast, or you ain't give time to learn it.

Their eyes tell you the story, same as they do with animals. I can tell you by looking in a sheepdog's eyes iffen he will bite or wiggle his tail. It don't mean, either, that biters is necessarily the toughest or the best for the job. Nor does it mean that the tail-waggers is soft nor yeller nor unfit. Same with men. No difference at all. Some biters are yeller'n hades. Some rump-wigglers will knock you down and stomp you senseless. Other bad ones are what I call 'snakebiters.' They ain't afeered of nothing that walks nor crawls nor flies, and that's the kind your pal was, kid. Snakebiters strike without no cause and give no warning. You hear tell that a rattler will always buzz his buttons before he hits you. You got to know that's a crock of clabber. They ain't no rightful idea when they're going to strike. It ain't no simple matter of shaking them rattlers to give the other poor devil his chance to get out'n the way. Horse apples!"

George Cassidy nodded soberly. The old man was getting his bad men and his sheepdogs and his sidewinders shaken up pretty good in the same blanket, but the boy did not miss his point. He had seen the killer kind for himself, and close up. Wonderful old Mike Cassidy, the bowlegged, quick-grinning little cowboy who had been more than a father to him, had bared his teeth against the boy as far back as the alder clump where they had left the Chunk horse on the Panguitch raid. He had seen Mike cold-bloodedly execute Deputy Stodenberg, and for no more reason than that the little outlaw did not want to go back to Panguitch for questioning in a bank job that never came off. As for Matt Warner, he was not so sure, but had been certain enough to jump at the chance old Hite had given him to desert the outlawed Mormon youth. Now he repeated his nod to the ferryman.

"I agree, Mr. Hite," he said. "There's them as will kill you for no decent reason, nor any rightful cause."

"That," said old Hite, "brings us to the other kind; your kind." He paused long enough to fire his cob pipe back into life. "Boy," he said, "looking you in the eye, I wouldn't pay you no second-time heed, insofar as fearing you'd cut me down, blindside. You ain't got it in you to kill heedless."

"I believe that's so, Mr. Hite. I surely hope it is."

"Hope ain't nothing to do with it, youngster. A man makes himself whatever he is. I don't have to be a loner and live out here with the snakes and kingfishers and coyotes. That just happens to be the way I want it. It's the trail I chose for myself. God didn't plant that decision in my daddy's seed. Folks are forever blaming somebody else for the bad they do in this life. But tell me the last time you heered one of them giving credit to somebody else for all the good luck he'd had along the way. Sure, you can't do it."

"Reckon not," admitted young George.

They talked some more, and of many things, for the old man was lonely and trusted few humans in the way he had trusted the boy from Circleville. George LeRoy Cassidy's charm was to see him through many a scrape and tight place in the hard years ahead. And at Dandy Crossing, Utah, in that winter of 1883, it was no different. The quick sunshine of his broad grin, the honest cheerfulness, the inner, essential good humor of the stocky youth, warmed the lonely man's heart. Neither Cass Hite nor George Cassidy could know of the years ahead. All that the old man knew—recluse, iconoclast, eccentric and misanthrope that local legend called him—was that he liked the sandy-haired Mormon boy and wanted to help him. As for the latter, he remembered enough of his early steeping in the Book of Mormon and the pre-Biblical faith of Lehi, Laman, Lemuel, Sam and Nephi, to believe that here at Hite's Ferry the Lord had sent him a sign. The sign said that old man Hite was right, that

George Cassidy could choose a new trail here. He could ride away from Dandy Crossing, north or south, good man or bad, just like the old man was trying to tell him. The boy suddenly realized that he had not yet irrevocably committed himself to the owlhoot, that he could still ride that other trail, that he had only to make himself do it.

"Mr. Hite," he said quietly, "tell me which way to ride out of here."

"In the morning," nodded the old man. "Not now."

PART FOUR

◆

The Trail
to
Telluride

25

◆

For four years and many a hundred hungry mile from Hite's Ferry, George LeRoy Cassidy followed the new trail. Turning away from the owlhoot was not easy, but young George was determined. He drifted and worked, worked and drifted. The wandering took him from Montana to Old Mexico and left him, in the spring of 1887, in the mining camp of Telluride, Colorado. He rode in on a morning late in May, when the mountains were greening against the coming summer; the sun, breaking free of the high meadow mists, brought the bird song and bustle of the new day with a gladness and good cheer not found in the lowland world.

Kanab, aging a bit now at nine years, still went strong and steady beneath his rider. He greeted Telluride as he did each new town, with ears shot forward and head alertly raised. His dark eyes scanned the dirt street, the sun-blasted false fronts of the stores, saloons and shady houses of the camp, all for any overt sign of danger to the cheerful boy upon his back.

Boy? Perhaps to Kanab. What changes for a
horse except the pasture, the stall, the water, the
day's work? But to Telluride, and to the legend,
George Cassidy was no longer the boy from Circle
Valley, nor any boy at all from anywhere. April lay
behind, and with it that birthday which the law
says separates children from grown men. George
LeRoy Cassidy was now five feet nine inches in
height, a bone-solid chunk of a man made only of
sinew and muscle and cartilage—a hundred and
sixty-five pounds of human rawhide and piano wire.
And yet, although he had hardened so outwardly,
the vital organ had never changed—in his heart, as
in Kanab's eyes, George LeRoy Cassidy remained a
boy.

But now, coming into Telluride, he was frowning.

The May sunshine and the mountain bird song
did not seem enough to lift his ordinarily buoyant
spirit. The trouble was the town, he thought. This
burg believed it was something, obviously. Set in a
bowl of gray granite peaks going up twelve and
fourteen thousand feet all about, it was a desolate
place which spring and sun could not quite soften
up. Yet the citizens were deluded, clearly. Between
the respectable buildings—and there were many of
them as big as anything in Salt Lake, including an
opera house—people were even trying to grow grass!
Yes, and doing it, even if their lots were no more
than postage stamp size, and the fine homes set as
close as three and four feet apart. Worse yet, the
grass was barbered. That was a fact. It was sheared
as short as a cropped sheep, and here and there a
sunbonneted lady sprinkled it with a watering can.
Still more incredible, now and again one of these
brave souls was tending an actual bed of flowers!
Now anybody who had ridden those parts of Colorado the past four years knew that growing flowers
where they would need to have been planted with a
bullprod mining drill, or a mallet and chisel, was
not the act of a sane person. Telluride was putting

on airs for certain. It was swarming with people. In just the few minutes he spent riding down Main Street, George Cassidy saw, on wagons or stages or the sides of buildings, the names of a score of mines and mining companies, which were known wherever gold or silver was dug for in the Rockies.

The Smuggler. The Liberty Bell. The Sheridan. The Emerald. The Ausboro. The Ajax. The Alta. The Tomboy. The Black Bear. The Union. The Nellie Bligh. There was no end to the big money operating in Telluride, that was plain. A man could not have come to a better town to find work, providing that was his game. That was precisely what had put the frown on the sunburned face of George LeRoy Cassidy. He had come here to find work because he knew the railroad had built as near as Silverton, only miles away, and he knew the mines of Telluride were booming. Well, that was fine for starters. But now, confronted with all the signs of prosperity and easy jobs in the rich camp, he was suddenly not at all convinced that he wanted to work.

He turned Kanab into the nearest hitchrail. It fronted the San Juan Feed, Grain and General Mercantile Emporium, and to get to it the big bay had to squeeze between a string of prospectors' burros and a mining company mule wagon loading at the Emporium's raised front walk. It was only midmorning, but the place was moving and the people hiving around as if it were high noon. It all looked far too energetic and well organized for the visitor. It reminded him, with some nostalgia but no great happiness, of the Mormon towns of his boyhood, especially the bigger ones like Price and Provo and Salt Lake. Everything seemed too much in order in Telluride, Colorado. There was a air of smug refinement about the settlement which Cassidy had never encountered in a mining camp before. Culture had struck here—and civilization. Both were advantages of a mankind too well gentled and persuaded toward law and order to suit any wanderer of the wasteland as traveled and adventured as the sandy-haired young man who now peered up and down the boardwalks with his quizzical frown.

The newcomer, without even getting down from his horse, decided that he did not care for Telluride. Who the devil did they think they were hoodwinking? Not him. He knew San Juan County. It was said that it was the only county in the U.S. of A. which did not have inside its corporate boundaries one single acre of tillable soil. It was all rocks and snow and pine trees and foamy mountain snow water booming down the hill at a hundred miles per hour.

It was a good game-hunting country, an extra fine mineral country; it had some fair grass and browse for sheep and cattle and was friendly territory to those who might not be exactly the leading-citizen-type themselves. With the railroad pushing into it, it might soon amount to about half of what it already thought it did. But that would never do away with the fact that it was ninety-eight percent rocks and snow, saving for the brief summer when the grass burst from beneath the boulders and the snowcaps melted and the birds came out to sing like they were doing right then.

"I reckon," he said aloud to Kanab, "that we will turn about and go on down into the desert. This here spring air has made me homesick. We could be at Hite's Ferry in no time, old horse. It's only cross the border and through the La Sals. Come June, we could be riding down off old South Table and along the Sevier to the homeplace." He paused, a shadow of the lost years passing in his blue eyes. "It would be somewhat to see Paw again, and to see the summer in Circle Valley, and maybe go and make it right with Sheriff Rasmussen in Panguitch. It seems we've rode five thousand miles, big horse, and all we've got is older."

He sighed like a man three times his age and started to lift the reins, backing Kanab out of the traffic at the hitchrail. He guessed that homesickness came up in the human trunk just like sap did in the trees—in the springtime. It had taken him hard about this time every year, but this was the first spring when it had hit him so sure and dead-center that it was time to go home again.

"Easy, big horse," he said to Kanab. "Don't crowd them mine-wagon mules."

The bay began to back, going daintily, quickly, like the trained cow horse he was. But he was not quick enough.

The teamster, coming out of the store, shouted a curse at the young stranger. It was a fine, round oath, complete with reference to the morals of the stocky rider's mother. In the spirit of the moment, the mule of the lead team reached out a leathery muzzle and bit a sample of hide from Kanab's crouching rear. The Utah horse, unaccustomed to such indignities, squatted like a rabbit and unloaded a set of iron-shod heels. Horseshoe and mule head collided with resounding impact. The miner's burros on the far side of Kanab at once crowded in toward the excitement, forcing Kanab into the lead mule team, where he fouled himself in their collar and trace tugs. The horse reared, trying to get free.

At this point, George Cassidy, who had been working to stay with his mount, left the battle. He was none too soon. As he lit on his feet and jumped for the boardwalk, Kanab went over backward and fell into the trampled manure of the rail's fronting. He took two burros and one of the wagon mules with him, and it required half a dozen bystanders twenty minutes of effort to get the various animals to their feet and separated.

Some harness had needed to be cut on the mules, and the teamster's temper was such that he felt called to look for the careless saddle tramp who had started it all. He had not far to seek. As he threw back his head and commenced to bellow out the details of what he would do to the "infernal no-good bum," a light hand touched his shoulder from behind and an arid South Utah voice inquired for a better description of the missing cowboy.

The mule skinner from the mines wheeled about to furnish the information, and found it unnecessary.

"Sir," said George LeRoy Cassidy in his friendly, cheerful way, "you done startled my horse, encouraged and abetted a mule to commit insult and perjury on my mount, and you desperated the memory of my mother. Ain't you nothing to say of apology?"

26

◆

They told of that fight in Telluride for thirty years. Children were born, grew up, married and went away, all to the tune of the morning in May of 1887 when big Buffalo John Scanlon questioned the antecedents of the smiling blond cowboy from across the Swell.

Buffalo John was earnest and mean and well taught. An out-of-work hide hunter and camp-meat supplier for the railroad crews building across Kansas to Colorado, he was a hairy dog of first reputation in the street-fighting folklore of the region. By the opposite token, no citizen of Telluride, at least none who was decent and paid his taxes, had ever heard of George LeRoy Cassidy. To the yelping pack of hardrock gophers, Micks, Bohunkies, muckers and Cousin Jacks which instantly surrounded the combatants, the soft spoken cowboy was nothing but the next victim.

But in less than three minutes, Buffalo John had been into the dirt eight times and was getting up somewhat slowly. His opposite was only breathing easily, grinning happily.

They fought from one side of the wide street to the other. They rolled in the mule marbles, rooted in the horse apples, furrowed up more honest soil with nose and ear and bloodied tooth than turned by iron plowshare in San Juan County since the Civil War. It was all over in five minutes, even so, and would have lasted half that time had it not been for Buffalo John's unbelievable strength and stupidity. Finally, however, the big man went down and could not rise again. He got as far up as to be braced on his elbows, looking up at George Cassidy. From there, he nodded in gallant admission of defeat, struck colors with a last gasp, heeled over slowly and sank among the wagon ruts and urine-puddled stale lakes of the gutter. There his recent supporters left him beached, to seize up the new champion and bear him into the Glory Hole saloon, to buy him refreshment until sunset or unconsciousness, whichever should occur first.

George LeRoy had never been a great drinker. To start on an empty stomach at break of day following strenuous exercise, and after receiving some respectable contusions, proved too much for the stocky cowboy. Within the hour he was tottering back out of the Glory Hole, pale and at the point of collapse. None of his merry men within the dank bar knew that he had departed, nor cared. They were busy with the bottle building a legend. George made it as far as the boardwalk's outer edge, his aim to get across the street and to the hitchrail in front of the San Juan Emporium, where Kanab still waited patiently. He got one stride into the road. Then his dragging feet encountered an obstruction, and he wavered and went down. He lay where he had fallen, no longer hearing the bird song or feeling the sunshine, directly across the stranded, still motionless remains of Buffalo

John Scanlon, in the gutter in front of the Glory Hole saloon.

The thudding of his limp form into Buffalo's back, however, forced a grunt of expelled air from the lungs of the supine gladiator and revived the big man. He came back to the world of the living, rumbling curses and shaking his shaggy head and rearing up out of the gutter like some antediluvian dinosaur from the muck of the ages.

When he had cleared his mind and freed himself of the body atop his, he recognized his bowlegged conqueror. At this point, those attracted by the sounds and movements of Scanlon's return to consciousness would not have given a pinch of dust for the cowboy's chances to ever wake up. But Buffalo John was a bigger man than any of them knew. Like Grizzly, he had developed an instant weakness "fer the leetle feller." Hoisting the inert form of George LeRoy Cassidy to his shoulder, he stalked across the street to his waiting mules and the parked wagon, the stenciled sideboard of which proclaimed it to be the property of the Upper Uinta Consolidated Mineral and Smelting Corporation. Into this vehicle, with the sacks of flour, beans, coffee, sugar, coils of rope, chain, bags of blacksmithing charcoal, boxes of blasting powder, fuse and general clutter of a returning mine wagon, he dumped the body of George Cassidy, even solicitously covering it with a canvas tarp against the glare of the mountain sun.

Tying Kanab to the tail-gate of the wagon, and making crude repair to the damaged harness of the lead team, the hulking skinner climbed to his seat-box and uncoiled the twelve-foot lash of the bullwhip. "Hee-yahh!" he bellowed at the mules, literally pulling them away from the rail with a mighty tug on the lines. "Lay to it, you sons of Satan! We're an hour late and losing time! Hee-yahh, hee-yahh!"

The mine wagon swung away from the rail with the sprint and dash of the Silverton Stage. The four mules hit their breastbands and collars with a will only lightly encouraged by the song of the black snake about their ragged ears and straining rumps. Behind the wagon, Kanab whinnied shrilly and broke into a lope to keep up. Within the vehicle the one hundred and sixty-five pounds of rawhide and piano wire, which ordinarily was George Cassidy, bounced limp and slack between the blasting powder and the dried beans. That is the way that the legend came to the employ of the Uinta Queen, at Telluride, Colorado, in the spring of 1887.

27

◆

Three clean-shaven hardcases, dressed well and with fine running horses tied at the rail of the Glory Hole, stood watching George Cassidy's departure from Telluride.

The first man was slim, dapper. His black hair was frosted at the temples. Bushy black brows shadowed a pair of piercingly pale blue eyes. He was deeply tanned. His companions, larger, coarser-featured men, were yet of the same lean stamp. There was an air about the three, an affinity both of look and behavior, suggesting common ties, and close. As they hesitated at the hitchrail, a fourth man strode up to them. He had come across the street from the direction of the Telluride *Journal*, the offices of which, interestingly enough, provided the best close-hand inspection station for the San Miguel Valley Bank building. He was not a happy man by nature, and now he was glaring about and shaking his head and kicking at the dirt ruts with his boots. "What's the matter?" the dapper leader greeted him. "Somebody recognize you?"

"Yes, blast the luck. I no sooner got set in the bay window of the *Journal* than in walks a Jack Mormon from Spanish Forks what knowed me as a boy. Ely Hofer. No chanct to bluff him. Heck, we was tads together."

"Well?"

"Well, what?"

"How does the bank look?"

"Easy. It's a tin box."

"Did you shake Hofer? He didn't see you come back over here? Didn't spot us?"

"Huh, you think I'm stupid, or something?"

"A leading question," nodded the slim man. "All right, you're spotted by a local. That lets you out. You might as well drift right now, this morning. We'll stay around a day or so, and see what we can see."

The fourth man frowned. "Where'll we meet?" he said.

One of the other men, a pleasant, bright-eyed fellow with golden brown hair, broke in. "How about that abandoned stope on the old Lucifer?" he said. "You know the one got flooded out?"

"Good idea," agreed the pale-eyed leader. "We'll be there tomorrow night."

The fourth man nodded, pausing a moment. "Understand they had a hell of a street fight here this morning," he said. "Too bad we missed it. They tell me over to the *Journal* that the town bully done got his from some wandering cow-waddy about one third his size."

"Seems so," said the remaining member of the original trio. A quiet man, he spoke slowly and diffidently. "Wisht we'd been here, too. In the saloon they say this toughnut feller was a drifter. Utah boy, they say. Mormon, likely. Always sort of like to cheer for the hometown boys."

"He was tough, all right, but he didn't fight underhand, they tell us." The leader spoke now; his pride in the moral prowess of another man not of large physique came from that natural quick sympathy of the underdog for his brave fellow. "We just saw him loaded into a mine wagon like a side of beef. He looked like something cut off a cow on the run. That big devil really chewed him up, but he couldn't spit him out."

"Yonder the wagon goes," said the man with the light-brown hair and cheerful eye. "Just starting the switchback up to the Palomas smelter."

The fourth man checked the distant wagon; his eyes narrowed. "That's one of the rigs from the Uinta Queen," he said, able to read the lettering even at that distance in the crystal air of the mountain morning. "Richest ore body since the original Smuggler, they say over to the *Journal*. Tellurous ore. Say it runs twelve hundred dollars a ton just the way they bring it out of the shaft."

"They still have to dig it," said the leader.

"Sure, but it's smelted right at Palomas. What goes down to the bank vault at Telluride, goes as gold-bar stuff. They say they just haul it down like so much coal, or cordwood, right in the damned mine wagons."

"Interesting." The leader was now watching the slow climb of the wagon up out of Telluride. "Ah, if we only had an inside man! Somebody planted at the Uinta Queen. Might be a cleaner way to retire rich than playing with giant powder and time locks. Wouldn't it be grand, now, to have the ear of the driver of that bullion wagon when it takes out to make that deposit at the San Miguel Valley Bank?"

"Maybe," said the dark-faced fourth man, "one of you three had ought to apply for the job."

"Gold bars, eh?" The leader spoke the words softly, almost reverently. "A mine wagon full of gold bars? My God, there has got to be a way! I had no idea they were freighting pure stuff out of here. How long has that smelter been operating at Palomas? Never mind. It is now, that's the case ace. Let me think."

"Go ahead," growled the fourth man, turning away. "I'm going to get me a bottle to take along to the Lucifer."

He started into the Glory Hole saloon, but had to step aside to make way for three very drunk citizens just then oozing out of the swinging doors. The conversation of the three, although badly slurred and scarcely elevating, caught the fourth man's ear. His dark eyes burned with sudden fire, and he crouched as though gathering himself to strike.

"You are crazier than a pickled toad," declared one of the inebriates. "I will give you Buffalo eight days a week and twice on Sunday, and I will still take old George to beat that overgrowed ape every time. That cussed Cassidy feller is the goldangdest fist fighter ever I see'd, and I see'd a few, in and out of the bottle. Put your money where your flannel mouth is!"

The dark-faced man backed slowly away from the saloon doors. He turned and went over to the three well-dressed hardcases, who were untying their lean horses from the rail.

"I just found you out something," he said to the leader. "The soused 'cowboy' you saw being dumped into that mine wagon is the same one that broke this here nose of mine over to Dandy Crossing in eighty-three. All bets are off, and I ain't spending no time in that Lucifer stope shack. I'm a'heading for the Uinta Queen, right now."

But the trim leader of the band spoke softly and cleanly. "You idiot," he said. "You're doing no such of a thing. Yonder up the mountain goes our 'inside man' on the gold-bar shipment sidetrack, and you talk of setting your nose straight? You'll never make it on your brains, brother-in-law, never. But, faith, then, you don't really need to, do you? For you always have me, and that's enough for any man, Jack Mormon or Mackerel Snapper. Bill, George, ride slow out south. Matt, you go north. I'll go roundabout. We will set up at the Lucifer and plan it from there."

The others looked at him a moment. Then all three nodded, got their horses and rode out of town. Watching them go, Tom McCarty laughed softly and swung up on his own mount. "Brains," he said lightly to the horse. "That's what separates me from the likes of you and Matt Warner."

28

◆

For a week nothing happened at the Uinta Queen. Given work as a stock tender and harness maintenance man at the minehead, George Cassidy made an easy and quick way for himself, as he did everywhere he went. Then Buffalo John took ill and the irrepressible Utah cowboy was put on Buffalo's mule-skinning run down the mountain with the highgrade for the smelter at Palomas. The mules took to him, responding to that magic he always held for livestock. They would sweat for him where they would sull on Buffalo John. Young Cassidy was able to make as many as three round trips to the smelter per day. The mine super took note of the fact, and put the new man permanently on the smelter haul. He also gave him the Palomas-Telluride weekend haul of the smelter's Saturday clean-up of rough-cast ingots made from the smelter metal. These extremely heavy gold bars, being impossible, it was assumed, for any bandit gang to handle, were transported to the lower town with no extraordinary precautions. Everyone in the area knew when

154

the goldbar wagon made its deliveries to the bank's vaults at Telluride. But who was going to run off with a short ton of gold blocks? Certainly not any horse-borne band of highwaymen, such as plagued the banks, stages and railroads of the Territory. The system was so lax that, at the end of his second week at the Queen, when it came time for young Cassidy to make the Saturday run with the clean-up to Telluride, it was not even considered necessary to send a guard force along.

True, a shotgun man from the smelter generally did ride down to Telluride with the clean-up, but he wasn't so much a guard as an invoice man sent to get the gold counted accurately.

The super at the Queen was a dour Scot named Mackenzie. He wasted nothing but wanted plenty. Even on Saturday morning he insisted that no wagon go down the hill empty. Hence, Cassidy, on the way to his noon assignment at the smelter, had to take down a regulation load of high-grade ore in the wagon to pick up the goldbar shipment in Palomas. Just above Palomas was a grade up to the pass, which dipped the road down to the smelter. It was the custom of the Queen's teamsters to pull over their hitches here and rest them before continuing the descent. On this Saturday morning, the first weekend in June, young Cassidy pulled his teams off the road as usual at the pass turnout. He wrapped his lines, set the brakes, rolled a cigarette and stepped down from the driver's seat to stretch his legs and soak up some of the fine summer sun and pitchpine-scented air. He had taken perhaps three drags on his smoke, when he heard the familiar ring of horseshoes on hard rock behind him. Turning, George Cassidy saw the three riders, black against the morning sun, emerge from the boulders of the summit. They cut between him and the wagon, and he halted where he was: he knew these three men.

"Good morning. Can I help you, Mr. McCarty," he said. "What can I do for you?"

While the slim leader of the horsemen blinked his pale blue eyes, and his two brothers opened their mouths in surprise, young Cassidy enjoyed the moment's pause. His mind had instantly clicked at the sight of dapper Tom McCarty. From the reward poster given him by old Mike Cassidy four years ago to the silent mountainside above Palomas, Colorado, was only a flash for the fox-quick eye of the young drifter. This instant, perfect recall was one of the qualities which were to shelter him where others fell.

"You're right cute," said Tom McCarty. "Or a wild guesser from way back."

"Well, I'm from way back," admitted the other with a ready grin, "but I ain't wild no more. Fact is, I've tooken the purity vows. Ain't had a mislaid thought since I left home to go to work for you in the banking business."

"Small world," the dapper Irishman observed. "You're a little late reporting, Cassidy, but I am pleased to tell you that the job is still open and is yours, if you want it."

"The job, Mr. McCarty?"

"Sure now, lad, don't tell me you're not interested in that line of livelihood any more?"

"That depends, I'd say."

"I thought that it might. Let me lay it out for you."

The McCartys, with Matt Warner, had cleaned out a hiding place at the old Lucifer mine in preparation for a "salting," which would pay off far better than any bank vault or railway express car job. The idea was so simple that it was scarey. All they needed to do was to reroute the gold ingot shipment from the smelter to the Lucifer, instead of to the bank at Telluride. Cassidy would merely pull off of the Telluride Grade at a place where another wagon would be waiting. The ingots would then be trans-

ferred to the new wagon, which would take them
up to the Lucifer. There, they would "salt" the old
stope with the ingots, dismantle the wagon, shove
it down the central shaft of the defunct mine into
four hundred feet of dark water. At any time in the
next ten years, or in two months, the gang could
return and "unsalt" the Lucifer. This done, they
had but to load the ingots on packmules and take
them over the mountain by the back trail to the
owlhoot rendezvous in Brown's Hole. If the fence
up at the Hole had upped his discount rate too
much, they could easily go south and sell the gold
to their Mexican outlet in Santa Fe. Granted, there
was a bit of common toil involved, but absolutely
no risk. And where could a young mule skinner
beat the pay? George Cassidy's one-fifth split could
run to ten thousand dollars, and for certain not go
under four thousand, all depending on the percent-
age required by the fence, the size of the Palomas
clean-up for the week, and other professional considerations. How did Cassidy feel about "them
apples"?

For once, the young Utahan was caught short
for pertinent comment. The plan was so bald, so
daft, so slap-dash daring, as to baffle any flip or
straight-out turndowns. He needed time, not to
decide on whether or not he would join the gang,
but to make sure his refusal would not wind him up
looking at the sky from the bottom of the nearby
gulch.

"Where's Matt?" he asked. "I'd of thought he
wouldn't want no more to do with me."

"Circumstances change plenty of brands,"
answered Tom McCarty. "Matt spotted you for us in
Telluride. He could easy have kept quiet and we'd
never have known it was you in that mine wagon.
Matt isn't exactly the greatest thinker to come
down the pike in recent ages, but he's quick enough
to want his share of salting the Lucifer."

"Where is he?" insisted Cassidy.

"At the stope. He was recognized in Telluride and we've had him to stay away from town since. What's your answer, cowboy? You in or out?"

When Tom came to it like that, his two brothers got down from their horses and moved a step toward George Cassidy. There they stopped, spread their feet a little and flexed their right arms, looking at Cassidy.

The latter shot a side glance at the granite fangs of the gorge below. He did not see a single jagged gray slab which he thought suitable for bearing the inscription, *George LeRoy Cassidy, R.I.P.* "Well, now," he said, forcing the grin, "I'll need to think it over. That's fair, ain't it?"

"Sure," said Tom McCarty. "You got ten seconds."

Cassidy took two of his ten seconds to consider the course of wisdom—to accept the proposal. It annoyed him to think that four years of hard work to stay straight could come down to ten seconds of enforced crookedness, however, and he used the remaining eight seconds to consider his options. "What about the shotgun rider from the smelter?" he said. "You know I pick him up at Palomas."

"Leave him to us."

"You mean to put him under?"

"I didn't say that; we're not killers, Cassidy. We'll just jump whatever guard you got along. Tie him or them up, use gaps, throw them in the smelter wagon and light out."

"All right," said Cassidy. "It's agreed, no fireworks."

"Agreed."

"There's just the one thing else, then: you got to understand I ain't doing this of my own free will, and that any contract signed under durast ain't legal and blinding."

He was grinning when he said it, and the McCartys could not tell if he was joking, or if he meant the limitation to protect his own conscience, or what. "You talk just like that damned old rascal,

Mike Cassidy," said Tom McCarty, eyeing him. "He taught you more than I thought. 'Legal and blinding,' eh? 'Under durast,' you say? Cassidy you're as ignorant as he was. I won't hold it against you, though, as there isn't time, and we can't all be educated."

Cassidy nodded. He knew the McCartys had had advantages not common to the frontier. Born in the East, the sons of a successful medical doctor, they were men of more than average polish. This was especially true of Tom. Indeed, the slim outlaw leader attracted the young Utah cowboy precisely by this patina of what old Mike Cassidy had taught him to think of as "class." Not many had it; Tom McCarty held it in spades.

"Thank you, Mr. McCarty," he now replied carefully. "I reckon I'd best be getting this rig on over the hill, before them boys down to the smelter get to fretting about where I am. They ain't educated either, and may just be stupid enough to come a'looking for me."

Tom McCarty shot him a pale-eyed glance. "Cute," he nodded, "real cute. You'll bear watching."

Cassidy climbed up on the wagon and unwrapped the lines. The mules hit their collars and the heavy ore wagon groaned into motion. Tom McCarty rode up alongside; above the squealing and grease-squeaking of the oak hubs, he asked the young skinner if he had everything straight in his mind. The latter answered that he believed he did, whereupon McCarty described for him the place on the Telluride Grade where the turnout would be made with the ingots from the smelter. Cassidy stated that he marked the spot from his memory of the route, and that he would be there, as agreed; but he still claimed duress.

"I don't give a hoot what you claim," said McCarty, regarding him piercingly from beneath bushy brows. "Just be there."

"Yes, sir, Mr. McCarty," said the substitute

mule skinner from the Uinta Queen. "That's one thing you'll learn about me, sir, even if I ain't had your advantages: when I make a deal, I don't never go back on it. I will be there just like I said, under durast."

Tom McCarty all too obviously did not care for the entire complexion of the avowal, but before he could examine the matter, the ore wagon had made the pass and was in full view of the smelter and of the small settlement at Palomas. It was too late for further discussion.

"Think of it in terms of improving the breed," the dapper bandit said. "Ten minutes on this job and you can send all your sons to the best college in the country. Why, you can buy the college. Just imagine it. You can stomp out ignorance in your family this very afternoon."

With these words, he turned his horse away from the ore wagon and back toward his brothers in the pass. George LeRoy Cassidy, the optimist, waved cheerfully after the departing outlaw. If he did not add words to the gesture, it was only because he felt them to be superfluous.

After all, the leader of the McCartys was substantially correct. He had strained no verities, offended no facts. Somebody *was* going to get educated that very afternoon—and maybe stomped in the bargain.

29

The gold ingots weighed lightly in the big ore wagon behind the six lively mules. Cassidy's shotgun guard bounced around on the seat, hung on in the curves, did not talk a great deal.

Down the hill they went toward Telluride from the smelter at Palomas, on down the hairpins and over the talus-slide trestles to the big grade. There they snaked precariously along the course of the stream which came down from the high, thin bridal-veil falls cross-canyon from the smelter. Down, down, through the silent stands of yellow pine and Engelmann spruce, off the big grade now and into the brief level of the flat created by the enormous tailings of half a dozen mines high on the mountain flank. No timber here, only an abandoned ore chute and snow shed at the foot of the Orpheus Number One's dump of medium highgrade waste. There, just beyond the gaunt buildings, the road went over the edge of the flat, on down into Telluride past the sluiceway take-off for the Matterhorn, the pump

161

spillway for the Utica, the boarded-up drift of the Lode Star's seven-hundred-foot level.

At the Orpheus chute, Cassidy shouted above the rattle and crunch of the wagon's wheels that he was turning in to check for a hotbox on the off rear side.

The guard, Allie Sugrette, said something which sounded like, "Thank God, I was about to lose my lunch," and thought no more of the detour until, rolling right on by the chute, Cassidy rammed the lead team into the dark tunnel of the snow shed, halting the mules only when the ore wagon and all three teams were engulfed in the bat-gloom of the rickety structure. By this time it was far too late for Sugrette to do anything but blink blindly and ask, "Now what in the heck you do that for?" A reply came not from his companion on the wagon seat, but from a small, slim fellow with a mask over his face and a long Colt's Revolver waving in his hand. The suggestion was to drop the shotgun, and Allie Sugrette froze up because the barrel of the Colt was compounded by the feel of a second gun muzzle nudging him behind the right ear. An eyetail glance in this direction revealed a second bandit. In the same instant, he was aware of a third masked figure on Cassidy's side of the wagon. Since this third highwayman was also brandishing a weapon, the smelter guard should have obeyed the first outlaw's injunction and dropped the shotgun, but he did not. Suddenly, Cassidy had the distinct and deadly premonition that the fool was going to shoot. The Utahan's big right hand instinctively shot up and then down across the wrists of the shotgun guard. Cassidy's forearm, thick and hard as an oak post, crunched downward with the hand. The blow paralyzed the guard's tensed grip for a fraction of a second; then his fingers spasmed open and he dropped the 12-gauge. Cassidy caught it before it hit the dashboard foot bar of the wagon box. As he did, Bill McCarty struck the disarmed guard over the head with the Winchester barrel; Sugrette pitched forward and hung, slack-jawed, over the dash.

Cassidy calmly leaned over his own side of the driver's seat and put the muzzle of the shotgun into the staring face of slow George McCarty, who was standing there with his six-gun down. The silence was instant and eloquent.

"Now, Mr. McCarty," the cowboy mule skinner called over his shoulder to the outlaw leader, "stop waving your pistol about and chuck it up here. You, Bill," he advised the second brother, "take care you don't tighten up on that rifle trigger. Happen you do, brother George ain't going to survive the shock."

The other two McCartys only stood and blinked a moment. But brother George, at least, was convinced of the stocky cowboy's sincerity. "For God's sake, boys!" he pleaded. "Do what he says!"

Tom stood and blinked some more. Bill watched Tom. Cassidy said nothing.

"All right," said Tom McCarty. "What does he say to do?"

Cassidy spoke to them in a way that left the McCartys with no doubt that they had tangled with a man who would go far, advantages or no advantages.

To begin with, he advised the three Irishmen that the borrowing of the guard's shotgun was no unplanned affair. In the exact way that it had come about, yes, it was. But in the essence of Cassidy's thinking, he had determined at the outset that when the McCarty's threw down on the guard and himself in the snow shed, Cassidy was going to take Sugrette's weapon and turn it on the outlaws.

Reason? Simple. George Leroy Cassidy didn't care for blackjack deals.

Next time the McCartys wanted to talk a job with him, they had better have it clear in their daft minds that Cassidy did not function well under threat. He could be led a long ways but not pushed one inch. Oh, and there was one other little thing which they had better understand. When Cassidy set out to do a job for any man, he did it. He had started out to do this job for the Upper Uinta Consolidated Mineral and Smelting Corporation, not for McCarty Brothers Limited. In consequence, the gold ingots in the ore wagon were going to be delivered to the San Miguel Valley Bank precisely as per the invoice in Allie Sugrette's pocket.

For purposes of facilitating this contract, Mr. George McCarty would continue to Telluride with Mr. Cassidy. He would continue in capacity of mule skinner, with Mr. Cassidy riding shotgun in place of the unconscious smelter man. It should not need to be belabored with men of advantages, such as the McCartys, that Cassidy would be guarding brother George, not the smelter shipment.

If any misunderstandings of the arrangement arose, whether on the part of brother George or brothers Tom and Bill, brother George would be forfeit.

In effect, brother George was in hock to the owners of the Uinta Queen. He could be redeemed only by the safe arrival in Telluride of the mine shipment, and the subsequent success of Cassidy in spiriting both brother George and himself back out of Telluride, while the good folk of the town were milling about in the excitement of the deductions which would certainly be made by somebody, and soon.

Mr. Sugrette, meanwhile, was stirring in his unconscious state. Time was becoming scant, but quick work could still save the day.

If brothers Tom and Bill would get in their rented rig and hightail it up to the Lucifer, they could almost surely collect Matt Warner in time to get over the mountain toward the Brown's Hole hideout ahead of the posse from Telluride.

What, the grinning Utah cowboy wanted to know, did the boys think of "them apples"?

Tom McCarty felt the sting of the question, as Cassidy had intended he should. But he played it straight, asking for time to think it over. Again the sandy-haired mule skinner grinned, again gave the natty bandit the backlash of his own sharp tongue.

"Sure," he said, "you got ten seconds."

Tom nodded and said quietly, "Good shot." He agreed to the conditions like the gentleman he was. Bill bobbed his golden-brown curls in like surrender. The two hoisted Allie Sugrette into the bed of the ore wagon, as directed by Cassidy, bid brother George scarcely any farewell whatever, leaped to the seat of their rented getaway rig—a light springbed mud wagon with a strong span of mountain stage horses—and applied the whip to the team.

The understanding was that Cassidy was responsible for the hostage's safety in Telluride, and the McCartys felt reasonably sure of the Utahan's word. As long as Cassidy remained determined to deliver Allie Sugrette to Telluride unharmed, Sugrette was going to tell all that he knew whenever he came around. And all that he knew was that George Cassidy suddenly had swung the smelter wagon off the road into the snow shed of the Orpheus, where three masked men had appeared with guns; when brave, fearless and loyal Allie Sugrette went to blast the trio with his trusty 12-gauge, driver Cassidy had slugged him and grabbed the gun away from him. Then all went black.

In owlhoot terms, this meant that George LeRoy Cassidy was all through in Telluride, Colorado, and would be lucky to get out of town a free man.

For his part, Cassidy gave the other wagon a decent start up the mountain, then backed his mules out of the shed and rumbled on down the hill, past the Matterhorn, the Utica and the Lode Star, over the creek bridge and into Telluride.

At the bank, he calmly went down the alley to the rear entrance and parked his rig by the door. "Brother George," he said, "pick up Mr. Sugrette and follow me."

George McCarty, very powerful and not too

quick, nodded and did as he was told. Inside the bank, Cassidy opened the door of the president's office and ordered George to bring in the unconscious shotgun guard. The president, waiting at the bank with his chief teller to receive the smelter shipment, was understandably upset when the bloody-headed smelter man was dumped unceremoniously upon his tapestried divan.

"Mr. Abernood," said George Cassidy, respectfully knuckling his sunburned brow. "I'm the new driver from up to the Uinta Queen, sir. I have got your load of gold out back, but there was a mite of trouble on the road, as you can see. I would appreciate it, sir, if you would go and fetch the doctor for this poor wounded feller. Meanwhiles, me and my staunch assistant, here, we will go and report the attempted crime to the town marshal. Here's the smelter invoice on them ingots, sir. We didn't lose a one of them to them dastardly outlaws."

President Pierre Abernood looked at the invoice, looked at the blood on his sofa and shouted for his chief teller. The teller came on the trot. Cassidy, not letting the latter come to a halt, took his arm and guided him through the rear door. "Right out here, Mr. Teller," he said. "You can see for yourself everything's in order according to the invoice. Oh, them was desperate men! But fearless Allie Sugrette, he just up and—" He broke off, an expression of abject self-incrimination on his honest face. "Mercy!" he cried. "We have plumb forgot about poor Allie! And him laying in there dying maybe, with us standing out here a'counting the gold, oh dear!"

He turned and sprinted back into the bank, the chief teller not far behind him. In the office they found President Abernood waving the invoice and demanding of his teller if the smelter shipment matched the paperwork from Palomas. The teller reprimanded his superior for thinking only of himself and wealth at such a time, but said that the shipment was intact, and evidently they could thank these brave men for bringing it through.

"Oh, yes, sir," assured Cassidy, his blue eyes wide with the excitement and nearness of it all. "That's the mortal truth, Mr. Abernood. Me and my assistant, here, we fit them devils off and saved brave Allie Sugrette's life. Leastways, I surely do hope that we have saved it. Howsomever, if you are a going to stand there instead of rushing out immediate for the doctor, then I ain't sure our sacrifices was in a successful cause, sir. Come on, Brother George!" he said, giving the slow McCarty brother a shove toward the office door. "Me and you must go quickly to notify Marshal Pettigrew, whiles there is yet time to catch them murderous McCartys!"

"The who?" demanded Abernood. "Did you say the McCartys? The *real* McCartys?"

"Oh, yes, sir, didn't I mention that? It was them, sir, no doubt of it. You see, I knowed their sainted maw over yonder in the Mormon country. They was good men at one time, sir. But, oh! the evil ways that they have come to!"

"My God," said Abernood. "The McCartys!"

Cassidy and Brother George were heading for the bank's rear door. Abernood dashed out of the office, following them with some added and pressing questions. But Cassidy wheeled upon him, thrust an accusing finger in his agitated face, and made testament that if the fearless and loyal wounded man on the tapestried settee was to die from loss of blood, the matter would be on President Abernood's head. The kindly and intelligent chief teller was staying with the injured hero. Cassidy and his assistant driver were trying to fetch the law as fast as they could. Only the bank president was failing in his clear and patent duty to go for medical help. In the name of simple Christian mercy, would he please, please go and find the doctor! Or, at very least, would he stand aside and quit obstructing those who were trying to do their civic duty!

The bank executive hesitated, turned away, and ran toward Main Street and the offices of Dr. Edgar Lacy.

"Now, Brother George," suggested Cassidy, "me and you had best scale this here back fence and hit right lively for the livery barn up the street. By great good outhouse fortune, I have my own horse down there to be hoof-trimmed and shod for the summer. I was to pick him up this afternoon and take him in another direction, and would powerfully urge you to hire yourself a suitable mount and do the self-same thing. One, two, three—run for the fence!"

They went over the rickety planks like chased tomcats. By the time Abernood had succeeded in telling the whole town about the attempt of the famous McCarty Gang to hold up the weekend delivery of bar gold from the Palomas smelter, they had rented a fine, fast horse for Brother George and were gone over the mountain from Telluride, Colorado.

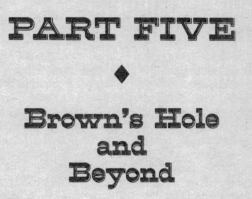

PART FIVE

◆

Brown's Hole
and
Beyond

30

◆

Brown's Hole, or Brown's Park, as it was later
called, lay in the extreme northwestern corner of
Colorado. Its northern fringes pushed into Wyoming, its western flanks encroached upon Utah.
This tri-region geography, together with the utter
remoteness of its locale and the semi-arid climate
of light snowfall and reasonable temperatures which
blessed it, made the Hole the favorite wintering
ground of the owlhoot breed. Nor was it deserted of
outlaw life in other seasons.

Brown's Hole was almost literally a hole. But
its depression was thirty-five miles long by six
miles wide. It was bisected by the Green River,
entering through sheer stone ramparts via Red Canyon on the north, wandering across the interior
"park" in gentle loops eastward, disappearing with
sudden, frightening cataract through the naked rock
portals of the Canyon of Lodore, south by east. Due
south, the hideout valley was cut off from the
outside by the virtually impenetrable mass of Diamond Mountain, cut only on the valley side by two

171

tortuous watercourses, Crouse Creek and Sears Canyon. Northward reared the immense barrier of Cold Spring Mountain, an even more total wall than Diamond's hostile bulk. To the west lay only badlands, where no water ran and no verdure relieved the naked sand and rock, rising canyoned flat after canyoned flat to the high Uintahs, blue upon the Utah horizon. Only eastward was the valley's wall breeched by reasonable entrance, where Vermilion Creek, already having cut its path through the Escalante Hills, sliced the heart of the Limestone Divide to empty into the Green two miles upstream of its wild-water plunge past the fearsome portals of Lodore.

The interior of the Hole was relatively level, composed of a complex of low cedar ridges and sagebrush upthrust flats spiderwebbed with arroyos and gulches. The Hole was mainly dry of live water, but it had useful pasturage and shelterland and comprised indeed, the greatest single "open winter" holding ground for cattle in the Northwest.

To this starkly grand and lonely gathering place of the wanted and the unwanted, George Cassidy brought Brother George McCarty in mid-June of 1887.

The nomad cowboy and Brother George had grown close on the long trail up from Telluride. It was impossible to dislike Cassidy, and George McCarty was the softest of the Irish brothers. He was a man of peace by inclination, an outlaw only through his kinsman's loyalty to his wild, high-rolling brothers. Taking advantage of his lack of enthusiasm for the owlhoot trails, Cassidy extolled his own four-year success in going straight and counseled Brother George to do likewise; at least to try the honest life. The Utahan's motive was not purely moral. He felt that by lulling the big man with tales of the simple life, he could keep his companion from thinking in terms of knocking his trail-fellow in the head some dark night and making it on up to the Hole alone.

The wonderful high country sunshine struck the two riders as they topped the last rise in the southern route and saw before them the walled park of their destination; it told Cassidy that his measures had worked. They had made the Hole and were firm pals and had the entire summer ahead of them in which to cement relationships with Matt Warner and the McCartys.

"Brother George," said Cassidy, as they paused to let their horses rest, "which part of the Hole do you reckon the boys will have picked to wait for us?"

"Likely Jim Warren's place right on down Diamond Mountain."

"You know the way?"

"Sure. Matt showed it to me last summer. You know, him and Warren was like paw and son. Warren give old Matt his first lessons in the rustling business."

"So Matt told me," nodded Cassidy. "Seems there's always a kindly old crook around to teach a boy how to defend himself from starvation."

"Huh?" said his companion.

"Never mind. Let's get on down the line, Brother George."

The big man bobbed his head. "Yeah," he said. "Happen I don't get lost getting down off old Diamond Mountain, we can make it in time for noon dinner. All we got to do is find that there Crouse Creek headwater and trail her down. We ought to be eating fresh beef for supper, even if we miss the first couple of casts to cut Crouse Creek."

"Take your best shot at it, pal," urged Cassidy. "I ain't et tame meat for so long I'm apt to bite inter the first cow critter we see, on the hoof, and a la carter."

"Huh?" said George. "Allie who?"

"Carter," answered Cassidy soberly. "Mighty fine feller I knowed whilst I was hacking ties for the D&RG the summer of eighty-five. Let's motate, good friend. Setting here ain't going to buy us no noon dinner at Jim Warren's."

"I knowed a feller named Carter onct," said big George, kicking his horse into motion. "It don't scarcely seem it would be the same one, though. This here hombre I knowed was strung up by a posse out'n Rock Springs, the fall of eighty-three."

"The fall of eighty-three? You don't say!" responded Cassidy. "Was he a dark feller with sort of green eyes and a pale face with a three-haired mole on the end of his nose?"

"Nope, he was a short, fat feller with a red face and a glass eye."

"Whicht eye?" asked Cassidy.

"It were the right eye, I recollect."

"What color was it?"

"Brown."

"Nope, that ain't the Carter I knowed," said the Utah cowboy. "Keep riding, pal."

True to his doubts, Brother George had trouble finding the Crouse Creek trail. By the time he did find it, the sun was sliding west. It was nearly dark when they at last rode into the hideout where Matt Warner had learned the rustling and horse thief trades, and where avowed cow thief Jim Warren had established his retreat for the fugitive kind.

But the slow McCarty clansman had been correct in his initial surmise; the other McCartys were there and waiting. They received the return of the two Telluride strays with creditable reserve. Bill seemed pleased enough to see big George, while Tom, dismissing the latter with a wave, turned his darting-eyed attention to Cassidy.

"Let's hear your yarn before Matt gets back," he advised the Utahan. "Providing it adds up, I will handle him for you. It if doesn't, you can handle him for yourself."

"I will do my level best to satisfy you," promised Cassidy. "I have tried my turn at handling friend Matt, and he don't handle worth a tinker's dam."

He told of his and Brother George's nip-and-tuck escape from the mining camp without embellishment. When he had done so, Brother George assured the two bright McCartys that "old George LeRoy" hadn't done halfway justice to the tale, and that if Tom and Bill weren't quick to see that, then they weren't the brothers he had sworn to Cassidy that they were.

Tom repeated that the story jelled well enough for him. He would not go into the sense of the thing—to an outlaw there was no sense in chilling a job where the payoff was so high and so secure—but would just say that if Cassidy wanted to stay on at the Crouse Creek camp for a spell, then that was all right with him.

Brother Bill bobbed his golden-brown ringlets, twinkled his light blue eyes, said that he was in general agreement. As a matter of fact, he would go further. "This boy," he said to Tom, thumbing young Cassidy, "shows me a lot of quality. I've given that Telluride job a good think since we been up there in the Hole, and I can see some mighty big gaps in it where we might very well have fallen through and broke our tails. I believe this here Mormon kid will do, and that we'd ought to take up with him where old Mike Cassidy left off."

"And where was that?" queried Tom alertly.

"This boy left home to hold the horses for the McCartys," replied Bill. "We know that from Matt, who got it from old Mike, Grizzly and the others. My vote goes for giving him the try at it, next job."

Tom McCarty nodded and turned to Cassidy. "Bill and I, especially me, are about old enough to be your father," he said. "When Bill refers to you as 'kid' and 'boy,' however, he doesn't mean it precisely. He does mean it about the vote. We vote on everything. It's the only way to stay solvent in this activity. Otherwise you are forever getting put out of business by your own partners."

Cassidy answered that he could see the justice and equity in this line of economic reasoning. He had, in fact, experienced its theory in operation a few summers back at Hite's Ferry, where Matt Warner had tried to knife him for saving old Cass Hite's life. Indeed, it was this same Matt Warner who now obtruded upon Cassidy's ability to judge the merits of the McCarty's assurances of peace and goodwill.

To this, Tom McCarty replied quickly enough that while the gang did take a vote on all issues of corporate policy, his personal ballot was used to break tie votes and to thus prevent stalemates or decisions adverse to the company health. "For example," the trim Irishman explained, "if there is a vote of five-to-one against pulling a certain job, and I cast my vote with the one, that's the tie-breaker."

"I see," said George Cassidy. "I must admit that I can't hardly imagine no smoother nor slicker way to get things did."

"Exactly," agreed Tom.

A good meal was prepared, and the brothers squatted down to it outside the doors of the shack Matt Warner had built in his first days in the Hole, so that he would always have a home to come to. They finished quickly. The last of the heavy biscuit-dough bread was used to sop up the brown blood-gravy of the fried steaks, the first round of coffee was being poured into the battered tin-can cups. Brother George, who had the feel for darkness of a vampire bat, held up a hand and said, "Tom, somebody's coming up the creek." Then, after a head-cocked moment, with all holding still, "One horse, going mighty heavy. Carrying double, likely."

"Douse the fire," said Tom McCarty quietly.

Bill reached for the water bucket and drowned

the coals. The men stayed on the ground, where their blurred forms could not be distinguished from the boulders which dotted the mountainside. Cassidy heard the clinking drawback of Colt hammers being put on the cock.

Five minutes of absolute silence followed. Then, from the canyon rocks below, a horned owl hooted four times. Tom McCarty answered with a perfect fox bark. Cassidy, straining his eyes through the gloom, saw the horse looming in the gray-black between canyon and shack. Even in the small moment of its approach, he marveled at George McCarty's skill at prediction. The horse was moving laboriously and was under double ride.

Matt Warner stopped the horse short of the simmering coals and blue smoke at the drowned fire. "Who's with you?" he asked. Cassidy shivered, remembering that cold, soft voice.

"A friend," answered Tom McCarty carefully.

"What friend?" Warner did not bring the horse on in. The man mounted behind him, who was only a murky blot, also sat motionlessly.

"An old friend of yours," said Tom. "One you haven't seen since Hite's Ferry."

"*Him?*" said Warner between his teeth, drawing it out.

"Him," answered McCarty. "Who you got with you?"

There was another silence. Then it was broken jarringly by Matt Warner's low laugh. The dark-faced outlaw heeled the horse on up to the men crouched in the darkness before the shack. "Oh," he said, "I got with me an old friend of that old friend of mine you say you got with you."

He got down from his horse, and the McCartys and Cassidy got up and stood peering at the stranger still on the horse. "Come on," said Warner roughly. "Get down, kid." He virtually pulled the raw-boned second rider off the horse and shoved him toward Cassidy. The Utah cowboy stepped back to avoid colliding with the newcomer; as he did, the latter uttered a gasp of recognition and reached out long arms through the darkness to seize him and to cry out in a low mutter, "My Gawd, is that you, George LeRoy!"

It was Dan Parker, his younger brother.

31

◆

Dan Parker's story had been told many times before in the folklore of the owlhoot. The younger brother, who believed himself to be the same thing the older brother was, and to be that thing because the older brother was that thing, was hardly new to the outlaw fraternity. Its legends were crammed with younger brothers of older brothers, and not generally to the credit of the junior relative. No men had better reason to know this than Tom and Bill McCarty. Thus they sympathized with Cassidy, adding the sympathy to the liking they already exhibited for the chunky Irishman. Cassidy was so near to them in spirit and good humor, and lacked only their experience, perhaps, to become both peer and partner in their chancey careers. They voted to forgive the Utah cowboy's act of strange faith to the Uinta Queen's smelter shipment; they voted to permit Brother Dan to stay along in the Hole, now that he had found George LeRoy, until the band might decide what best to do with him. This, of course, would depend greatly upon another decision which would soon confront them. Funds from the last job down in Arizona Territory were running low; a new employment must be planned.

Matt Warner refused to cast any vote upon the peace agreement, saying only that what lay between George Cassidy and him was their affair and would be settled by them in its due time. Meanwhile, he could not with conscience vote to make Cassidy a member of the gang. Nor could he, with courage, vote against the stocky cowboy. That would look like sour apples, and he felt he owed his Mormon cousin something a deal stronger than that.

It was not possible for Cassidy to hold a grudge. He was sorry Matt could not forget the broken nose at Dandy Crossing. As for him, all of that lay four years behind and was not meant as harm in the first place. Any time that Matt wanted to make up, that would be fine with George Cassidy. Any time that Matt wanted to take a swing and try for eveners on the beak of the Utah cowboy, fair enough. Cassidy would do his best to duck. They left it there.

In the remaining weeks of the brief summer of the Colorado high country, the gang loafed about Brown's Hole, fishing, hunting, highlining the lookout ridges and peaks to be sure no enemy drew near, and in general lazing the sweet-scented days away after the timeworn manner of pausing outlaws. It was the way such men balanced their lives, retained their reason, restored themselves in flesh and spirit for the dangerous trails and riotous times of the autumn to come.

The fall of the year was their harvest time, as well as that of the honest homesteader and the granger. Then the streams were at their lowest, the roads and getaway trails hard and dry, the mountain passes into and out of Robber's Roost and the Hole open and snowfree. Then the money of the honest men grew fattest in the banks and railroad express cars of the land. And it was then, too, that the instincts of all men warned them to save a little

something for the hard weather ahead, to squirrel-
up a few nuts for the deep snows of December. For
the McCartys, as for other thrifty men, the nuts
were gold coins, and the somethings were crisp,
fresh bank notes and unsigned bills raided skillfully
from the miser's hoards of banker, railroad magnet,
express company tycoon, either from fixed vault or
from rolling treasure car, it mattered not to the bold
robbers from Roost or Hole. When September's frost
silvered August's golden grasses, when the blue
wood smoke of pine and cedar hung pungent and
exciting in the mink-sharp bite of the mountain air,
over forest clearing shack and remote mesa cabin
alike, then the masked riders would come down
from the high country and commence their levies
against the fat and the faint of heart cowering with
their ill-gotten gain in the flatlands and the valleys.

It was a pattern as old as the Assyrians, the
learned Tom McCarty assured George Cassidy. And
it was as valid in Colorado of the eighties as it had
been off the coast of Africa in the days of the
Barbary pirates. It was called collecting the tribute,
and it beat the entire whey out of hard work as a
way to make a living.

Danger there was. Who could deny the damage
of a bullet in a bad place? If your number was up
and your name on the rounded nose of that particular lead pill, however, that was the price of the
game. You paid it, and your pals rode on without
you. But ah, compadre! If all went well and you
scooped up the yellow coins and the paper certifi-
cates by the sackful, then you learned something
about life and the way she ought to be lived, something that ninety-nine years in the lowlands couldn't
teach you.

What for sure did the honest farmer, rancher,
logger, tie hack, miner, prospector or town mer-
chant ever find out about wild women and the high
life that *real* money could buy in the sin spots like
Cheyenne, Denver, Santa Fe? The honest man worked

his life away for wages. He got up with the sun, went to bed with the sun, was born broke and died the same way. But most of all, God knew, he didn't have any fun in between. He never knew what fun was. And nobody ever told him.

Tom McCarty knew what fun was. And he had been told where to find it, and how to buy it. You bought it with money, mister, and nothing else!

"I believe you," said George Cassidy seriously. "I believe the heck out of you. And I'm four years sick of trying to prove it the other way around. But I've tooken my own oath that I ain't going to go in that direction, and I will be blacksnaked if I am going to start out lying to myself at this stage."

"Think about it," the dapper bandit suggested. "It will come to you."

So while he fished and explored and hunted and lazied around with his brother Dan, and with Brother George McCarty, Cassidy thought about it. He thought about it from mid-June to the end of August, and then he went to Tom and Bill McCarty and said that he was ready to talk.

He said that what the gang needed was unity and trust, a combination hard to achieve with Matt Warner feeling the way he did about George Cassidy. Hence, the best thing for all was for Cassidy to get out and go his own way. This he was ready to do. But before he went, and in repayment of the good treatment given him in the Hole, he had worked out a plan for another sort of a hideout than the Hole or the Roost. Cassidy believed that with the coming of the railroads, and with many new towns springing up along their lines, simply to run off and hide in the high rocks was not going to feed the sheepdog through many more winters. There were too many people crowding into the country. The wild places might be good for a few more years, but wise heads would be thinking about tomorrow.

Tom McCarty nodded and told him to get on with it. He wasn't too convinced so far, he said, by talk of tomorrow. Tomorrow didn't fit into the McCarty philosophy, nor indeed into the realities of the bank and train robbing business.

Cassidy agreed in theory, but maintained that what he had in mind would work out in practice. The idea, he said, was to set up a hideout that was right in the middle of things, not way out on the edges of nowhere. That way, the gang could go to this place and cool out right in among the respectable folks, while the hunt for them was being pushed into the old, familiar owlhoot strongholds like the Roost and Brown's Hole.

"Ah, sure now!" interrupted brother Bill, his handsome Irish face lighting up with the brilliance of the Utah cowboy's bandit thinking. "What we must do, Tom," he explained to the intent leader, "is bust a bank in, say, Laramie, then loaf on down to, say, Cheyenne, and spend the loot there. As the two places are connected by the Union Pacific, we can ride the cars. No use bothering with horses and with running for the high rocks, not with Cheyenne so close by rail."

"Yes," said Tom McCarty. "And another nice thing about Cheyenne being so close to Laramie is that if we get scooped up in Cheyenne, they got only to ship us back on the cars to Laramie, as that is where the state pen is. Why, faith, the whole thing might be done—bank, train ride, hoosegow— in no more than two, three days at the outside. I think it is admirable. Maybe even insane. Cassidy, you were right the first time. What we need is for you to ride on out of here the first good, dark night, and never to come back."

Cassidy, never one to heat up when he knew he was right, grinned and agreed that it sounded crazy the way they had just spread it around. But since they were educated men and he but a Utah ignoramus, they could understand he might have failed to make his point, and so would surely grant him further chance to do so. Both McCarty's eyed him at this juncture. The brothers were of high temper, and both liked nothing better than a good Hibernian brawl. In the bull-necked, bullet-headed, blue-eyed and always cheerful stock rustler from Circle Valley, they recognized a fellow soul, and a man who unquestionably would give them as much as they cared to try to bite off of him, and do it with a laugh back of two fists like locomotive pistons.

In this case, Bill was eyeing brother Tom for the sign to start swinging, but the older man had the insights of a thrice-trapped wolf, a mind as resourceful and keen as a hunting cougar's. "Wait along," he counseled. "Let's see what the Mormon brother has in mind."

What the Mormon brother had in mind was what he had been talking about with Brother George McCarty all summer long; Brother George had expressed a distaste for the undue exertions of the robber's life, but he was reluctant to leave his brothers, whom he dearly loved and admired. On the opposite hand, Cassidy's "big" brother Dan Parker also posed a problem. While he had unlimited enthusiasm for the idea of being a highwayman, he had precious small talents for the work.

George Cassidy's idea had begun to ferment here.

Then, when Brother George McCarty had spoken with some longing of a years-ago trip to the green forest lands of the Oregon country, the entire solution had occurred to Cassidy. Why not encourage Brother George to go out to Oregon and take up land? Once established out there as a respectable rancher, what better place in the outlaw world for sweating bank or train robbers to cool off in, than in Brother George's bunkhouse? Who would look for fugitives from that Laramie robbery in the hinterland of Dalles, Portland or Eugene?

Bill McCarty unballed his fists and blinked. Brother Tom nodded, his blue eyes blazing. Cassidy swept on.

"Now to sew up the idea," he concluded airily, "we just throw in my boob brother, Dan. He can tag along with George for company on the trail and to wash the supper dishes. We can sell the both of them on the trip without letting them know that they are being sent out to set up the gang hideout. We get shut of two square pegs, and at the same swoop we stake out a hiding place that nobody, not even the Pinkertons, will ever suspect us of having the handle to. What you say?"

Bill looked at Tom, Tom looked at Bill. Both nodded on the exchange. "We think," said Tom McCarty, "that you had ought to change your mind about not being a member of the gang."

"Oh?" said George Cassidy. "How is that?"

McCarty explained quickly that he and Bill had just taken a silent vote. It had come out two to nothing in favor of Cassidy joining up as one of them. Since Brother George McCarty and brother Dan Parker would not be voting, that left only Matt Warner. Whatever Warner's vote would be, it would not be to cut himself out of the loot on the next job—a job which had already been set up in the summer's planning. Tom and Bill wanted Cassidy in on that job. Matt could sull all he wanted, but he wouldn't balk in the end. He liked that yellow metal, and the wild times in town that it would buy, too much. So forget Matt Warner.

Cassidy nodded, thinking hard, trying to think true. But he could not manage the latter task. He looked at the callouses on his palms and fingers. He thought of the four years of honest toil, of cutting ties for the railroad construction crews, of herding cows, breaking horses, digging fence holes, bucking a crosscut saw with timber crews up in the big tree country, of mucking out mineshafts and shoving ore carts, of biting the crimp of blasting caps onto quick-running fuses, of camp cooking and bunkhouse swabbing and a score of other jobs given to drifters in that time and place. The end of the thinking was that Tom McCarty was right—honest work only wore a man's life away; there was no real money in it, and surpassing all considerations for George LeRoy Cassidy, no fun whatever.

Again, the dapper McCarty brother scored dead-center. Fun was all there was in the world. Cassidy looked up from his calloused hands, and from his back-trailing thoughts. And he nodded once more to Tom McCarty. "I will go and lay out the Oregon bait to Dan and Brother George," he said. "Old Matt was right, after all, I guess." He shook his head and finished, almost wistfully, "Another Saint gone sour—"

32

◆

But neither Brother George McCarty nor young Dan Parker took the Oregon bait. Brother George simply doubted his fitness for the assignment. Dan Parker, after four years of trying to find his older brother, was not prepared to surrender the reunion. Moreover, Dan had powerful urges to be an outlaw and no whim to return to the ranching life. Here things came uneasily to a halt. However, Tom McCarty told Cassidy not to fret. There were ways and ways, he said, to influence the pure in heart and empty of head.

Presently, Tom wrote a letter to his father in San Juan County, Utah. Cassidy was given the chore of taking it into Rock Springs, Wyoming, for secret posting. It was a long ride to mail a letter, the Utahan thought, but Kanab needed the exercise, and so did he.

After his return to the Hole, however, the weeks ate through September with nothing happening. When half of October had gone, he really felt that Tom McCarty had lost his nerve for the big fall

187

heist. But he was to learn again that the jaunty little Irish outlaw knew well the subtleties and subterfuges of his chosen way.

On October 23, a rider came into the Hole from Rock Springs bearing a letter for Tom McCarty among other information for the residents of the owlhoot settlement. The letter was from Tom's father in Utah. The good doctor had decided to move, with all his belongings and what remained to him of decent children, to—imagine where, of all places—yes, Oregon! There was even more that proved specifically useful in that letter. Big George McCarty's plump wife sent her love and warning notice that she was getting mighty lonesome in that empty bed. Also, Dr. McCarty expressed compelling need for one of the boys to come home and help him settle up affairs and get the family on the way. He even thought George might be the best for this task, being strong and pacific of nature, but, of course, this was a matter for the three brothers to decide. Their father could only ask.

Brother George furloughed, next trick was to induce Dan Parker to leave with him. This was Cassidy's turn. He performed it by pining out loud for home. Oh, if someone could be found who might scout the way for him—making sure the law was no longer waiting for him in Circle Valley— George LeRoy Parker could be home for Christmas!

Christmas, heck. If someone who *really* knew Circle Valley could be found to do the scouting, old George LeRoy could be home by Thanksgiving! It took Dan Parker two days to realize that he really knew Circle Valley and might be just the one to serve as the advance man for his brother's first return to the homeplace since the killing of Deputy Orville Stodenberg.

When Dan so informed Cassidy, the latter was soberly grateful but doubted that leader Tom McCarty could spare as good a man as brother Dan. Dan selflessly insisted, however, so they went directly to

McCarty. There they learned the worst. Dan *was* too valuable for a one-man decision. A ballot would have to be taken. The members of the gang were at once called in and the vote counted. There was no horseplay. This was deep stuff. Young Dan stood by, nostrils distended, proud, fearful, prayerful, all at the same time. The vote went unanimously against permitting the fledgling outlaw to deprive the gang of his outstanding services on the eve of the "big job." The verdict struck Dan into speechless gratitude and dismay. But Tom McCarty proved equal to the disappointment.

"This one time," he said, "I am going to break the vote because I have such faith in this boy. Kid," he said, placing his hand on Dan's shoulder, "you get on over there to Circle Valley and scout it out for old George, here, and we will just hold up on the big job till you get back. I wouldn't think of pulling off a heist like this one without you along."

Of course, it would have taken a team of broomtail broncs to keep brother Dan from departing after that. He and Brother George McCarty left the Hole that same night bound for Rock Springs and the stage to Salt Lake, a route chosen for them by their leader.

"You might as well case that stage run while you're traveling," ordered Tom. "I've had it in mind for knocking off for some time now. You can give us your professional opinion, Dan, when you get back. As for you, Brother George, goodbye and good luck and God bless mother when you get home."

The following morning Tom and Bill McCarty, George LeRoy Cassidy, Matt Warner and a young rider named Elza Lay, unknown to Cassidy, rode out of Brown's Hole, Colorado. Their course lay eastward along Vermilion Creek. With sundown they were through the Limestone Divide, making south around Douglas Mountain, toward Greystone and the Yampa River. Camp was on the open plateau in a beautiful little draw containing good grass, a few

low cedars and one of those clear-water springs
mapped only in the minds of such far-eyed, watchful
horsemen as these who came down off Douglas
Mountain. Supper was a quiet, grateful time, given
to eating and to thinking, each man to himself in
the spare-worded western way. But with the coffee
and the rice paper cigarettes and the restful easings-
back against the saddles, came the expectant crin-
klings of the crow's-feet at the eyes, the relaxing of
the wide, good-humored mouths, the moment for
which these hardened men endured the dangers of
the owlhoot and the highline.

All relished the pause, savoring it like a fine
cigar. Then Bill McCarty grinned and bobbled his
golden-brown curls. "Well, Tom," he said, "whereaway
this trip?"

The older man drew on his cigarette, inhaling
deeply. "The D&RG," he said. "Mainline, east."

"Of where?" squinted Matt Warner.

"Grand Junction."

Warner nodded, dark face intent. "When?" he
said.

"When I say," answered Tom McCarty, and
George Cassidy noted that neither Matt Warner,
nor Elza Lay, nor light-hearted Bill McCarty did
other than to nod as if to say, "All right, that's that."
Then they fell at once to laughing and joking and
trading lies about liquor and women and winning at
cards.

Cassidy, having no great supply of such experiences, took out his harmonica and began softly to
play "Shenandoah." It was a part of his particular
nature, gay and spirited as he was, to withhold
certain sides of himself for revelation when mood
and time and fall of wilderness firelight might pluck
the chord within him. Not one there had known
before that instant that he owned the instrument,
let alone that he could wring from it such poignant, sad-sweet strains.

The boasting fell away, the laughter softened,

the eyes dropped to the fire, the heads were bent to hear.

> Oh, Shenandoah, I long to see you,
> Away, you rollin' river . . .
> Oh Shenandoah, I love your daughter,
> For her I'd cross the rollin' water,
> Away, we're bound away, across the
>   wide Missouri. . . .

Cassidy tapped the mouth organ on his palm and put it away. One by one, the riders sought their blankets. When Cassidy was wrapping his frayed bedroll about the weariness that suddenly pervaded mind and limb, he felt a hand touch his shoulder. Kneeling beside him was the slender figure of the newcomer, Elza Lay.

"Thank you," was all the other man said.

33

◆

It was over one hundred miles, crow's-flight, from
the first camp to Grand Junction, Colorado, and
Tom McCarty rode the distance in a wary, circling
way. He quartered the country like a wolf working
up the wind toward the bait. He would not be
hurried, would not be cajoled to "move on down
the line." It was the final week in October before he
led the gang into view of the selected town. Even
then it was a distant vista. From their base camp
set on canyon edge in the rough breaks south of the
Colorado River, Cassidy considered the scenery not
only distant, but dim. He had seen better pictures
on Bull Durham sacks, or in Monkey Ward cata-
logues. Twinges of original doubt returned.

Presently, Tom McCarty called the group about
the fire. Unfurling a greasy map which none of
them had seen before, he said tersely, "Cluster in
here. Pay close heed." The men drew in, peering
curiously. All sensed something.

When he had taken his look, Matt Warner
whistled shrilly between clenched teeth. "That's a

company survey chart of the whole D&RG," he said. "Where'd you come by that?"

"Direct from the Denver office. Cost me five hundred, but original art comes dear. Isn't it lovely?"

"Why," exclaimed Bill McCarty, "lookit there; it's all mainline clean over the Divide, no more narrow gauge!"

"Just drove it into Grand Junction this summer. This route map's hardly dry. Denver man got it to me in the same mail as the letter from Paw. But faith now, lads, don't look so glum. Did you think we rode all this way to celebrate the arrival of the mainline to the forks of the Gunnison and the Colorado? Well, not quite. The rest of that note from the front-office man was to the effect that the first general payroll for the big new division shops at Grand Junction would be sent over the new line from Denver right after the first."

"Of what?" It was Matt Warner, quick and cold.

"Of November."

"Cripes, that ain't far off."

"Neither is that new mainline track, Matt. We can hit it from here and be back in this base camp, where lion dogs couldn't track us, before daybreak. We lay up here one day, then slip back over the river and hit for home the next night."

"Where you mean to make the stop?"

"The Whitewater Grade."

"That will be east of town, right?" Bill McCarty asked the question, intent like the others, eyes glued to the survey of the D&RG's trackage. "Say, five miles, maybe six?"

"About that."

"How you figuring to make the stop?" Warner spoke again.

"I'll let you know when we get there. I wouldn't want any of you losing good sleep, meanwhile."

"Like that, eh?" It was still Matt Warner questioning. "That rough?"

Here George Cassidy raised his eyes from the magnet of thin spiderlines on the railroad map. "Hold it," he said. "Rough, you say, Matt?" He turned to McCarty. "What does that translate to in uneducated cowboy talk, Tom?" he asked. "Somebody getting it in cold blood?"

Tom McCarty shook his head. "Look," he snapped, "how many times do I have to tell you we don't work that way?"

"Well, I don't," Cassidy told him. "And I don't care how many times I got to tell you. You forget that part of it, and I'm out. On the spot, boys." He turned, bringing them all in on it. "The first time somebody kills senseless with me along, and that's as deep as the shaft sinks."

Elza Lay, the gentle, slender youngster who said so little and seemed so soft, broke in diffidently. "You can't work in this line, Cassidy," he said, "without you sometimes get boxed and must shoot. We've all did it, and will again."

Cassidy instinctively liked Lay. There was something about the new man which attracted his sympathy. He felt, perhaps, that Lay, like himself, was a drifter with the wind, that he had not selected the outlaw life, but been driven to it by the whims of fate, or led into it by artful currents of persuasion. "Elza," he said, "you saying you done already kilt somebody?"

"Sure. Ain't you?"

"No."

"Well, it's easier than you'd think. The first one's the worst."

For a moment Cassidy believed the other was stringing him along. He began to spread a relieved grin across his friendly face, then decided not to. Elza Lay wasn't grinning back. "You kilt others?" he frowned. "Deliberate a'purpose?"

"Look, Cassidy," Bill McCarty interrupted, "it ain't like you make it sound. Men get killed breaking broncs. Or punching steers. Why, you can get your neck broke falling off the back stoop full of whiskey."

"I told you dumb buzzards," said Matt Warner.

"Yes, we know." Tom McCarty's pale eyes burned from beneath their black brows. "But we didn't bring Cassidy along for his gun. He can think, Matt. Now don't try to figure out what that means. Just lay off Cassidy and mind your own assignment. Moreover, you know I agree in theory with peaceful means where practical. Gunfire rags me something fierce."

"You should have been a sawbones like your old man," growled Warner. "Then you could have croaked people legal."

Tom nodded and tapped the map. "Somebody," he said, "has got to go into Grand Junction and meet with my front-office man. He will tell our contact the schedule, number and running time of the payroll train. I don't cotton to this last-minute timing, but it's the only way to make sure we don't miss the shipment." He paused, looking around the firelit circle. "Now we need a man for the meet-up in Grand Junction. Should be somebody that isn't known in these parts, and whose picture isn't on the jail wall or in the sheriff's top desk drawer. I reckon that simplifies it. Cassidy, you're tagged."

That night, George LeRoy slept uneasily. He was awake with first daybreak. Getting up, he rekindled the fire and put the coffee water on. Before it boiled, Tom McCarty had joined him. The others were still not out of their blankets when Cassidy left the camp.

With his departure—a new man going into a new town in a new country, for Grand Junction was only some six years old—the other members of the gang would know no ease until his safe return. Not safe from Cassidy's standpoint, but from their own. Safe in the sense that their message boy would not talk loosely, would not lead any law back to the base camp.

They all understood the risk. Despite its tender-
ness of years, Grand Junction was the largest town
on the western slope of the Divide. There was
nothing larger than crossroads or cow camp size
within one hundred miles of it in any direction. It
was already headquarters for all of the Gunnison
Valley activity—mineral, lumbering, railroading,
ranching. And in such a boomtown, the patent
dangers—lures—of painted lady, round brown bottle, green felt table and celluloid eyeshade were all
too plain to the waiting veterans of the easy haul
and the high old time.

When three days passed with no sign of George
LeRoy Cassidy, Matt Warner went to Tom McCarty
and said that he was all done stalling around; he
was riding into town.

McCarty faced him down, saying he had instructed Cassidy to stay in Grand Junction until
one of two things happened: either the front-office
informer from the D&RG Denver headquarters
showed up for the meet or sent word by some other
way to call off the meet, or the payroll train made
Grand Junction without word from the informer.

"Now," he said to Warner, "how the blazes you
going to change any of that by galloping into town and
yelling, 'Anybody here seen a square-faced Mormon-
cowboy with blue eyes and stubbly blond-sandy
hair, that's been waiting for schedule confirma-
tion for a train robbery on the Whitewater Grade'?"

"I don't care how you twist it!" scowled Matt.
"I still say that bandy-legged, bull-necked Circleville
bronc stomper is going to get us all in trouble. He
can't be trusted."

Tom McCarty flicked him a birdlike, swift dart
of the pale eyes. The bushy brows gathered themselves. "Matt," he said, "listen careful to what I say.
If you live to be a hundred, you'll never see the day
you're as steady as that cowboy, you hear me?
You're Teenie's brother and I will hold with you as I
would my own son, or Bill's. But you better get over

your mad at George Cassidy. You're beating too much bulldog. Next time he won't stop with just busting your nose."

"You think I'm afraid of him?" Matt Warner, if he respected any man, respected Tom McCarty. It was more than respect, it was outlaw loyalty. Tom had given him sanctuary when he fled home at thirteen, had guided his way, counseled and sheltered and taught him. But now Matt Warner's courage seemed to have been questioned. No man could do this and fail to answer for it. "Well?" he demanded. "I'm waiting. You think I fear this Cassidy kid?"

"He's no kid, Matt."

"Answer me, blast you! You think I fear him?"

"I think you'd ought to fear him," said Tom McCarty quietly. "And don't cuss me again, Matt. You know better than that."

Matt Warner stood with his head down, lips moving soundlessly. After a moment, he nodded and left.

The waiting resumed. October 28th. The 29th. The 30th, 31st. November the first. Still no George Cassidy. The second of November dawned and dragged into afternoon, sunset, the swift plunging darkness of the autumn. Neither Cassidy nor any word from Cassidy had come.

"In the morning," said Matt Warner, "I'm leaving."

"Me, too," said Elza Lay.

They ate their suppers in silence, went to their blankets tight-lipped. Bill and Tom McCarty sat over the coals, warming their hands, drinking coffee, watching, listening, exchanging looks to save words which might be overheard and misunderstood.

Finally, Bill could bear it no longer. "Tom," he muttered, "the boys are right. We'd ought to get of here." He blinked the smoke out of his eyes and lowered his voice still more. "What you reckon has happened to Cassidy?" he said.

"Nothing. He's doing what I told him."

"Maybe. I still don't like it. This camp is spooking me. We've been here too long. We'll be spotted by somebody."

"What's to spot? We're ten miles out of Grand Junction. Only thing running by us is that wagon road to Rifle, yonder in the canyon. We have the Colorado to one side, the Gunnison to the other. Nothing but the stage coach and two ranch wagons been up the Rifle road in six days. Relax. Rest easy."

"Can't do it. Come morning, I'm pulling out with the boys."

Tom eyed him. The blue eyes were alight, but not with anger. They were close, these Irish brothers. It was thick blood between them. "Likely you're right, Bill," he admitted. "It does seem Cassidy ought to have got that schedule information by this time. There's been five trains over the line, judging by the smokes we've counted from up here."

"I reckon," said Bill, "that your contact didn't show. I don't think Cassidy would shy off. But he could have been scooped up. Them dirty Pinkertons always shadowing a town on the jump like this one."

"True. But he's not on their sheet that I heard of."

"He's friendly, but close," said Bill. "Who would know?"

"Was that a train whistle?" asked Tom, starting up.

"Naw, just the wind whining high in them Gunnison rocks."

"I'm getting triggery, too. What's the date today, the second?"

"Till midnight," said Bill.

"We'll hold one more day. You game, Bill?"

"Son of a gun, I dunno."

"Come on, shucks. Cassidy will show. I hate to run out on him."

"Well, we sure can't afford to go down there

looking for him, Tom. You want to winter here, up on that coldwind point?"

"I have had this hunch digging at me all day long. He'll show. Tonight. We won't need to argue about tomorrow, Bill."

"You'll die busted betting hunches."

"Well, I'll die betting, anyway."

Bill nodded, understanding the way his brother felt. It was the owlhoot way. You kept your eye on the main chance. You never let the ball ride free. You always kept your money down. The ones who took up all the time lost. Tom seldom did that. Tom was a winner. A money-down man. Quality. "I'll back your play," said Bill.

Tom McCarty cocked his head, listening. He leaned down, putting his ear to the rocky earth. "Somebody coming," he said. "Douse the fire."

Bill, who had as quickly laid his own ear to the ground, grinned and shook his head. "No need for that. Cassidy's big bay comes late with his off-forefoot on the lope. I could pick him blindfolded out of a cavalry charge. I'll rouse the boys."

A moment later the drumming beat of a horse's hooves could be heard; then the pace slowed. Gravel slid off the canyon wall out in the darkness. Iron shoes clinked on trail stone. Cassidy came up to the fire on Kanab, slid off the tall bay, let the reins drop, rolled in his bowlegged walk over to Tom McCarty. "You doing anything special tomorrow night, Mr. McCarty?" he asked. "Say along about eight P.M.?"

Bill was back now, flanked by Matt Warner and Elza Lay.

"Eight P.M.?" said Tom. "No, I don't think so. We're free, far as I know." He turned to the others. "How about you, boys? Can you make it?"

"Make what?" growled Matt, rubbing his eyes. "What the devil you talking about?"

"Robbing a train," said Tom McCarty. "Eight P.M. mountain standard time. Tomorrow night."

"The payroll train from Denver?" asked Lay softly.

George Cassidy bobbed his round head. "As ever was, Elza," he answered. "Tom's contact showed up tonight. I just left him. He was late, but, mister, he wasn't light."

"Come again, and say it slow," said Tom McCarty, licking his lips. "I want these rustlers to hear it real good."

He looked at Matt and Elza Lay. They caught the look but jumped their own eyes to George Cassidy. "Go on," said Matt, "start clicking your key. We're on the line."

"Take this down, then," said Cassidy, eyes shining. "The train is Number 329. The express messenger is T.C. Tillingsworth. The money will be in his safe, all new notes and local mint gold pieces. No marked or signatured stuff at all."

"Well?" said Tom, bending forward with the others.

"Sixteen-thousand dollars to the dime," answered Cassidy.

34

♦

Tom McCarty picked a spot where the tracks came out of a low-banked cut at the top of the Whitewater Grade. Just outside this cut, the gang went to work.

Picks and shovels stolen from a nearby section shack were used to loosen six ties beneath a rail collar. The collar was swiftly unbolted, opening the rail connection. Heavy ropes, saddle-packed all the way from the Hole, were fastened with a modified diamond hitch about the loosened rail and two of the freed rails. The ropes were then tied to the saddlehorns of Bill McCarty and Matt Warner. The latter eased their mounts into the slack of the ropes, told Tom they were ready.

"What time is it?" asked Tom. Strangely, among the five of them, there was only one watch, Cassidy's old turnip given him by Mike Cassidy.

A little elevated by the importance assigned him by accident, the keeper of the clock pulled out the instrument. Its loud ticking could be heard in the silence. Elza Lay, standing with Cassidy, took out a sulphur match and struck it on his raised leg. As the match flared, the watch whirred slightly, then made a grating noise. "Son of a siwash," said the proud owner, "she has quit on me."

"Seven fifty-three," said Elza Lay, spinning the match away. "That's where she was."

"All right." Tom's voice seemed too tight to Cassidy. "It doesn't matter. All we got to do is wait."

The men knew the train should have been on the grade before this. Tom had cut the time too close, fearing to be spotted loosening the track. No, that didn't make sense. It had been dark for two hours. Tom knew what he was doing. But where was Number 329? The unspoken question was answered by a lonesome wailing from beyond the cut. Again it echoed through the valley—hoarse, plaintive, ineffably sad—the lost-soul keening of a steam locomotive's whistle.

"You can set your watch now, Cassidy," nodded Tom McCarty. "It's eight P.M." The gang laughed, a little too loudly, but nonetheless the spirits revived. Sixteen thousand dollars was coming 'round the bend.

"Pull up your blinders, boys," said Matt Warner, with his wolf's grin. "We may have to shoot somebody we know."

He and Bill McCarty again eased their crouching horses against the ropes. Up the track now, along the rock walls of the cut, the shimmering dance of the engine's headlamp was flashing and jumping. In the shadow of the exit boulders, Cassidy and the others pulled up and adjusted the blue polka-dot bandannas furnished from Tom McCarty's saddle bags. The engine was through the cut then, and they could see the glow of its firebox staining the night. They watched the swing and jerk of the following cars pounding up the grade, heard the cast-steel drivers of the locomotive bite into the slight curve of the exit, and heard, too, the warning shriek of the whistle as the engineer picked up the two horsemen in the jolt of his headlamp.

"Pull!" yelled Tom McCarty, and Bill and Matt Warner put the spurs to their mounts. The fear-crazed horses leaped outward, away from the harsh screeching of the whistle. Behind them the ropes sang tight, stretched, held; and the loosened rail sprung outward and peeled away from the trackline. Number 329 hit the makeshift switch, left the rails, ground to a bumping, steaming, grating halt, upright on the rocky ballast of the roadbed. Behind it, the string of cars shuttled their couplings, banged their steel trucks, groaned, squealed, tightened couplings again and stood still upon the gentle grade sealed in the cut. Only the engine, the coal-tender and the express car stood outside the cut. And the locomotive's cab had come to its final grating halt exactly where Tom McCarty had stationed Elza Lay to handle the engineer and fireman.

Cassidy, posted at the cut exit to keep any passengers or train crew from coming forward, understood that he had just been taught how to stop a train.

No one had been hurt. The rolling stock of the railroad hadn't even been appreciably damaged. Yet it was all done in less than thirty minutes, from first swing of pick and jab of shovel. No time had been given the train crew to react. No piles of burning ties across the right-of-way. No water-tank stop to alert them. Nothing. The express messenger hadn't even had time to think about locking the connecting doors of his car. Matt and Tom McCarty had already disappeared into the express car, leaping to its platform from the backs of their horses. Even now, Bill McCarty was riding up with those horses and handing them, with his own, to Cassidy and saying, "Hold them; I'm going through the cars and see what the suckers have brought along to put in the pot." He had an empty flour sack in his left hand, his Colt revolver in his right.

Cassidy had never seen a happier man, nor one who behaved so precisely like he knew what he was doing and was satisfied with the work. He was not given long to savor this thrill. He had only gotten a good hold on the three spare mounts when two shots in close sequence came muffling from inside the express car.

Cassidy's grin faded. God punish the traitors. They had said there would be none of that. The Utah cowboy drove his spurs into Kanab. The tall bay leaped down the line toward the express car, dragging the other horses in his wake. As he came up to the car, Elza Lay, also pulled from his station by the gunfire, was just running his horse up to the car platform. Cassidy shouldered Kanab into the other rider's smaller mount, virtually pinning Lay's animal to the side of the express car.

"Here!" shouted Cassidy. "Hold these horses, or let them go, I don't care which."

Lay scrambled to clutch the tangle of reins which the Utahan flung at him. Before he could reply in anger or denial, the stocky cowboy had leaped from Kanab's back to the car platform and disappeared into the lamplit, gunsmoking interior.

The scene inside the car sealed Cassidy's anger. The express messenger was on his knees beside the company safe. His scalp was cut. Blood ran down his face and dripped to the car floor. Over him stood Matt Warner, pistol held by the butt for "buffaloing" the messenger. Even as Cassidy broke into the car, Warner cursed and struck the man again. As the latter sagged groaningly, Warner fired a shot so close past his head that Cassidy could see the new blood spurt where the bullet plowed along the jaw and took away a piece of the right earlobe. He didn't remember what happened next. He only knew that when the fog of his senses had cleared, Tom McCarty was shaking him by one arm and Matt Warner was on the floor beside the express messenger, and the outlaw's face was adding its share of blood to the public gathering in front of the unopened safe.

"Lay off!" roared Tom, "whose side are you on? You like to beat Matt's head in. Listen, you dumb Mormon ape, this imbecile guard won't open the safe. You think we'd ought to ask him nice? We're losing sixteen thousand dollars a minute here!" a belated realization struck him. "My God!" he cried. "Who's holding the horses?"

"Elza," said Cassidy, completely in control now.

McCarty leaped to the side door of the car, forced it open, leaned out bellowing into the night. "Lay, get Bill and come on up alongside with the horses!" Then he was back at the express messenger. Cassidy meanwhile had picked up the latter and sat him in a rickety, wire-braced chair. On the floor, Matt Warner was shaking his head, pushing himself upward with his white-knuckled hands. Distinctly and monotonously he was repeating aloud, "I will kill him, I will kill him, I will kill him...."

Cassidy reached down and picked up the fallen outlaw's Colt. He shoved it in his own belt. "What do you intend to do?" he asked Tom McCarty.

"What do *you* intend to do?" glared McCarty, blue eyes wild. "Take over the running of this gang?"

"Not ever," denied the Utah cowboy. "But I had your word on no rough stuff. So what *are* you going to do?"

McCarty here understood that his husky Mormon recruit was not acting now from temper, outraged sporting blood, or personal animus toward Matt Warner. This young cowboy meant exactly what he was saying, and not an eye blink less.

But Tom McCarty had cut his even white teeth on hardcases. He, no less than George LeRoy Cassidy, was fearless, and a tough fighter. "What I am going to do," he gritted, "is take a vote of the whole bunch on whether to blow out this stupid messenger's brains, or let him and the money go." He flung a glance toward Warner, now on his feet and braced against the safe. "You all right, Matt?"

Warner nodded to him, but looked at Cassidy. "I'll kill him," he repeated. "I'll kill him."

At that moment Elza Lay and Bill McCarty rode up with the horses outside the opened door. Tom told them the situation and they voted instantly to kill the express messenger if he would not open the payroll safe. It was four to one. But when Matt Warner seized the messenger and held his arms from behind, while Tom McCarty put his Colt beneath the expressman's bloodied ear and demanded that he open the safe, the bowlegged drifter from Circle Valley pulled out his own Colt. Cassidy shoved it between McCarty's shoulderblades with the soft-voiced suggestion that the weapon's presence there represented the tie-breaking vote. No D&RG payroll guard was going to get murdered that night, unless Tom McCarty wanted to try for a unanimous vote by turning around and taking away George LeRoy Cassidy's blue-steel franchise.

The silence in the car then made the labored breathing of the beaten express messenger sound like thunder under the canyon rim. Murder did indeed glare from the glittering eyes of Matt Warner, and black Irish anger choked the lively face of Tom McCarty. But Cassidy held the Colt. It was the case-ace, and no men knew it better than these who now waited for Tom to speak.

But Tom did not get to speak. The stillness in the car was suddenly shattered by a series of piercing shrieks from the engine's whistle. The engineer had discovered that he still had boiler pressure, and was yanking on the whistle cord with the wailing, wild regularity of a mine disaster or a prison break. Back along the halted string of cars in the cut, conductors' and brakemen's lanterns commenced to bob and flash. The D&RG was no stranger to night stops that were not on the printed schedules. Those crewmen could be coming out of that cut with

Winchesters any minute. The incessant, nerve-tearing shrieking of the whistle continued unbearably. Now voices were heard from the cut.

Outside the car, Bill McCarty stood in his stirrups for a last, hard look down the line. He did not like it, and turned back to his furious brother. "Tom!" he yelled. "For God's sake, forget it! The cut's swarming with people and that idiot whistle is going to rouse up the whole valley. We got to go, Tom. Right now!"

Tom knew it. Even Matt Warner understood that his own life was in balance now. Panic had set in. It was a thing known to the outlaw breed—it happened. Jobs went haywire like this. When they did, smart men did what Bill McCarty was advising from outside the car—they left.

Matt was the first. He released the messenger and leaped for the door and the horses. Tom McCarty was next. Cassidy was left in the car with the messenger He patted the dazed man on the shoulder, leaned down and said earnestly, "I'm sorry as can be about this, partner," and then ran for the connecting door and the between-cars platform. Kanab, trembling and walling his eyes, was still standing where his rider had left him. Cassidy dove for the saddle from the platform. The big bay flinched but did not go out from under him. Next instant Cassidy had clawed his way into the seat and was fanning the tall horse into a wild gallop after the dim forms of the scattering gang. As he did, the Winchesters commenced to bark from the cut. The Whitewater Grade job was over.

35

♦

At camp a fire was built and a blanket spread to count the haul made by Bill McCarty in the passenger coaches: eight pocket watches, three gold elk's tooth fobs, five Masonic rings, two diamond stickpins, one platinum toothpick, one nickel-plated .36 caliber Spanish bulldog pistol, not working, and $163.77 in small bills and coin. The stillness closed in like quicksand about the grim riders.

Cassidy would have made light of it, but these hardened bandits were not merely angry, they were ashamed, shaken. To poke fun at such men would be no more profitable than jabbing a stick at a mud-dobber's nest.

After a long strain of staring at the miserable gains spilled upon the blanket, Matt Warner stood up. He went to the camp picket line, followed by Elza Lay. They untied their horses, mounted and returned to the fire. Warner halted his mount, looking down at George Cassidy. "I'll be seeing you," he said. Without another word, he and Lay rode out of the camp.

After the coals of the fire had popped half a dozen times, Tom McCarty spoke. He told Cassidy that he could not say what his dark-tempered brother-in-law now intended to do. But his best guess was that Matt would be looking for the Circle Valley cowboy from that time forward.

Cassidy answered that he had understood very much the same thing, and that he thought this was the time for him to leave the gang. Matt Warner had been a boyhood friend of his, and had also befriended him years later in Robber's Roost. What had happened between them at Hite's Ferry and again this same night at Whitewater Grade were things which Cassidy regretted, but he would handle them in much the same manner if he had to live them again. His way was not Matt Warner's way, it was as simple as that.

Both McCartys urged him to ride back to the Hole with them and reserve his final decision. Cassidy shook his head, saying Matt had been in the gang before him and held prior place. To this the McCartys replied that Matt and Elza Lay worked together and independently of the McCartys, who were by no means bound to Warner or to anyone. Tom and Bill both liked George Cassidy and would not hesitate to work with him again. Despite the fracas in the express car, they were impressed with his nerve and his quickness. Given a little more experience, they were certain Cassidy would make an owlhoot rider second not even to Matt Warner.

The Utahan was grateful for the Irish warmth of the two brothers. As quick to forgive as to flare, Tom and Bill McCarty looked at life, and lived it, much as did George Cassidy. But the latter was without deceit. He repeated his intention to quit the outlaw life, but did agree to ride back to the Hole with the McCartys. This, he said, was because he had set out from the Hole with them to do a job, and the job would not be done until he had returned to the Hole with them.

"Maybe," he said, throwing them his quirky grin, "you will remember that what I start, I finish."

"It would seem," Tom grinned back, "that you have that inclination. It cost us a load of gold ingots in Telluride and a sixteen-thousand-dollar payroll at Whitewater Grade. You'd better make a good rider, kid, for your services certainly do come high."

Cassidy shook his head. "I doubt I'll ever make it as a bandit rider," he said quietly. "At least not in the McCarty gang. I don't think you operate smart."

Tom and Bill straightened. "What?" they both said at once.

"Maybe," nodded the stocky Mormon cowboy, "you could tell me the answer to one simple little question; you was going to stand by and see that express messenger killed—you actually voted to do it. Right?"

"Right," replied Tom, blue eyes darting glints of gathering storm. "Make your point or pass the dice."

"My point," said Cassidy slowly, "is this: How was killing that poor little confused feller going to open that safe?"

The McCarty brothers, both with their mouths opened to come down hard on the upstart, now shut those mouths with common, gulping muteness and exchanged brow-cocked, quizzical looks. Tom turned to Cassidy and put it to him with outlaw honor. "I will be double blasted," he said, "if I know."

And there they let it rest for the night. In the morning and all of the long following hours of daylight, there was little talk. With dusk they were saddled and riding for the shallows of the Colorado and the crossing at Palisade Wash. By next dawn they were far up toward Black Sulphur Creek, in Rio Blanco County. Two days later they were back in the Hole.

Here, more than a little news awaited them. Matt Warner had been to the Hole before them. A visitor from his past had come into the hideout during the gang's absence, a man named Hendrickson, brother of the lad whom Warner had assaulted ten years gone. Hendrickson had a message from home: the injured boy, while still alive, had become helpless mentally. There was talk of putting him away. Hendrickson, once close to Williard Christiansen—Matt Warner—in the old Utah days, had thought that Matt should know.

Why Hendrickson thought this, why he had ridden the long, dangerous way into Brown's Hole to find Matt, was never known, or known only to Matt. The result of the meeting, however, had been that Warner, pausing only to change horses and sleep one night, had gone back out of the Hole with Hendrickson. Where they were bound, neither man said, and no one in the Hole asked them. In the lexicon of the owlhoot, curiosity was defined as fatal to more than felines. Matt Warner, however, had left a message for George LeRoy Cassidy. "He said he would be seeing you," shrugged their informant at the Crouse Creek outlaw camp. "He said you would understand."

"I reckon," Cassidy nodded, "that you might say I do."

But his sad tale from the Utah past was not the only disquieting intelligence borne by Hendrickson. He had come in by way of Rock Springs. There he had taken a few too many and landed for the night in the local hoosegow. The man with whom he had shared his cell had seemed a likeable chap, if not bright. When he learned Hendrickson was from the Mormon country, he had said that he, too, was of Saint persuasion in the beginning, although he had fallen on hard times and become an outlaw. At this, Hendrickson had brightened and asked if, by happy chance, he might know of Matt Warner. And if, by even happier chance, he did, where might Warner presently be found? The man answered yes to both questions, and proceeded to give Hendrickson the

directions for getting into the Hole and on down to
Crouse Canyon and Matt Warner's camp. In exchange for this information, the poor fellow had
begged but a single favor. He had, he said, an older
brother who was also an outlaw, and also residing in
the Crouse camp. Would Hendrickson please bear
to this older brother a letter given by hand and in
brother-Mormon trust? Hendrickson had done so,
turning the letter over to the Crouse Creekers for
delivery when Matt Warner had so suddenly decided to ride out of the Hole and away to God knew
where.

The Crouse Creek man updating the McCartys
and George Cassidy on all of this paused at this
point to rummage in his duffelbag for the entrusted
document. "Got it here summers," he said, leaving
Tom and Bill McCarty to share a mutual heavy sigh
and the unspoken wonder as to what Brother George
had done this time. But when the brief pawing
through mildewed socks, patched shirts, gray wool
underdrawers, Ned Buntline yellowbacks, Denver
newspapers, bunion plasters, horse liniment bottles
and boxes of Hinkle Pills was successfully concluded, it was not to the McCartys that the searcher
turned. "Here," he said to Cassidy. "It's for you."

The latter, sensing something undue, took the
envelope and walked off a ways. Picking a sunny, flat
rock overhanging the brawling course of the creek,
he opened the letter. A lip reader and tongue furler,
the Utahan frowned his way through the nearly
illegible scrawl, suffering as much from the deci-
phering as from the content:

Dear George Leeroy,

I have tooken the trubble to writ you
becost they have me in the Rock Sprigs
jalehouse. I am wandering iffen you will
come and git me loost, otherwise they

*plane to transfur me to Laramy City in 2
weaks. The bale is $200.000 and they wont
taken no cheks, nor draffs, so it will need
to be hard muny, whicht oughtent to be no
problem with the big job pullt off by this
timm, and you having your cut.*

*The thing was that it lookt to me like
a easy haul to take that stage from inside.
So's when we wuz on the way outside
Rock Sprigs I putten a gun on the drivur.
You'd shud have seed old Bruther George. He
never had no idee I wuz a'gong to do it.
Hah! Hah!*

*Well, anyway, the drivur hit me a lick
whenst I wuzznt looking, and I fell offn
the box and waked my hed hard inter the
grond. Next thing I knowd, I wuz here in
the jale. I rekon old Bruther George went
ahed to Salt Lake, as I ain't herd no diffrunt.
Iffen you cain't get me out, all rite. But I
thot I'd ought to tell you abot the job. Ift
youd bin heer, we cud have did it easy.
Leave me know ift your cuming to help.
Wuzznt thet sum laugh on old Bruther
George! Oh boy.*

*Yr. Lovng bruther,
Daniel*

Cassidy slowly folded the letter, put it back in the
envelope and threw it into Crouse Creek. "I sometimes wish," he said to the rocks and the rushing
stream, "that I had been borned a only child."

At the cabin he made it as direct as he might.
Brother Dan had botched a job in Wyoming and was
in jail. Cassidy must go and see if he could hire a
lawyer to bail out the boy. Brother George McCarty,
so far as Dan knew, had made it safely on to Salt
Lake, as planned. As for himself, if all went well,
Cassidy might come back to the Hole, and he

might not. He honestly didn't know. Many thoughts were churning in his mind, including those of home and heritage. "It's been a powerful spell," he said yearningly, "since I seen the Sevier, or old South Table, or sat with my paw and shared the sunset."

Tom McCarty offered him money for the lawyer, but it was refused. "I will earn it somehow," said Cassidy.

That afternoon he took Kanab up to the blacksmith at the Bassett Ranch and had him reshod. He spent the night there, and rode for Wyoming with daybreak. How he "earned" the money for Dan's bail was never documented. But it remains a favorite of Sweetwater County folklore that at seven P.M. of the night of November 11, 1887, the Salt Lake stage was stopped just outside Green River, Wyoming, and the passengers relieved of approximately two hundred dollars and what the masked bandit in his cheerful, friendly manner described as "costs." The driver had between his feet a metal-bound express trunk containing nearly three thousand dollars in cash, and this he threw down to the outlaw without being asked. The latter picked up the trunk and returned it to him, saying he wanted only what he figured Wyoming owed him. "Drive on," he instructed the grizzled stager. "And remember to be kind to mothers, Mormons and small children."

The following day Attorney Malachi Ernshaw of Green River was retained by a most pleasant suntanned stranger to drive up to Rock Springs and bail out one Daniel Moroni Parker, a citizen of Sister Utah. When Ernshaw returned to Green River with the freed felon, the "happy cattle buyer" who had employed his services said that he would return in the morning so they might discuss the further defense of the case, agree on fees, and similar decisions. Ernshaw was more than pleased to be of help to such a clean-cut, personable and forthright young man, although he failed to understand the latter's interest in the dull fellow whose release he had effected. In either event his opinion proved academic. After the hearty parting handshake, he never again saw boot nor spur of client or culprit.

Indeed, hours before good lawyer Ernshaw had lathered to shave next morning, George LeRoy Cassidy and Dan Parker were across the Utah line and riding hard for home.

In Crouse Canyon the McCarty brothers waited a week, and then another, and even after that until the first hard snow of winter had blocked the northern trail. Then, while the southern trail was still open, Bill said, with sudden Irish fervor, "Faith, Tom, and what are we thinking of? Let's light our shuck out of here too!"

And with that, they saddled their best horses and pointed them up and over Diamond Mountain. For that moment and place they disappeared, with Elza Lay and Matt Warner, from the memory of the legend.

Cassidy and Dan Parker came into Circle Valley the back way, detouring up the Sevier from the main road, planning to spend the final night at the South Table Mountain lineshack. "For old times' sake," said Cassidy, "and to give a man the feel of being home, without his actually being there yet." His real reason was that, only miles from his father's ranch, something had compelled him to turn aside. It had seized him without warning, deep and chilling. He could put no name to it, nor did he try. All he did manage in the moment of the warning was to think of and suggest the delaying last night at the lineshack.

Dan, however, far from being displeased or curious, thought the idea a capital one. "Why," he said enthusiastically, "there ain't nobody that I know of been up there since me and you and Mike. Paw, he wouldn't even go in the shack when he come up the hall with the posse from Panguitch. You know, George LeRoy, Paw was sure funny about the whole thing. Hah, hah! Why, he never would admit you'd had a thing to do with murdering old Orville. He even told Sheriff Rasmussen that if there was a innocent or decent man's blood in there on the lineshack floor, he knowed his boy LeRoy couldn't never have had nothing to do with it. And you know that he wouldn't go in and let hisself be showed where the bullets struck, or where old Orville had bled all over the dadblasted place, or where me and you had drug him over to the—"

"Dan," ordered Cassidy, gray-lipped, "for God's sake, be still."

At the shack, where the sun was going swiftly and the cold of the November night was closing in, the cheer did not increase. The stains on the planks of the bunk where Orville Stodenberg had been laid out seemed to Cassidy as fresh and fearful as the night of their making. He even imagined he could see the blood marks on the dirt floor still wet after four winters. When, following a particularly eerie cry of wind and rattle of shack door, he shivered and glanced up to discover the dead deputy standing just within the door, snow-covered, Winchester in hand, vacant eyes fastened on him; the returned cowboy knew that he had made a serious mistake: no man who had departed with the mark of Cain upon him could come home again.

If George LeRoy Parker were to wait another fifty years, the ghost of Orville Stodenberg would still be standing just inside that rickety door, looking for the ones who had taken his life.

Cassidy knew then where he was, and what he must do. He was twenty-one years old this night up on the mountain. Boyhood lay beyond his reach, down there in the valley, sleeping with his father, peacefully along the grassy banks of the Sevier. He wished mightily that his father's dreams were good, and he thanked the Lord that his father still believed in him. But he knew what he was, even so. Perhaps he had to come home to find it out. It did not matter. Whatever he might have been, or done, or hoped to do, rested with his father down there. He could not pick it up again, nor carry it if picked up. No man could. Yet if a man would not lie to himself, nor to those who believed in him, then he was still some part of a man. So it was with Cassidy. He must travel on. His home was not here, but out there.

When Dan was safely asleep, Cassidy arose and went out of the shack in his stockingfeet, carrying boots, gun belt and carbine. He saddled Kanab, put a lead rope on Dan's horse, mounted up and walked both animals quietly for half a mile. At the Sevier, he turned upstream along the dim track of the owlhoot trail old Mike had shown him so long ago. Sniffing the icy wind, tasting the stinging melt of the new snowflakes on his lips, he spoke to Kanab and to the other horse, and they responded, sensing the same urgency. The big snows were moving down from the north. The time for riding any far trail was narrowing; and it was a very far trail they would ride from Sevier River to Robber's Roost— even without the ghosts.

When the gaining flakes swirled in behind Cassidy, filling the tracks of his horses, putting their clean whiteness over the last small sign that he had been there, it was the end of the boy from Circle Valley. He came no more to Table Mountain, nor ever again to Sevier River.

About Will Henry

Henry Wilson Allen (best known by his pen-names Will Henry and Clay Fisher) was born in 1912 in Kansas City, Missouri. He worked as a gold miner, house mover, sugar-mill operator, small-town newspaper columnist, General Motors assembly-line laborer, stablehand in Hollywood, contract writer for Metro-Goldwyn-Mayer, television script writer *(Tales of Wells Fargo, Zane Grey Theater)* and, since 1950, with publication of *No Survivors*, novelist.

Among his fifty-three books are *Pillars of the Sky, From Where the Sun Now Stands, The Gates of the Mountains, Alias Butch Cassidy, The Tall Men, One More River to Cross, Chiricahua, I, Tom Horn, Who Rides With Wyatt, Yellowstone Kelly, Mackenna's Gold, Warbonnet, Red Blizzard, Yellow Hair, The Fourth Horseman, San Juan Hill, The Brass Command*, and *Apache Ransom*.

Will Henry has earned a record five Golden Spur awards from the Western Writers of America, Inc. He was the first recipient of the Levi Strauss "Saddleman" award for career contributions to Western literature, and has earned the Western Heritage Wrangler Award and Outstanding Service Award from the National Cowboy Hall of Fame.

Two Will Henry novels, *From Where the Sun Now Stands* and *I, Tom Horn*, have been named as among the greatest Western novels of all time.

An estimated fifteen million Will Henry and Clay Fisher books have been sold by Bantam Books alone.

Eight motion pictures have been made from Will Henry's novels, including *The Tall Men*, *Santa Fe Passage*, *Mackenna's Gold*, *Journey to Shiloh*, *Yellowstone Kelly*, and, in 1956, the Universal film *Pillars of the Sky*, starring Jeff Chandler, Dorothy Malone, Ward Bond, and Lee Marvin.

Will Henry (the name he prefers, personally and professionally) is the most honored and respected of all Western writers, and is widely regarded as the most significant author of historical novels of the West in American Literature.

Will Henry is one of our most respected novelists of the true American West, and ALIAS BUTCH CASSIDY is one of his most popular novels. Over the coming months, Bantam Books will reissue a number of other magnificent Will Henry Classics.

Turn the page for a preview of the next outstanding frontier saga by Will Henry:

NO SURVIVORS

A powerful saga of the legendary White Sioux.

This book will be on sale in December 1991. Look for it—and other Will Henry novels—wherever Bantam Books are sold.

Hₐ ISTORY talks with many tongues and they are not all straight. Captain Keogh's horse Comanche may indeed have been the only living thing found on the banks of the Little Big Horn "forty-eight hours" (as the books say) after Custer's last battle, but the implication that the horse was the only survivor of the general's immediate command is not true. There was another survivor, though, to be sure, "forty-eight hours later" found him riding far out and away from the stark windrows of tongueless dead. And riding far out and away from the remembered pages of history. I was that survivor.

It is not the purpose of this journal to dim the memory which General George A. Custer enjoys among our people as a hero. But I saw him die, and the tragic knowledge of the detail of that final hour will not rest in me. I write with the hope the heroes may stay alive in legend, while their dead rest in peace.

I was sixteen when the War between the States burst into bright flame. Within the year I was brevetted a captain, and, following Chickamauga, one year to the month later, I was promoted to field grade. I spent the next eight months under J. E. B. Stuart, and was again brevetted, this time at Spottsylvania, to full colonel. My age at the time: nineteen years, seven months.

I was twenty-one, a full Colonel of Confederate Cavalry, the night Lee called his last war council in the wood outside Appomattox.

As these words fall onto paper they appear all too simple. But I had found the war a fierce crucible, it being my fortune to be continually in its highest heats. As a result, if I wasn't the hardest of the forgings dropped from its metal, I wasn't the softest, either.

This statement will appear immodest. Well, to one who hasn't ground his teeth on a pistol barrel while a dirty-fingered army surgeon digs a .50-caliber Yankee slug out of his groin, it may. Or again, if one hasn't enjoyed the pleasures of biting his own arm to keep from screaming like a woman while an orderly pours fuming nitric acid into a saber cut across the great muscles of the back, he too, may be excused his dubiety.

But to a boy who experienced such things at an age when most youths are pondering school sums or giggling with girls over a church supper, the accounting seems bare enough.

At the time I would have thought I could take Appomattox without the quiver of a face-muscle, yet to watch Lee that night, as he read the requiem mass of the Confederacy, would have broken the heart of a rock.

Our forces were chopped to pieces. Yet they were fighting furiously when at 3:00 A.M. General Lee sent to know what progress we were making. I was with General Gordon as cavalry liaison officer when the message came to our front. I heard his reply.

"Tell General Lee," he stated, quietly, "that my command has been fought to a frazzle and unless Longstreet can unite in the movement, I cannot long go forward."

Colonel Venable, Lee's aide, later told me that when he delivered his message, the old warrior stared into the morning blackness, soundless for a full minute, then slowly announced, "There is nothing left for me but to go see General Grant, and I had rather die a thousand deaths."

In the following reaction on our immediate front I had my first contact with the man who was to prove such a fateful factor in my later life, and who was to furnish by his strange death, one of the greatest military mysteries of all time. My first sight of him was as he came riding into our lines from the Union side in company with our Confederate truce officer, Colonel Green Peyton.

Our message to the Union commander had read: "General Gordon has received notice from General Lee of a flag of truce, stopping the battle." The Union commander opposite was the hated Sheridan. Hence, all of us on Gordon's staff were prepared for the awkward task of responding gracefully to "Little Phil's" approach.

Imagine our feelings when we saw, not Sheridan, returning with Peyton, but an unknown Union general whose appearance was so remarkable as to keep us all in silence as he drew up.

The man's posture and motion in saddle were faultless. Accustomed as were all us Southerners to fine horsemanship, none of us had beheld a more thrilling rider.

He was a thin man, as gracefully slender as a woman, yet with the impression of whipcord in that slenderness. He wore his hair falling in great flat curls to his shoulders, and in the coming sun of that funeral day, it gleamed with the brightness of yellow-gold.

A nervous private, standing close to me in ranks, muttered aloud, "Look at his hair. Yellower'n field-corn in August."

This compelling officer galloped up to General Gordon, halting his charger with a beautiful flourish of horsemanship a scant foot from the nose of the general's mount. Presenting his saber in salute, he announced: "General Gordon, sir, I am General Custer and bear a message to you from General Sheridan. The General desires me to present you his compliments, and to demand the immediate and unconditional surrender of all the troops under your command."

Gordon, white-lipped, replied, "You will please, General, return my compliments to General Sheridan, and say to him that I shall not surrender my command."

Unperturbed, the Union officer concluded, "General Sheridan directs me to say to you, sir, that if there is any hesitation about your surrender, he has you surrounded and can annihilate your command in an hour."

General Gordon remained adamant, saying his position was perhaps better known to him than to Sheridan, and that if the latter wished the responsibility for further slaughter, it was his.

Custer now saluted, wheeling his horse as if to depart, but instead edging the nervous beast along our lines until he halted him in front of me. Looking intently at me, he saluted. Puzzled, I returned the salute and we both sat looking at one another.

My mind raced in search of an explanation of his singling-out of me. Then, even before he spoke, I had it.

When Custer had approached our command, while he was still seventy-five yards out, an ungallant Confederate private had half-raised his musket as though to fire at him. Guessing the fellow's intent, I had struck his piece from his hand, ordering his arrest in a back-flung sentence without taking my eyes off the approaching Union officer. The private was a hill man from Tennessee, one of the deadliest shots in the company. I was satisfied Custer had been a trigger-finger twitch from death; the honor of the Confederate Army equally close to lasting disgrace.

But the action had been so swift, so completely trivial to the major drama, that men in our own company had not noticed its occurrence. That Custer might have seen this by-play seemed incredible.

"Colonel"—his voice had a disturbing depth—"my compliments. You have doubtless saved my life. Should our paths cross again, I shall remember you."

Turning to go, he gestured toward the soldier who would have shot him., With a nod to me, he queried, "May I issue an order, Colonel?" I nodded back, perfunctorily, and he immediately called to the corporal whose detail stood guard over my glowering trooper. "Corporal. Release your prisoner, please. Give him back his rifle." Then, wheeling his horse in a sharp, near-foot spin, he presented his saber to the entire line. His parting words were all the more memorable for the deep hush in which they were delivered.

"My compliments to the incomparable Confederate Army." He was gone in an instant, dashing off to his own lines.

I shall recount nothing further of the death of the Confederacy at Appomattox. Such accounting as has been given, may be regarded as the preface to the real saga of my life, its westward course following my abortive attempt to "go home" after the surrender.

My sole assets at the outset of the journey west, beyond a personal hardihood already described, were my horse and an old Colt Dragoon revolver. I assume the three of us made something less than a reassuring picture.

Hussein, as the foundation of this dilapidated trio, contributed his full share to our appearance of villainy. A magnificent bay stallion, reputed to carry in his veins, undiluted, the blood of the original Barb, he had been presented to me by my troops after Chickamauga.

He had somehow miraculously survived the last two years of the war, but at what price! A Union Minié ball had ploughed a crooked furrow aslant the last five ribs of his near-side. To balance this, he bore half a dozen foot-long, saber scars on the off-side, these diligently appliquéd there by various Yankee students in sundry cavalry-crocheting bees. His off-ear had been inletted by a charge of Union grape, that I believe was looking for me, and, as a result, it flopped down with all the elan of a Georgia jackass's. His winter coat half shed out, his mane and tail splintered alike by bullet and bramble, his numerous battle wounds and picket scars grown-in a ghostly white, his general condition that of a coondog fed on creekwater, he was indeed as lordly a Rosinante as ever Confederate Quixote bestrode. Withal, he was so thin his shadow had holes in it.

Nor was his appearance alone wicked. Hussein's happiness of spirit lay somewhere between that of a wounded grizzly and a rutting elk. He hated mankind in general, womenkind in particular, would kill another horse quicker than look at him. Two things were sound about him: his lungs and heart. The former had never known exhaustion, the latter was as big and strong as a nailkeg, containing in all its iron-bound stavings, one sentiment only—an abiding love for me.

I was fit companion to this beast. My outfit was not gray simply from the colors of my beloved cause. Over all my person, from the crown of the rim-crimped stetson to the worn-open toes of the high cavalry boots, lay a film of powdery dust. This deposit did nothing to enhance my features, none too graced by nature in the first place. I once overheard a private of my command describe me to a courier.

"Yew'll find Cunnel Clayton on the left front up ahaid. Look fer where the Minié balls is thickest and the most Rebel yells comin' from. He'll be the one 'bout three ax-handles tall and one broad acrost the shoulders. If yew cain't find him from that, look fer a face like a Cherokee's standin' ahint a mustache black as a yankee's heart and stiffer'n a bobcat's whiskers in squattin' time. If yew still cain't spot him, give a Johnny-yell. The fust officer which hollers, 'Forward, men!' is him."

This sketch of my charms, while florid, need not be greatly footnoted. A union of black Irish and deep Creole blood in my ancestry had conspired to leave me with a face and complexion more designed for a murdering aborigine than a Georgia gentleman.

One would not think a mere gun could claim a personality warranting description. But the Colt Dragoon which had hung at my side since First Manassas, defying all replacements by later models, had earned that distinction.

Dubbed "Ol' Cottonmouth" by some forgotten soldier, it had gained that title in my command because of the number of Yankee visitors it had welcomed with true Southern courtesy. It was credited with having struck down more Yanks than the dysentery.

It was this tender trio which favored Market Square in Kansas City with its appearance in the spring of '66, a little over a year after Appomattox. It had taken me that long in the South to learn that the Yankees spelled reconstruction and destruction the same way.

First, I had found the Clayton plantation effectively dedicated by Sheridan to Sherman's proposition that war was hell. My mother had died: my two sisters "gone Nawth."

I hung around below the Line, working the cribs and card games from Macon to Mobile, from Augusta to Austin. I went up the Mississippi on a river boat, gambling. I got shot in Memphis, losing my roll and thirty pounds of good weight. I drifted back home, crowding twenty-three, a border-tough, cardsharp, bordello client, general all-around ruffian. I'd been out to Texas and hadn't liked it. But I'd been "up the river" and heard talk of Kansas City, the Oregon Road, and California.

Kansas City of the late '60s was the head kettle of the frontier fleshpots. And Market Square was the raw heart of the red meat in that kettle. Here came the off-season scourings of the frontier to "simmer in the sun and summer in the sin." Here were the cowmen, traders, trappers and buffalo hunters of the West, in town for a hot summer before another hard winter. Here were the emigrants, teamsters, scouts and wagon captains, drawing a last safe breath before sailing their prairie schooners out into the perilous Indian sea, beyond.

Here were all the refinements of the effete East laid out for sale to the grimy buckskin brigade whose members were following spring down the Missouri from Montana, and up the Red from Texas. Here a buffalo hunter could buy one of the new Henry rifles for $100 or seventy-five prime robes. Here a horn-fisted trapper from the Upper Snake could sell fifty winter beaver for $200 and buy a woman for one dollar. Here cowmen picked up herd-delivery checks of $85,000, following sixty- or ninety-day drives from the Staked Plains, and left half or all the money scattered around Market Square and its sub-arteries of sin, in less than twenty-four hours.

My problem was where and how to get an outfit. A pressing problem, too, but in the interests of candor I must admit an ace-in-the-hole.

The day after Appomattox I had sold my saber to a souvenir-hunting Union lieutenant for twenty dollars. This precious blade was, I informed my benefactor, General Gordon's personal property, given me by him in gratitude for my faithful service. The fact I had taken it no earlier than the day before, from a luckless Yankee officer in no way diseased my conscience. All's fair in peace as well as war. Caveat emptor.

The money still held lonely vigil in the breast pocket of my tattered army jacket. It must be admitted, too, the thought had crossed my mind that should this golden ace need a blue-steel "kicker," such a card hung low and handy in the worn holster at my side.

Thus, the old Colt, the lieutenant's goldpiece and I set out from Market Square to improve our fortunes.

I dropped the reins on Hussein, leaving him standing amidst the teeming activity of the square. I had no worry he would not be there on my return. It would have been worth any man's broken bones to touch him, much less take him off.

I shall always maintain it is the "s" of Southern to partake properly of spirits, and the "g" of Gentleman to know the spots on a pasteboard. My education in cards and whiskey had begun early and run late. I fancied that among other of the little polishes of self-preservation, I could take care of myself in a poker game. My first thoughts of multiplying the twenty-dollar goldpiece turned around visions of straights, flushes and fours-of-a-kind. I thought I was old enough to know a bust from a bobtail when the chips were down.

It did not take long to locate as chancy a game as a man would care to buy into. Even from ten feet away, the deck looked as cold as a clam in an ice-cake.

Five men, all hard cases, had a saddle blanket spread on the ground in the shade alongside a livery barn. The play was table stakes and, as in all camp games, the stakes were running high. A gallery of frontier riff-raff circled around the players. Elbowing my way forward, I watched the play for several minutes.

Chief of the camp scavengers who preyed upon the free-spending buffalo hunters were the deliberate cardsharpers. These airy-fingered gentry ran a pose of being honest trappers or prospectors but in reality were on the range for one purpose: to sweat the spendable suet off the hard-fatted calves of the frontier. They worked in pairs, a skillful team making enormous profits in a good season; a good season being any one they happened to survive.

Still, by the very nature of their profession and of the rawhide gentility of the clientele upon which they practised it, these sharps were nearly always gunfighters and killers. Their routine never varied: build a game to a point where they were losing, then set in to fleece the honest players unmercifully. The answer to any and all objections to the style of play from this point on, was the six-gun. The clean player who opened his mouth to question any deal would be summarily shot out from behind his hand. Few were those who cared to declare for sweet fairness under such rules.

Three hands were enough to let me know where the spots were on this leopard. The game was crooked as a hound's hind leg and twice as dirty.

Stepping out of the circle of onlookers, I slid the old Dragoon out of the holster, spun the cylinder, flexed the hammer, eased the gun gently back into its worn resting place. When I had made my way back into the circle, one player, white-faced and shaking, had just risen and left the game. I stepped into his place, dropped to one knee, asked for cards. As these were being dealt me, I gave my holster just a suggestion of a forward shift, observing calmly, "If no one has any objections, we'll play honest poker."

Not a word interrupted the soft fall of the cards. The two men who had been rigging the game, and opposite to whom I had been careful to place myself, looked across the blanket at me for a brief moment after the last card fell. Then, not troubling to regard me again, they picked up their cards and the play continued.

In a few hands, with a luck not inherent in an honest deck, I had won a considerable amount. Now came the hand for which I had been waiting. From the betting it was evident everyone had been dealt a big hand. The man on my right opened; I raised. The man on my left, a small, simian-eyed prospector, raised. The first of the two riggers did likewise and his partner raised him. The last man dropped. The game getting where it was, it was time to take a last sizing of the opposition.

The man on my left front, the smaller of the two sharps, was exceedingly thin, shallow-eyed, nervous and quick, with a mouth almost lipless, above a sallow, weedy goatee. His clothing was stylish, of good quality. It would be fatally easy to underrate his hypersensitive type in a gunplay.

The other man was big, quiet, compelling, not quite the picture of the conventional cardman. I got the feeling, watching him make his lazy, slow moves handling cards and money, there was in him some animal strain of vitality. In the entire play he had not said a word, making his bets and requests with monosyllabic grunts.

It would be a hazard to fix his age, but it was probably no less than thirty-five. His dress was that of a buffalo hunter. Two late-model Colts hung low and far forward on his massive thighs. At variance with the custom, he wore his mustache trimmed close and was otherwise smooth-shaven, while his hair, which was the most singular hue of ashen-gray, escaped in thick growth from beneath his black slouch hat. His skin was prairie-burned almost mahogany. This, with his strange, pale eyes and silver hair, presented an unforgettable contrast. In build he was heavy, yet one knew before he moved just how he would be; light, easy, deceptive, blindingly fast.

We now all took cards. The man called Slate was dealing.

I held three queens, drawing the fourth and a jack. The only sounds came from the watchers, an occasional cough, the nervous clearing of a throat, the sibilant movements of many feet in thick dust. I knew, without looking, that those behind me were drawing back and away.

"How much left in your pile?" My words, directed to Slate, broke the richest silence I'd ever paid to listen to.

Without moving his head, which was bent in study of his hand, he raised his pale eyes until they met and held mine. This was the first time our glances had met directly. I confess to a momentary nervousness and, had wishes been wings, I would have been soaring far away from there. The feeling passed and, since under the rules of a table-stake game, a player must answer the question. Slate told me what I wanted to know.

"Three hundred." His voice was as flat as the click of a cocked trigger.

"All right, my friend." I hoped my voice wasn't shaking any worse than a wet hound in a hailstorm. "I'll tap you."

In a moment, every dollar in sight was in the middle of the blanket. The little man looked repeatedly at Slate, but the latter's field of vision never wavered from my mid-person, a field which included, very nicely, my cards, my hands, my gun.

The play had now reached the point of no return. To the crowd it must have seemed I was playing squarely into the hands of the crooked gamblers. I had built up a big pot, betting into their combined hands, and had cleaned the table on the last raise after the draw.

"You're called." The big man's deep-grunted phrase had all the salutary effect of a tumbler of ice water thrown into the small of the back. Let no one tell you the hairs at the nape of the neck cannot rise; human hackles literally lift.

"Queens. Four of them." The cards accompanied my words.

"Full," said the smaller man. "Tens over jacks."

The big man seemed to hesitate. My whole body was singing-tight. Then his cards came down. "Four aces."

My left hand was on the ground in front of me, my right free, carried lightly across my right knee. "I reckon you didn't hear me when I said we'd play honest poker." I scarcely recognized my own voice.

Slate's hand froze in mid-reach for the pot.

In gentler times and places the charge of cheating at cards has proven the most reliable percussion for the cap of gunplay. Both my men wore double pistols. I made no move for my own.

The little man went for his and I shot him in the stomach. He had his guns out, though their muzzles never pointed higher than groundward. From the tail of my eye, my gaze and gun now covering Slate, I saw the other gambler slide slowly forward, eyes wide, his body following his guns down into the dirt of the stable yard. He rolled partly on his right side, started to say something, hemorrhaged and died.

Slate's hand remained in mid air.

"Any more bets?" My voice rasped with tension.

Slate's hand drew back. His eyes on mine, as they had been from the onset, he grunted very softly, "I'll pass."

With that he was on his feet in a motion which defied any definition of starting and stopping. No further word or glance did I get. He simply turned and vanished, the crowd drawing back to admit him, closing again to swallow him.

But there on the blanket in front of me were nine hundred hard Yankee dollars. All mine by Colt-induced default.

Rising to go, I felt a hand on my shoulder. Tensing, I glanced at it, finding it more nearly resembled the paw of an old boar grizzly, than any human member. The owner of the hand redeemed the note of its bearlike promise.

WILL HENRY

When it comes to Western historical fiction, Will Henry is a literary legend. A five-time winner of the coveted Western Writers of America Golden Spur Award, the recipient of the Levi Strauss Saddleman Award for lifetime achievement and a host of other honors, he is held in awe by his colleagues and beloved by fans around the world.

☐ **WHO RIDES WITH WYATT**
25002-7 $2.95/$3.95 in Canada

☐ **JOURNEY TO SHILOH**
28798-2 $3.50/$3.95 in Canada

☐ **PILLARS OF THE SKY**
28878-4 $3.50/$3.95 in Canada

☐ **ONE MORE RIVER TO CROSS**
28988-8 $3.50/$3.99 in Canada

Buy Will Henry's novels wherever Bantam Domain Books are sold or use this page for ordering.

Bantam Books, Dept.   WH   414 East Golf Road, Des Plaines, IL 60016

Please send me the items I have checked above. I am enclosing $_____
(please add $2.50 to cover postage and handling). Send check or money order;
no cash or C.O.D.s please.

Mr./Ms._____

Address_____

City/State_____ Zip_____

Please allow four to six weeks for delivery.
Prices and availability subject to change without notice.   WH -- 5/91

TERRY C. JOHNSTON

Winner of the prestigious Western Writer's award, Terry C. Johnston brings you his award-winning saga of mountain men Josiah Paddock and Titus Bass who strive together to meet the challenges of the western wilderness in the 1830's.

☐ 25572-X **CARRY THE WIND–Vol. I** $5.50

☐ 26224-6 **BORDERLORDS–Vol. II** $5.50

☐ 28139-9 **ONE-EYED DREAM–Vol. III** $4.95

The final volume in the trilogy begun with *Carry the Wind* and *Borderlords*, ONE-EYED DREAM is a rich, textured tale of an 1830's trapper and his protegé, told at the height of the American fur trade.

Following a harrowing pursuit by vengeful Arapaho warriors, mountain man Titus "Scratch" Bass and his apprentice Josiah Paddock must travel south to old Taos. But their journey is cut short when they learn they must return to St. Louis...and old enemies.

Look for these books wherever Bantam books are sold, or use this handy coupon for ordering:

Bantam Books, Dept. TJ, 414 East Golf Road, Des Plaines, IL 60016

Please send me the items I have checked above. I am enclosing $_____
(please add $2.50 to cover postage and handling). Send check or money
order, no cash or C.O.D.s please.

Mr/Ms _____

Address _____

City/State _____ Zip _____

TJ–9/91

Please allow four to six weeks for delivery.
Prices and availability subject to change without notice.

ELMER KELTON

☐ 27713-8 **THE MAN WHO RODE MIDNIGHT** $3.99

☐ 25658-0 **AFTER THE BUGLES** $2.95

☐ 27620-4 **HANGING JUDGE** $2.95

☐ 27467-8 **WAGONTONGUE** $2.95

☐ 26147-9 **THE BIG BRAND** $3.50

☐ 25716-1 **CAPTAIN'S RANGERS** $3.50

Bantam Books, Dept. BOW2, 414 East Golf Road, Des Plaines, IL 60016

Please send me the items I have checked above. I am enclosing $_____ (please add $2.50 to cover postage and handling). Send check or money order, no cash or C.O.D.s please.

Mr/Ms _____

Address _____

City/State _____ Zip _____

BOW2–9/91

Please allow four to six weeks for delivery
Prices and availability subject to change without notice.